A FALL IN AUTUMN

A FALL IN AUTUMN

MICHAEL G. WILLIAMS

❀ Created with Vellum

To my husband Michael, for encouraging me at every turn.

To Josh, Kat, Corwin, Joe, Mike, Brian, and the many other creative friends who played in that game of Microscope or listened to me blather about this world since then.

1

When Buttercup saw me, I had a glass of air-reactive sake in one hand and, in the other, a bean pastry so tough it tried to take my lunch money. I tracked the big lug for an hour before he finally made me, right there in the middle of Lower Market Market. Yes, that's its name; it isn't *my* fault the Empire breeds creativity out of the bureaucratic class. Buttercup—the big lug—gave me a look from under the brim of his hat, one that said in no uncertain terms he would very much be looking forward to my funeral. I thought—mistakenly—I would be undetectable in the middle of all the glow splash and the condensation mist and the hundreds of meters of low market stalls heaped against one another like drifts of filthy snow.

I don't know why I named the guy "Buttercup," but I did, and it stuck. I bestowed that moniker on him a couple of days before when the client showed me a likeness of him and told me where to find him on Saturday afternoons. The client wanted him tailed to see how he was passing his time. I figured she was a jilted girlfriend or maybe a wannabe with a little cash to burn, throwing detectives down the wishing well. Find out where he hangs out, what he does, and *just happen* to be there herself next time. You know, the usual.

I don't have time to go into greater detail as I write this, or to start earlier in my career—earlier than these, the case I *thought* would be my last, and the case that really was—but if I did, you would see what I mean.

A detective's job is not glamorous. We spend a lot of time finding married ladies' lost kittens and washing them off in enough coffee to make them stand up straight before we bring them home. Buttercup was yet another of these: a woman wanted me to find a man, so I found him. It's never a happy task, but at least the dogged pursuit of unhappiness could mostly pay the bills.

Buttercup rang in at three hundred kilograms of uncooked beef, maybe more, and not all of it the lean stuff, but as they say, it takes all kinds. The client was a Mannie, raptor leanings, with the iridescent eyes and the peaked, glinting, halfway-to-talons fingernails to prove it: made for detailed work in the dark. I didn't ask her how she earned her birdseed, but I figured something in the middle: good enough to hire me but not good enough to hire someone better. Buttercup, on the other hand, shouted fisticuffs and heavy lifting. Opposites attract, right? You never know in my business, which is simply the business of trying to find things out. The funny thing is, half the time, when it all comes together—when we answer the client's question, when we reach wrist-deep into the muck and pull out the truth with a stream of something that smells bad running off the corners—they wish we hadn't.

Knowing—knowing a thing, knowing a person, knowing a secret—can hurt worse than any patch of briars you have to wade through on the way there.

Not a lot of detectives will take a Mannie as a client, but not a lot of Mannies were interested in hiring an Artie, so I figured we were even on that score. I'm not picky about my clients, personally, and not merely because I'm, by nature, such a big-hearted egalitarian guy either. I like to think I take people as I meet them rather than trying to shove them into the nearest box, sure, but that isn't the point. Mainly, I'm not picky about clients because I can't afford to be. Here I am, born the old-fashioned way from people too nice and too dumb and too infuriating to know better, but I live in the City of Autumn anyway. By that fact alone, I am already kind of a freak. I will always look different, sound different, and think different from the rest of the people who've been built for a place like this. No one in either end of the social spectrum ever quite knows what to do with me.

Sometimes, when I stare into the reflecting pool that is every single glass of hooch ever poured, across the whole history of people deciding to bottle up ways to get stinko, I know in my heart I like it that way. Autumn, last of the great flying cities of the ancients, is a freak show through and through: antiquated, idolized, hated, mocked, resented for its wealth and for the disparities of wealth and power evident at even a cursory glance. It's beautiful, careworn, crowded, lonely, cosmopolitan, and suffused with a certain kind of *knowing* the City itself will surely never last forever. The whole place is waiting for some other shoe to drop, a shoe it can't describe, can't name, can't explain. But it knows that shoe is out there all the same, and the City hopes to the gods that shoe is not the City itself. We find solace in the groupthink of living in a place so many others live, and we find ourselves annoyed at the traffic. We find fear for its future when we read the histories of its dead sisters from the past, and we find ourselves wishing something would come along to clean it out a little but maybe not a lot.

So, here we all are, every last one of us feeling like the rat with the nicest cage and every last one of us wishing he had it to himself. I figured out a long time ago the biggest freak in the whole show gets two things: spat on and space. I could handle one if it got me the other, no problem, and thank you kindly.

Buttercup's demeanor went from grim to worse as he looked at me, and he turned away from the market stall where he was eyeing bales of hay like he might take one home for supper. He started making his way—slowly, at first, but he was picking up steam as he went—toward the Pearl Street gate. When he got there, Buttercup looked to his left so he could turn right out onto the sidewalk, which would put him going in the direction of the downtown steerless. It was a smart move: the carriages are too small for a tail to jump on without being in fairly close proximity. If I jumped on with him, he'd know for sure I was a tail. If he wanted to question me in a public place, he'd have his chance. If I didn't jump on, he could shake me at any stop from here to Autumn Center.

On my way to the gate, I downed the sake and tossed the bun to a clutch of street kids. I wasn't hungry—I hardly ever was anymore—but that didn't mean it had to go to waste. Those kids could have the luxury of fighting over who got to chip a tooth.

I decided to let Buttercup think he'd gotten the best of me for now. When I reached Pearl Street, I turned left and crossed instead of following him, but I let him see me looking back over my shoulder. Might as well feed the myth of being a shaken tail, right? Let him think I was grumbling to myself over his clever escape, let him get a little room to loosen the belt on his confidence so his guard could sag. Once I was across the street, I fell in behind a troupe of Sisters of Sincerity and let my own crumpled cap give me a little cover. I walked thirty meters right behind them, then forty, shrinking behind their ridiculous wimples, then turned at a lamp post and made my way back across. A short row of dingy yellow mag cabs always lined up near the Lower Market Market, and I hopped into one near the back with a Rat for a driver.

"Hey, buddy," the guy chattered at me. "Front of the line, right? We got rules!" I ignored him and pointed at the bus up ahead, the one Buttercup was about to board.

"You can make it up to the rest of the guild next time," I cooed, trying to help this go fast and easy. "I need you to tail that bus, and I need it discreet."

Ratface looked at me in the rearview mirror, twisted his whiskered cheeks this way and that in consternation before saying, "Forty on top."

I shook my head, but I didn't laugh. "Twenty. That's more than the going rate, and it's plenty to split with the other guys. Five will stuff plenty of orange rind in those handsome cheeks."

The guy didn't even bother to negotiate further. I was right, and he knew it, and anyway, the other drivers ahead of him had started to notice he was picking up a fare out of turn and raising a ruckus. Ratface checked his side mirror, twisted the steerer, and the mag shot away from the sidewalk and around the rest of the queue. The cabbie in front actually stepped into the way, bringing my driver to a sudden stop. I bounced off the smoked glass partition covered with stick-on advertisements of interest to libertines and last year's chewing gum. I cried out in pain, but the Rat ignored me. He had his window down to yell at his guild brother.

"What, you trying to get run over?" He sounded like annoyed family: concern and anger in equal measure and well accustomed to one another through long affiliation.

"What's this, grabbin' a fare out of sequence? You know the rules, Fay. You know I get first crack, then Scram, then Langley, *then* you." The other Rat hitched his pants up in the back like he was getting ready to do some sort of manual labor.

The driver hitched a thumb at me. "I'll split the fare later," he barked. "This guy's a religious devotion. Take a walk, bro. You need to cool off." I could hear the wheel in his head squeaking as he thought while talking nonsense. "Says he always takes the fourth of anything."

The "bro" looked in the window at me, squinted his big round eyes and then leaned back. "Hey, you didn't say you had an Artie," he said, then to me, through the walls of the car, "No offense meant, you know, just, it's what they call the vernacular on the street, you know?" He doffed his big straw hat. "Fourth of everything? Learn something new every day. What's the word? Numeralolololology?" He slaughtered the pronunciation, running the syllables together languidly across the top of his palate like they were pushing to get out of his mouth.

I looked at the Rat in the front. "Unless I'm mistaken," I pressed the tips of three fingers to the pad to link him to my account, tapped a rhythm, and with my fingers still held to it subvocalized *tip twenty,* "I've paid you to drive the car?"

"Easy!" they both said at the same time, but the driver shot forward again, joining the flow of traffic at the tail end of a light and maybe running it a little bit. Buttercup's steerless had pulled away from the raised platform, but the driver told me it wouldn't be a problem to catch up.

"That's the 9," he said. "I know its route like the back of my own paw."

He probably did, too. After all, learning his way around the City of Autumn was what he was designed to do.

The Route 9 steerless autobus went downtown, but Buttercup stepped off it before it got there. He jumped the line for the 27, earning a few shaken fists, and rode it away on a tangent, headed sidewise for the Down Preserves and a bit of fresh air. He was good at getting away from people, I could tell that: he knew to get in a crowd and then to get out of the crowd. If you want to stay clear on who's been around for a little while, you have to shuffle the deck of faces and see if any come up twice. Unlucky for him, I was better at my part in the game than he was at his. Ratface wanted to cut a corner here and there, take a shortcut, leap the walls of the maze Buttercup was trying to run, but I wouldn't let him. I needed eyes on that steerless at every stop in case Buttercup did another jump and dash.

He didn't. Twenty-five minutes after he stampeded the platform at Pearl Street, I saw him duck out the back of the steerless right before it pulled away from the next stop past the entrance to Down Preserves. That put him walking back this way, able to watch to see if anything was still following him—such as the bright yellow mag cab in which I was sitting. I dropped flat across the back seat and told the Rat to keep driving. "Turn down a side street," I barked, my voice muffled by the coat

I threw over my own head. I crumpled against the slightly sticky upholstery and tried not to think about what might have made it sticky in the first place. I didn't want to consider my Artie immune system going up against whatever was now on my face and the palms of my hands.

I felt the mag cab twist a neat little turn, and the shadows of a narrow street fell over us. I counted to five, then to ten, then lifted up in the seat to peek out the back screen. Buttercup was walking in the entrance to Down Preserves, ducking so his horns barely missed the arched sign over the entrance: wrought iron, painted black, and draped in antioxidant smart moss. Some people believe that kind of moss—common as dirt—was one of the first of the protean plants. Seemed like a stretch to me, but then, everything's a stretch in a place like Autumn.

I pressed my fingers to the pad again to finish paying for the cab even as Ratface started up the sputtering hostage negotiation patter of cabbies the world over. He'd gone out of his way, he'd lost a lot of fares at the Lower Market Market, he might not be able to find his way back—

At that, I gave him an unimpressed look. "Argue all you like. I made you an offer and you took it and the deal is done."

"I bet you got some paper to slide me, too, right? You don't look so clean you don't have any." Ratface licked his chops, and the cab's doors remained resolutely locked.

Paper money was illegal, of course. The only hard Imperial currency left was all in museums, but people with no money tend to work out their own medium of exchange. Usually, that was what you might call "goods and services," but sometimes, it's something more tangible and transferrable: local scrip a gang or entrepreneur prints up to circulate without the Empire logging every transaction. The Empire tells us making up our own money is a kind of rebellion, a form of disloyalty we ought to avoid. I think all that does is give some people the idea in the first place.

I didn't have any on me—at least, not any I was going to give this guy—so I shook a finger at him. "Do your job like you were made to do, sure, but don't insult my intelligence, Mannie." He didn't like me using that word, and neither did I, but it got his attention and it made him ready to cut me loose. The doors unlocked. I slid out and took off down the sidewalk toward that same moss-covered, wrought-iron entryway.

My hat cleared the sign with a good meter to spare. Like I said,

Buttercup was big. I rounded the corner to see a group of people loitering in the small gravel parking area, either about to go in or coming out. They looked at me and then looked away, some of them a little sheepish—not literally, mind you; that's another word I should have felt bad about—though their kids stared at me in earnest and with simple curiosity. I winked at one of them. I didn't blame them for being curious. Arties like me are easy to spot, what with the old scar down the right side of my face, the nose I broke years ago, the ear half-chewed off from that time in Sunrise, the widow's peak. I'm not subtly imperfect the way some Artisanal Humans are: I'm beaten up, dented and scratched, with holes in the toes, and showing it. Everything about my face screams non-designed. Even if I'd been a cheap Man Plus knockoff from a back-alley retrogeneticist, I, at minimum, wouldn't have the scars or the bags under my eyes. That stuff is foundational for designed humanoids. I stood out like a moldy orange in a bin of apples.

Mom and Dad got me the old-fashioned way, and I've been fending off insults and adulation ever since.

Walking into Down Preserves felt good, the way I imagine it feels to walk into church with a clean conscience. It also felt like—well, not like coming home, because this felt good—but I felt less out of place. For once, I wasn't the only natural thing around. Oh, there are always plenty of proteans around in Down Preserves, sure, but it's one of the few places in Autumn where wild things are allowed to grow. At the entrance, there are grasses—actual grasses, trimmed once they reach a certain height by real Sincerity monks with glinting silver scythes and the black cowls and the whole shebang. The land there slopes upward ever so slightly, enough to let you know you're going to work if you keep walking. There's real earth, rich and brown, tended into perfection by those same ascetic brothers, mute in their devotion to the perfect world they say came before the Rise. I love walking there when they've been working. The powerful scent of tilled soil, the bright green smell of that hand-mown grass, the thick perfume of heavy blossoms letting it all hang out, all come together to make a lurid cocktail of aromas reaching deep into the experience of our ancestors and reminding us we once always walked in such places. It's enough to get a city boy high for a week—or to remind a former country boy like me of the best features of a place I came to Autumn to forget.

I've always thought it weird to have the Sinceres in Autumn at all, given their position on modern society. But if my history teacher back in school taught me anything, it's that we—humanity, in all its manifold forms and branches—have spent forever telling ourselves life was better yesterday while looking forward to tomorrow. We're addicted to a past shrouded in the mist of fiction, one where we didn't have so many mouths to feed or decisions to make. The Sinceres—I've never thought about it until now while writing things down, but when you say it aloud, it sounds like "sin seers," which they probably think is pretty fucking clever of themselves—make hella bank on that. They sit around spinning tales of the wonders of humankind, of the time when we all looked more or less the same, before the Mannies, before the Plusses, before the whole human buffet.

Don't believe them. Their stories are self-evidently lies. My profession has taught me nothing is ever as simple as it seems, and nobody's pure, no matter how pretty they are. Usually quite the opposite, in fact.

Right after the ground rises a little, it levels out, and a gravel and sand trail emerges from the manually tended grass. The gravel is a mix of shades of beige and white and gray and red, all different kinds of rocks jumbling together, but slowly, like pixels in a painting shifting together to present a larger image. The rocks resolve into stones and then into small boulders, stepping stones, and bigger outcroppings as the crust itself rises out of the sand and soil. Down Preserves is way in the back end of Autumn, near the Inner Edge. The angle of elevation is partly to give us more natural space to run around in—useful when the City drives us too fucking nuts to stand each other another second longer—and partly to hide the massive exhaust and thrust portals. Instead of the sight of yet more machinery, no matter how vital it is to things like navigation or braking or whatever, Down Preserves gives us something like Terra Firma to look at out the windows of our homely hovels. It's a little bit below to remind ourselves what life is like in normal places, a corner of open green we can scurry to when we need it.

Walking into the woods on that slowly forming path, surrounded first by large ferns and the tropical flora of North America and the desert scrub of the Mediterranean, it's easy to feel like you're everywhere and nowhere: for all the Sincerity monks say they're keeping things "natural," it's as unnatural a mix as you can imagine. No geography in the world contains that botanical mix on its own. That's religion for you. Heading up the hiking trail, though, into the simulated higher elevations, you start to find deciduous forest and deer and Scratch Ivy, and the mosquitoes fall away: all the stuff you're used to if you were lucky enough to be born north of forty-five degrees. I like it in that part of Down Preserves.

It would have been easy to get lost in letting my mind wander, except I wasn't dressed for a hike—ratty slacks and the dress shoes I needed to replace a year ago, the ones with a hole in the sole right under the pad of my foot—and I was busy tracking a third of a ton of likely very angry meat. This whole case was starting to smell bad, too. I was supposed to be seeing whether Buttercup was visiting a milkmaid on weekends. If he was, she picked a hell of a place to ply her trade. If he wasn't, I was supposed to tell the client what he *was* doing. The rational part of my mind told me to turn around, go back and call off the case, give the client back her retainer and invite her to take a long walk to a different detective. Something about this didn't add up. The client didn't want pictures, and they always want pictures if they think there's actually a case. The cobwebs in my cupboard and the late rent notice in my mailbox urged me forward, though. If I was going to eat this week, I had to know what Buttercup was doing on Saturday afternoons in Down Preserves. I could only hope it didn't involve giving one of his mittens a quick sniff.

Down Preserves is the largest open space in Autumn, but that doesn't mean it's actually very big. Designers modeled it on a place from ancient times. The Americans had a place called Golden Gate where they preserved a section of carefully tended nature in a large and largely artificial urban landscape. There's a whole thing in the visitor center about how they borrowed this and that from Golden Gate for the design of Down Preserves. This version is more extreme, though, and if you go high enough up the back, you make it into the Alpine zone. When Autumn travels to the right places for it, we'll get snow down in the City, but here, it's winter all the time with white-furred rabbits and the like to give it that touch of Mother Nature.

I climbed, breathing hard but not breathless, pulling my jacket around myself against the constant wind. It probably wasn't all that cold out, but the slightest breezes cut right through me these days. In the higher elevations of the park where you're above the Fore Barrier, you start to get a taste of real weather. For once, I was glad I quit smoking a few years ago: I could breathe, and I could smell the wet chill of some distant winter in the colder air blowing down the hill at me. It felt glorious, if only because I wanted to savor every sensation I could and this one was so starkly different from the uniform pleasantness of everywhere else in Autumn.

Back when I quit smoking, I pretended I did it for health reasons, but the truth was, I was tired of the stares it got me. Arties aren't supposed to do a lot of the fun stuff other people get to do. That's true for all kinds of things, of course, and normally the judgment of strangers doesn't bother me. Smoking was different, though. I gave it up after a Sister of Sincerity walked up to me on the bus, slapped the reef out of my mouth, and dragged me off the bus at the next stop. I decided maybe it would behoove me, if not entirely to *respect* some people's views on my status as a living historical artifact, at least not to *aggravate* them.

The trail through the middle elevations in Down Preserves is, of course, impossible to use for tracking: all gray rocks and brown mud. All that is covered in a uniform blanket of gold and brown and red leaves dropped from trees perpetually bursting with the colors of fall foliage. It would make a hell of a place to have to run away from someone: even at a walking pace, I had to step carefully and look where my feet were going rather than up ahead. I was hoping Buttercup would go as high as the snowline so I could find his prints there. The standard attire of a working detective wasn't exactly hiking boots, but having a trail to follow would be worth picking twigs out of my loafers for a week.

As I rounded a curve, a frigid gust came shooting down the path to greet me. Maybe this could happen according to plan! Maybe I would actually get to sneak up on him. Maybe I was *not* being led directly into a trap. Maybe I would get to close a case and get paid in full. *Maybe today would be okay after all.*

The snowline was right there, maybe thirty meters from me, then twenty-five, then twenty, then fifteen—and then Buttercup stepped out from behind a tree. He balled up one fist and rubbed his knuckles against the palm of the opposite hand like something out of bad theater.

"Okay, Buttercup." I held my hands out at my sides, clearly unarmed, clearly no match for his massive bovine strength. "So you made me. But please tell me you didn't lead me all the way here so you could teach me not to follow you around. You could have done that with a kind word—even an unkind word, maybe even a cruel one—way back in town, saved me a cab fare, saved you a bus ride or two. I mean, really, seriously, please do not beat me up and leave me to sleep it off."

"I'm not going to." Buttercup's voice scraped and banged, something heavy being dragged on stones. It suggested the shaking of ancient flanks in the golden light of a primitive morning from a simpler time. His eyebrows slowly inched closer, like each had an uncertain crush on the other at an old school dance. "Did you call me 'Buttercup'?"

I shrugged at him. "It seemed to fit somehow. No offense intended, of course. I'm glad to hear we can talk this out. You're my last job. I'd like to conclude this as tidily as possible."

His eyebrows finally got together, and he shook his massive head. "Not gonna talk, neither."

"Okay, but that doesn't leave us a lot of options and, to be honest, I'm a pretty lousy dancer." I was simply producing words, trying to keep him occupied. Something was about to happen, and I was pretty sure it wouldn't be good.

I was right.

Fingers—talons—tapped me on the shoulder from behind, and when I looked back, it was the client. She hissed at me. "He's not going to beat you up. I am."

That was the last thing I remembered for a while.

It didn't matter. Nobody in particular needed me awake.

While I took a long nap on the side of an artificial mountain at the back of a sculpted landscape, Autumn flew on through the daylight toward a zone of night. As I write this, it's sometimes hard to recall the fine details, but if I remember correctly, we were moving from South American highlands toward Africa. I always enjoyed it when we went to Africa: lots of fresh food and a few new faces around town. Things would be looking pretty good on the dinner front for the next few weeks.

The next thing I knew, the golem shook me gently awake. He had a little snow in his hair, having blown in from above the snowline a few meters away, but my vision still blurred a little when I tried to open my eyes, so the rest of the details were hazy. My head ached and my face felt like Buttercup danced on it, which was not necessarily outside the realm of the possible. More than anything, though, I was surprised to see a golem: one of the *actual* Living Metal themselves, with dark hair and artificial skin and all the complex mechanisms of the face that let golems toe the rim of the forbidden Uncanny Valley of Lore.

"Are you alright?" The golem asked it in that gentle voice they all have —the tones I once read were selected to make them seem trustworthy.

"I don't know," I mumbled. "I don't suppose you've seen a bird and a bull pass that way, laughing up each other's sleeves, have you?" It had started to get dark, which meant it had been a couple of hours at least. I was probably concussed, but I needed the rest, whatever the source.

"I'm afraid not." His eyes narrowed in mimicry of relaxation. "I'm glad I found you, though. You need medical attention."

"No," I groaned, trying to sit up. "I'm fine. I'm really fine." I got up on one hand, then the other, then managed to stand with his help. I dusted myself off and shook my head back and forth. "I guess I'm not getting paid for that one." I sighed it to myself, but the golem smiled a little. He started to say something pitying or placating, but I waved it off. "Never mind. Thanks for stopping when you saw me. It's more than most people would do."

The golem ducked his head and shrugged a little at me. "Sadly true."

I sighed a second time and looked around. "Worse places to get beaten up, I guess." I patted my pockets: my wallet was still there, which was something.

Of course, they hadn't robbed me. They wanted me to know it was something personal.

"True," the golem said. "It's going to be a beautiful day tomorrow, but I wanted to catch the forest today before the colors change."

"Oh?" I looked up. "Are they going to change?"

"Haven't you heard? We're going to have spring tomorrow." The golem smiled. "I appreciate it, but I'm not quite ready for everything to be green again for a while."

I nodded at him. That's life in Autumn for you: envy of the world, object of hate, and we complain about the weather being too predictable. I tipped my hat at him. He was beautiful, if a little too sincere, which is what you always hear about a golem after somebody gets a look at one up close: more human than you'd expect, maybe too human. I'd seen them before, from a distance, but I'd never met one in person like this. "Sorry to hear that." I rubbed my temples. "Thanks again."

He stopped me, holding out a hand to shake. "I'm Alejandro."

I took his hand and met his eyes. They clearly weren't human: the irises spun, concentric rings of flexible materials rotating in opposition to one another around pupils obviously Other in origin. They weren't from the right color palette, either, and in my memory of that moment—that pivotal moment, when a simple introduction eventually changed everything I understood about myself, about the grand flying City of Autumn, about the Empire, and about the world—his pupils glowed a faint electric blue from within, striking both in their obvious artificiality and their very human softness. Alejandro had eyes that said more to me of compassion, of understanding of the human condition, of hope and loss and regret and persistence, than any other set of eyes I'd seen in a long time.

So, of course, I walked away and forgot to give him my card or tell him my name or anything useful and didn't turn around when he called to me to ask if I needed help. Instead, I staggered back down the trail and out onto the street, back across town, out of the green and brown aromas of night flowers opening and tilled earth, and into the miasma of bodies and sweat and damp fur and old food the City offered the nose instead. I couldn't afford another cab. If Talons was stiffing me on the job, then she would shut me off from her accounts as part of whatever this had been as soon as they laid me out and beat it. Eventually, I dragged myself up in front of my office door an hour before midnight. Stenciled letters declared VALERIUS BAKHOUM, QUESTIONS ANSWERED, and behind that door was a desk, a couple of filing cabinets, a few purpose-driven proteans to keep the air from going stale, and a couch I could unfold into a bed.

I did exactly that, stripped to my imperfect Artisanal skin, and fell dead asleep before I was even flat.

2

"Bakhoum! Bakhoum, you lousy son of a bitch!"

That's how I awoke three days later. I didn't continuously sleep for the better part of half a week, but I might as well have for all I got done. The client—you know, Talons—canceled the open line for this job, so that was that: my last entry in the ledger for this gig was a big fat goose egg. I got a retainer, I got a few of the expenses covered but not nearly all of them, and I got nothing for finishing the job. I had basically no money and no prospects. The cupboard in the kitchenette was pretty bare, and I was a week and a half late on the rent. The voice on the other side of the door was my landlady. She was neither an Artie nor a Plus, but I didn't know anything about her genetic baselines beyond that. Whatever engineering produced her did not make her especially solicitous toward the idea of accepting excuses in lieu of rent, which I guess is good if you're a slumlord but lousy if you're a penniless tenant. I stayed very still on my futon, afraid to breathe lest she hear the frame creak and kick the door in to get at me.

Of course, she would never do that. She knew she would never get the cost of a replacement out of me.

There was more pounding, then: "I know you're in there, you rat. Don't think you can impress me with your fancy historical genes. You know, I could have you thrown out anyway, and that's what I'm going to do on Fireday if you don't get your shit together. You've got three days.

You hear me? Three. Days." Then, she stomped off down the hallway, her footfalls echoing off the plaswood and cement. My office is in a building constructed for durability and stability, not fashion. The plaswood floors were a later addition intended to class the place up, but it turned everyone into a tap dancer.

After she was gone, I let out my breath and sat up, pulled on trousers, and stretched to the sound of a hundred popping joints. Whatever kept the landlady at bay was good enough, even if that meant hiding and holding my breath. I cared far less about paying her rent than where I would get food or smokes—oh wait, I'd quit smoking—or a cup of coffee.

Coffee, I thought. The memory of the stuff was almost enough to wake me. I ran out of Buenos Dias Blend the day before, and I didn't have a penny to spend on more. I inspected a bottle of Old Indefatigable on top of the filing cabinet. Whiskey in a coffee cup wouldn't be anything new, and neither would whiskey first thing in the morning, but something about whiskey from a coffee cup first thing in the morning seemed unacceptably perverse.

I lifted the bottle and put my hand on the stopper, but there was a second knock, one much quieter and more reserved. It sounded an awful lot like a customer's knock: the sort of knock that said they were sorry for bothering me but sorrier for having a problem in the first place, and still not as sorry as they would be to pay. I put the bottle back on the file stand and nudged the button to unlock the door.

Alejandro opened it and stepped inside as quietly as a cat in a bassinet, then closed it behind him with a click the baby would have slept through. Normally, the hinges squeaked and the door took jiggling to get closed. I'd always heard a golem's senses were way beyond ours, but I had no idea. I blinked and set down my coffee mug, still empty of whiskey or coffee or anything, and nodded. "Well." I tried not to look surprised. I probably failed. "Okay."

Whereas it had been dark and dramatic a few days ago, Alejandro's skin was an off-white with hints of gray where an egg's shell might have shades of beige or tan. His hair changed to a deep reddish purple. I had assumed golems were fixed in their appearance, and in that moment, it occurred to me to wonder why I ever assumed that in the first place. No reason they can't swap things around like any Plus.

Taking in his choices of colors, my mind kicked around words like "eggplant" and "burgundy" before deciding they fell short. The golem's hair was pulled back and tied into a neat ponytail. It hung so that it hit the middle of his back exactly between where his shoulder blades would have been if he were a living man. He stood maybe two meters tall, maybe taller, easily several centimeters taller than I am, so I had to look up a little to meet his eyes. It had a sobering effect: he seemed instantly superior in the social hierarchy.

I reminded myself everything about a golem is literally by design. If he was tall enough to make most people look up to him, it could only be a deliberate choice, almost certainly meant to convey authority—one I found, ironically, a little off-putting.

Alejandro had good cheekbones, a pair of pale and expressive lips, eyebrows that jutted at a barely noticeable obtuse angle over his eyes, and a prominent Adam's apple. I thought that was an unusual touch of mimicry for something otherwise obviously constructed. Why bother with the laryngeal prominence if anyone could tell he was made of some kind of cellulose and bioplas? The various design choices taken together suggested ambivalence: maybe a team expressing in their work some internal conflict about how human he should or shouldn't be, or maybe a Doc Frankenstein somewhere who was never quite at peace with the idea of his or her creation.

My initial over-analysis of his design and execution bothered me in the way I was always bothered by my detective's reflex of seeing motives behind every detail. But, I also knew a part of what bothered me about him was what bothered me about the *idea* of golems in general: no one knows who made them or where they came from. All anybody knows is they're ancient. Sometimes they're very kind, and sometimes they're assholes, and sometimes they're just sort of there, dissociated and distant in a way some people read as snobbery, and regardless of what they're like socially, absolutely none of them will admit their origins. They've been asked plenty of times, of course, and the urban legend goes that once in a while one of them will open up enough to say she or he doesn't know whence they came. I never liked that answer. It's the sort of non-answer politicians give when they want to make you *feel* like they answered your question. It's a deflection. I hate people who play that sort of game.

The fact Alejandro was drop-dead gorgeous—as walking, talking kewpie dolls go—didn't help me get over my prejudices. If anything, it made me wary. The most dangerous thing in the world is a good marketing campaign, and he looked like a doozy.

"I hope you don't mind I'm here." He murmured it with a small smile that seemed genuinely apologetic rather than the cocky sort of ironic I would have expected from some biological Casanova. "I was concerned about you."

I arched an eyebrow. Neither of us moved. I stood between the cabinets and my desk, Alejandro right inside the door, maybe five meters away. A little sunlight slid down the slats in the still-closed blinds in my window, and I still stood barefoot in dingy denim trousers and no shirt. "You figured out who I am." I pointed a thumb at the handset on my desk. "You could have called." I picked the cup back up. Perverse or no, I was going to fill it with whiskey.

Alejandro paused, something I assumed was an intentional effect since his brain probably ran ten thousand times faster than mine. "Once I knew who you were," he replied carefully, "I found out what you do and, it turns out, I need your services."

I set the cup down on the desk again, this time with a thud. "A golem needs a detective? I thought you guys knew everything." I tried to smile a little at the end because I sounded like an asshole when I hadn't meant to —well, not entirely. "Each the wise elder at the top of a mountain of secrets even their prodigious memories outlive?" I spoke it as a question, but it was a direct quote from the Spiralist texts, where it appears as a statement of self-evident fact. I am not a Spiralist, and I don't have much use for their religion, but at least they're forward-looking. I might occasionally have worn one of their St. Haraway medals solely to see scandal on the face of a Sincere, sure, but provoking offense is the extent of any dogma I might possess.

Alejandro didn't blush—maybe he couldn't—but his eyebrows sagged, and his eyes dimmed a little. "I'm sorry," he near-whispered, and his hand was on the knob again. "I shouldn't have bothered you. I'm glad you're well, M. Bakhoum." He twisted the knob in perfect silence, opened it impossibly smoothly, and turned.

"Wait." My voice surprised me with its urgency. All I did was crack a joke in the presence of a golem. I know that is—to Two-Truth Spiralists anyway—like farting in front of the Hexagonal Pope, but people had undoubtedly done worse, right? Still, I felt like a heel. "I was simply…" I struggled, caught between the desire to be true to my offense-provoking reflexes and the need to sell exactly enough of myself to pay rent a little longer. I looked at that empty coffee cup and I thought of the landlady and I knew I couldn't pay bills with pride. "I'm kidding. Come in." I nodded at the client chair—only one because no one comes to a detective's office in any state other than alone—and walked around to my side of the desk. I still didn't have a shirt, and I didn't care. Rent didn't matter *that* much. "I happen to have some room on my dance card, Alejandro. Please, call me Valerius."

Alejandro turned, not quite looking at me, as though considering something far away. I'd seen plenty of visitors to my office do the same. Lots of people have second thoughts right before they spill their guts to me. He nodded to himself, closed the door again, strode over in near-silent and perfectly paced steps, and sat down. "I need you to solve a murder." His eyes met mine, and he had that look of grim determination one gets when they know they want revenge more than justice.

"Who's the victim?" I leaned forward, putting my forearms on the edge of the desk to show I was taking him seriously. "This might be a job for the police."

"I am the victim," Alejandro softly replied. "And no, I do not mean someone is going to try to kill me, M. Bakh— *Valerius*. I mean that this is not my first body. My last one was—" In my imagination, his voice clicked mechanically when it caught for a moment. He skipped whatever the finish to that sentence might be. "And I need to know why and by whom."

"I see," I lied. I blinked my lids in rapid succession, something I could do with my face for a few seconds while that sunk in. There were a lot of potential ramifications to those few words he'd said and, like viewing a sculpture that relied on some trick of the light, I was worried focusing on any one detail in particular might make the others fall out of view somehow: like maybe if I let myself get all the way through thinking *golems have more than one body*, I would forget also to file away the memetic tendril on which was written *a golem did something bad enough to get killed for it*. "I see," I lied again.

"I doubt that," he replied, but he had a small smile that spoke to me with a gentle sort of sadness. Ancient and awed, sometimes fearsome, occasionally worshipped, always seeking to avoid being understood too well, as though allergic to the notion of becoming familiar: golems are *something else* all right. No wonder we have so many plays and stories and legends about them. They're like cats who can talk.

"Well," I went on as my usual cynicism crept back in and tried to shove aside the moment of pure fascination, "here's the thing." I nodded toward the door. "It says 'questions answered,' which is a polite way of saying 'detective,' which is itself a polite way of saying 'a lady thinks her boyfriend is stepping out,' or vice versa, and they'd like me to do the dirty work. I learn things, Alejandro, and sometimes those things are about a subject as heavy as murder, sure, but the victim has never before been the client, so we're in uncharted waters. Further, if you don't give me some significant details to start from, then I'm afraid I must confess I will quite happily take your retainer with a guarantee I will never in a million years find anything out." I smiled at him, hands open, shrugging. When it came to honesty, I had an office so clean you could eat off of the floor. I would have been a rich man many times over if I were a little bit dirty, but I was sure I would also have been dead.

Alejandro smiled again and the simskin around his eyes crinkled with precisely the right amount of genuine-seeming amusement to warm the cockles of my heart. Whoever built this guy put a lot of love into it. I won't lie, some animal part of me wanted to get all that love back out, maybe in a single go. "Okay," he murmured after a moment's consideration. I didn't let myself wonder how many operations his brain could perform in the time it took him to emote something on a human scale like that. I probably couldn't afford to count that high. "I'll tell you this: I died in Splendor." He looked off to one side, remembering, the way you do. His gaze shifted back to look me dead on. "I died when Splendor fell."

I didn't suck in a breath, didn't whimper, didn't cry out, didn't order him out of my office, but I did stare back at him in stupefied silence for a very long time. "The Fallen Ghost," I breathed. It wasn't a question.

He nodded at me. "I died when she fell, and a part of me—it's hard to explain why, but it feels very distant—a part of me remembers what it felt like when she fell. A part of me can still feel the end of gravity in Splendor and how it felt when I realized we were falling, all the way down, all the way to the end."

The Fallen Ghost.

I shuddered all over.

Ghost Drives are how we have the Cities at all. They tell us in history classes there used to be a bunch of them. Now, there's only this last one, the City of Autumn, flying high over the Global and United Empire of the Vrashabh, which everyone politely does not mention is neither global nor united. In this late and deprecated age, there are plenty of Ghost Drives in other things, too, but the engines of this City are the greatest things humankind has ever built. Tucked behind Down Preserves, Autumn's engines are the apex of engineering in the whole history of Earth. The ancients supposedly had technology, of course, but look what they did with it: they blew it. They got everything wrong. They failed to prepare for the changing world in which they lived. They were ignorant and primitive, and they didn't make good use of what they had. Overpopulation and filth are the two best controls on human populations, and the ancients manufactured both like they were going out of style.

Autumn's Ghost Drives are more than the engines of the City—more than mere locomotion or steering. They are also the brain of this vast, highly automated place. The people who built and launched the Great Cities understood human nature well enough to know we would fuck up whatever was left to our care. If everything about the maintenance of this place, its day-to-day operation, et cetera, were left to humans, it wouldn't have stayed in the air a week. Instead, it's been afloat for—well, gods, I don't even remember how long. Centuries, at least. It's been so long, it's one of those numbers we gloss over in school as kids. Anyway, the Ghost Drive manages a lot of things. It runs a lot of the City's automated systems, maybe all of them. There are smaller Ghost Drive devices here and there in the City—gyros and hovers and a handful of mag cars and some corporations own a few Ghost Drive delivery trucks as a show of power and wealth. They're specks compared to the intelligence contained in a Ghost Drive like the one running Autumn. Every city worth the use of that word feels like a living thing and, in fact, by many measures is exactly that.

A real city develops moods and tells itself jokes in the pantomime of traffic patterns and abandoned projects. A city like that becomes more than the sum of the people inhabiting it. They become networked in a way they can't quite put their collective finger on, but that doesn't make their finger any less collective. Those cities still have nothing on Autumn. Knowing there's that much Newron™ power (I always hear that trademark symbol in my head when I say it) humming away somewhere underneath our feet makes the City feel alive in a way a regular city—a patch of convenient geography, any of the many mundane land-bound lower-case-c cities—can never match.

The Great Cities were launched into the air long ago, when humankind was just starting to emerge from the Darkest Ages. Flight was being rediscovered. The Empire was young and ambitious. The Empire ran into the Eastern Expanse and their Ghosts Drives, and one thing led to another. There was what they call a *confluence,* though I suspect was more like plain old industrial espionage, and here we are: living on the back of the Great City herself like ants on the back of a turtle, like fleas on the back of a dog with nothing but charity in its heart.

Ten years ago, though, there were *two* of the Great Cities: Autumn and Splendor.

I surfaced again from my own thoughts and blinked at Alejandro. "Tell me what Splendor was like," I challenged him. "Prove to me you were there."

And that's exactly what he did.

Splendor was a lot like Autumn, by all accounts: that same sense of the City being truly alive, a feeling of the people in it being watched over. There's a feeling in Autumn, sometimes, that she's looking out for us, guarding us like a mother hen sitting on three-quarters of a million tightly packed eggs. Some of that sense of maternal affection comes from her flight patterns. She tends to stick to places experiencing the eponymous season of the year. When the southern hemisphere begins to fade into winter, she often glides into the far north of the northern hemisphere, where spring is starting to take the edge off of winter and it feels a lot like fall.

There's a practical reason, of course: those are times of the year when it rains most. Autumn's programming is a complete mystery—there's absolutely no one alive who could even begin to map the unknown trillions of lines of instructions and connections she must have been given at launch—but she exhibits patterns and must satisfy specific needs. Otherwise, the City is a sealed box, one of the locked-room mysteries writ large on a chunk of airborne landscape. One of the patterns she follows is to seek out fresh water, so we never have to worry about that. It's usually cool and often wet in Autumn. Even when it isn't actively raining, it's almost always foggy, and that fog is wet and dense because it's actually clouds. It can be cold in the City, but the wind is kept in check by the presence of the Fore Barrier. That doesn't mean we don't get breezy, but it does mean we don't all get peeled off every time she's moving at full speed.

When we glide into yet another rainy season somewhere so the water washes over us, and the trash and some of the people get dragged down the drains so the sidewalks gleam again in the moonlight, it's hard not to think Autumn loves us—loves us enough to put on a show, to take care of us, to wash us off like a mother cat and her kittens. She also warns us in advance. A literal ticker tape emerges from a machine in City Hall, and the Lord Mayor's meteorologist tells us the score for the next day or two or three. She's rarely wrong, though once in a while, a storm catches her off-guard. Whoever built this place had a lot of things thought out ahead of time. I feel like maybe the sense of companionship we all need, hovering a mile above the Earth with nothing but an ancient set of mysterious devices no one would know how to repair if they broke, was one of the things Autumn's makers considered before they cut her loose.

The thing about the Fallen Ghost, Splendor, is that she was supposedly like that but *more*. People felt at home in Splendor, whereas in Autumn we always at best feel like we've *made* a home. Splendor wasn't necessarily all streets of platinum and sterling silver trees, either. It had slums, it had rich assholes, it had cops you could buy and politicians who'd sold out. It had all the things you'd expect in a City that massive—seven hundred thousand according to official census results, and everyone guessed that was short by at least twenty percent—but it had more than that. There was something in the air in Splendor. The things written about Splendor have almost all been written in the decade since she fell, so they run toward aggrandizement, toward overstating her grandeur and flattering her the same way we flatter any dead asshole whose parents or kids might overhear what we say. Still, through all of them, there is a single thread of honest sentiment. If my so-called career as a detective has taught me anything, it's that the theme that keeps coming up, the one consistently appearing somewhere in every Splendor story, is either a willful lie or honest to gods *truth*, and it's nothing short of love. People *loved* living in Splendor. They loved visiting her. She was the last of the *nice* Great Cities, the ones people would seek out as a tourist knowing they would have a lovely time.

Plenty of people visit Autumn, but it isn't for the hospitality. People visit Autumn the same way they visit one of the Sincerity Church's monastic Pax Americana reenactments: it's one of those things they should do while they can. They visit Autumn like they're visiting the surviving and somehow lesser half of a set of elderly twins.

"So, you lived in Splendor," I admitted, and I managed not to put air quotes around *lived*, but I suspected his golem hearing could detect it in the subharmonics of my voice or something like that.

Alejandro hesitated. If he were a human, I would have said he was trying to find a way to answer the question without quite telling a lie. "Yes," he finally replied. His eyes fell a little when he said it, too, and they got a little sad, and for the first time in my interactions with him, my gut read it as nothing more than a touch of honest emotion on an expressive face. It can twist me up sometimes to see a human suffer emotional pain or distress, sure, especially when things are so bad they're showing it despite an upgrade that's supposed to make it impossible—a Plus with an entertainer template, or a Happy Housespouse who's been taking their microflora every day per the autopharm instructions.

Seeing it on a golem was *awful*. Somewhere in my psyche, I, too, was carrying around all that cultural programming about golems always being friendly or gentle, the way you tell kids if they're in trouble they should find a cop even though by the time they're a teenager they'll have learned better. Seeing those beautiful eyes—dangerous, artificial, falsely expressive, and inescapably, undeniably gorgeous—turn sad at the memory of a place he loved and by all accounts probably loved *him* was like a kick between the legs.

"I'm sorry to bring up a bad memory." I made an automatic apology, reflexive in my attempt to wipe the sadness from that face, even though he was the one who'd told *me*. I felt a need to make it up to him anyway.

Alejandro waved a few fingers, a delicate movement and at the same time the most human thing I'd seen him do so far. It was meant to sweep away an ugly moment, a throwaway gesture by someone whose every movement I imagined to be calculated and overt, like the way he'd opened and shut the door without letting the hinges squeal. "Having lived in Splendor is why I'm here. Please don't apologize for my experiences," he murmured after another of my heartbeats had passed. His eyes met mine. "Please don't apologize for anyone's experience. Surviving a tragedy beats the alternative." The corners of his mouth twisted up, and I hated my heart for the way it melted a little bit.

"But you didn't survive." My own smile was a little warier. My nose crinkled at the approach of a laugh that never arrived. "Technically, *that* is why you're here."

Now he did smile, and it almost made it all the way up his face. "True." He paused. "So what do you need to know?"

I looked around for a moment, considering how to answer him. I needed to know all kinds of things: who built him, how many spare bodies did he have, where did he keep them, what was his purpose, and how long had he been here? Those would have been the tip of the iceberg, as the ancients used to say, whatever an iceberg is, and I wouldn't even have been warming up. To buy myself some time to sort my thoughts, I looked down at my bare feet, at my bare chest. "Do you mind if I get dressed? If you're here to hire me, I ought at least shower and put on a shirt."

Alejandro smiled a little and nodded. "Feel free," he said. "You needn't be shy around me. I have no sense of shame about human nakedness."

I blushed at him. "Uh, thanks for the assurance," I muttered. "But I'm going to step down the hall."

Twenty minutes later, I was in a tie and a shirt that probably buttoned at the collar, and I had on the same mud-caked shoes I was wearing three days before when he found me at the edge of the snowline back in Down Preserves. My hair was combed back and parted on the right so it would eventually fall across my face if I moved right, the way I like it—the way I've liked it ever since an old lover told me it made me look like a star from the prehistoric age. He said I had an ancient's name and an ancient's look and they fit one another. I've always held that compliment close to my heart. It was the only thing he gave me worth keeping.

I sat back down at my desk. Alejandro sat politely, perfectly still as I moved around the room after I returned. When I eased into the chair across from him, he seemed to come back to life like a handset powering back up from sleep mode. I wondered how he powered himself, and I wondered how he recharged, and I wondered if I would ever know him well enough or long enough to feel comfortable asking.

"So, it sounds to me," I rubbed my hands together as I spoke, "like you aren't looking for someone who killed *you*. You're looking for whoever brought down Splendor. Is that correct? Because that's a much more interesting question, and you don't seem like the kind of guy to dick around with the small stuff."

Alejandro nodded his head, but he also waggled it back and forth on his neck. He sometimes used odd body language, nothing I'd ever seen a person do, and this seemed to communicate some sort of ambivalence in his response to the question. His hand also swiveled back and forth at the wrist, like a raft bucking from one side to the other on choppy water. I wondered if that was how they indicated things wherever he was built—whenever he was built. "Yes and no. I think whoever brought down Splendor did it to destroy all the artificial intelligences managing, working in, or resident upon that City."

Splendor's destruction had always been officially classified as a catastrophic failure of her Ghost Drive, but nobody really believed that. It felt like taking the ancient myths and saying Osiris had a heart attack or L'Oswalt had really been a magician. Everyone knew deep in their gut there was more to it than that.

We all saw the video of Splendor's demise: the line of thin smoke from the middle of the aft engines followed by the eruption and jettisoning of one and then two and then five of her tremendous exhaust jets. Splendor tilted to one side like a mag car with a faulty charge, began sinking, and finally crashed in the center of the Gulf Desert in the middle of one of that region's torrential seasonal rains. She came down both too far from people to hurt much of anyone and too far from people to get much help *from* anyone. In the videos, she seems to fall slowly, more like she's trying to land, but, of course, it's deceptive. If the moon smashed into the Earth, it would probably look comfortably slow if you stood back far enough, but it would be a catastrophe all the same.

Everyone knew the fall of Splendor was no accident. She flew too long, saw too much history, to fail as a *fluke*. There was nearly a war with the Eastern Expanse over it. A Legion threatened to go rogue and launch an assault on an Expanse perimeter base because so many people were sure the Expanse was behind it. The Vrashabh Emperor held his forces in check, barely, and the rogue general was hanged on video to emphasize the virtue of obedience, but people still said he was right to rebel.

"So you subscribe to theories of terrorism or war or some other sort of sabotage?" I clasped my hands together over my stomach, my thumbs up, the way life coaches do on videos. It's a way to look comfortable and confident without using their other favorite trick: mimicking the body language of the client. That's usually my gambit, but I figured a golem could probably pick up on it better than a human.

"Of course I do." Alejandro sounded certain. "Don't you?"

"I'm a detective. I always assume both that things are never as simple as they sound and that things are way simpler than people tell me." I shrugged. "I don't try to make too many assumptions without some facts to push around the plate. The *facts* are that Splendor fell and many people, perhaps most, assume it was more conspiracy than accident. Beyond that, there isn't a lot in the way of agreement to go around."

That's when Alejandro slipped. Maybe I bugged him with my resolute skepticism and my refusal to take gossip for argument. Maybe a golem is capable of petty resentment, like a child yelling *nuh-uh* over its shoulder as it runs from an argument. Maybe it was calculated.

I've spent a long time ever since pondering that last one.

"I was there, I know what I saw: an an—," Alejandro started, but he shocked himself—or seemed to—and paused in the middle of the last word. His eyes didn't leave mine for a moment, a mere fraction of a second, and then they looked at the window and the flat blinds covering them and the honey light of morning trying to seep through.

I sat up a little straighter in my chair and ran a hand through my hair to push a lock out of my eyes. "Okay. Sounds like there's plenty for you to tell me." I reached out and fiddled with my handset. It lit up red as it started to record. Alejandro looked at it and opened his mouth to object, but I cut him off. "This is Autumn, Alejandro, not Splendor. You know the rules. 'All activities may be documented.' It's written right into our charter. Don't play dumb on me."

"There was a time," Alejandro said, "when humankind valued freedom to speak over the freedom to record." He sounded a little sad and a little wry when he said it.

"Sure, and we used to fly to the moon in tubes of silver and gold." I smiled a little. "Tell all the Sincerity fairy tales you want, mister, but they probably wouldn't let you in their church, and they sure as hell won't solve your murder. That means we stick to the facts."

Alejandro regarded me with eyes I knew, had they been human, would have played for pity: maybe squinting, maybe tearing up a bit. He searched my face for something he wasn't finding, looked disappointed at its absence, regarded his own beautiful hands folded in his lap, and then nodded. "I, of course, require client confidentiality." His voice was pitched low, a hint of resignation mixed in.

I nodded. "I offer it for free."

"I'm willing to pay the standard confidentiality fee in order to be sure," he replied, mouth twisted a little sourly. "I'm a wealthy being."

I arched an eyebrow. Another item to tuck away in the woefully slim file on golems: not so much that they might or might not be wealthy, but that they had a sense of pride, and it could be wounded. "Like I said," I countered, "I don't charge a confidentiality fee."

"That must make you pretty unpopular around the guild."

I shrugged again, but this time with only my thumbs. "I need customers, not colleagues."

Alejandro smiled for a flicker of a second and then paused in exactly the way a human would have done were they clearing their throat. "In the City of Splendor, I had a job."

My other eyebrow went up this time. A golem with a job—a clock to punch, a bill to pay, a role like the rest of us—was unheard of. That's one of the things "everyone" knew about them for some value of "everyone."

Alejandro went on. "Splendor didn't have cabs." He lifted a hand to gesture at something he saw only in his memory. "No rats to drive them. There were rats for other things, but not to drive. The City's transportation network was entirely automated. Recall that Splendor was the City of a Million Souls, though the exact mathematics were debatable, and yet nobody owned a mag car. Instead, we had a vast armada of linked mags running on a neural network. Each car operated as part of an autonomous cluster controlled by one Ghost Drive. It worked like cells in a body. The Ghost Drive coordinated the routes of the nodes in appointed areas and the delivery of cars for maintenance." Alejandro shrugged a little. "I worked in maintenance." He smiled again, this time at me. "Machines caring for machines so they can in turn care for people," he said. "That's how I thought of it, and it felt good and right. There are things I don't remember because the trauma of my own death and the circumstances in which I worked prevent me from recalling any number of details, but that's the rough shape of things: I was caring for transport.

"There was a typhoon." Alejandro looked away again, into the world of memory. "Splendor operated in much the same way as Autumn in regard to water. They all did, in fact." He looked back. "The Great Cities, I mean. They all would dip into fronts, localized rainy seasons, storms, whatever was needed to keep their water supply topped off. We were suffering an unusual dry spell, and Splendor's gardens started to show it." He paused and gestured with one finger. "Water reserves were only about a third of normal. I remember getting the notice we had to reuse water to wash the mag cars." He laughed suddenly. "There was a sense of shame to that. *Shame*. We were so wasteful. I find myself embarrassed to think about it now. At any rate, we needed water, and Splendor detected a typhoon moving toward the Gulf Desert. The more accurate term was 'hurricane,' but no one uses that anymore." He shrugged, again surprising me with the naturalness of his body language. "Normally, we would fly in front of it, wait for it to pass, drop into the back third, and fill up the reserves in a matter of hours. It could be dangerous for the people of the City, so Splendor issued a general quarters announcement. The living populations were ordered to shelter. The streets were cleared, the mag cars were all brought in, the steerless busses were all parked and immobilized, the gyros and hovers all strapped down, and we waited for the storm to pass.

"Everything went exactly as planned. The streets were emptied. I remember waiting with the equipment, strapped in place, feeling lucky the typhoon formed when it did. Then I had an idea: why not use the rain to wash the mag cars, too? I wanted..." He paused and smiled at me. "This is going to seem sentimental, perhaps, but I wanted the good feeling I got from this lucky storm to wash over everything and...bless it. So I opened the vast street-level doors at each end of my sunken garage, did some calculations, and figured I could effectively turn the garage bay—the size of at least four or five tournament fields put together—into a giant washing bin. I even opened up one of the soap dispensers, vented it right onto the floor. As water rushed across the garage in great pounding waves, it picked up the soap and created a scrub cycle."

He smiled again, and I would have sworn there was something like joy in those beautiful, artificial eyes of his. I wondered whose hands had shaped them. I also laughed because the image of a garage the size of a palace turned into a massive washing machine full of soap and water was genuinely funny to me. I produced a little chuckle, nothing hysterical, but Alejandro picked it up and threw it back at me, and I was so shocked I laughed harder. A golem laughing! Now that was like hearing the Hexagonal Pope himself fart.

Alejandro's smile lingered as he went back to speaking. "During the storm, when things were supposed be so pure and beautiful and cleansing, the men entered." Alejandro stopped, and his voice caught for a second. This was the part I needed to hear. The client always hesitates to tell me the thing I need them to tell me more than anything else.

"The men were in a heavy hover, one of the ones that carries dozens of standard persons. Those hovers are huge and can withstand the winds in a typhoon." Alejandro ran his dry, artificial tongue across his dry, artificial lips. "The hover had chromatic skin shifting to match the color of whatever was behind it—sky, cloud, ground, whatever was opposite any given observer. In a place as flat and gray and violent as the edge of a typhoon, that meant slate and white and black, swirling as the massive cloud system around us twisted up and wrung itself out. I think a human could not have seen them, or would have had to look very closely. I could detect them because..." He paused. "Because my eyes were different then." He waved off any thought of explaining. "Gods below," he said. "I'm saying way too much."

I didn't say anything to encourage or discourage him. I wanted him to feel like he was expected to keep speaking.

"Anyway," Alejandro said, and he sounded more human the more he spoke, "the hover landed hard, with a massive splash, outside the garage. The doors opened on the side of the hover and out the men came. There were only a few of them: a squad of five and their escort. They carried weapons, wore suits of body armor, and each had a rucksack with something heavy in it. They had an escort who led them to the edge of the garage—right up to the door—before descending into the water. The men stepped in very gingerly, testing their footing. The water was up to their knees and getting higher, but that didn't matter. The men waded in right up to their chests while that escort led the way at the front. The whole group marched through like nothing was happening." Alejandro looked back at me, and anger glinted in his eyes. The way that anger flashed left no doubt in my mind as to his sincerity. This wasn't a calculated conveying of false emotion: the way his hand twisted up on itself in his lap as he spoke looked to me an awful lot like someone who wished he could choke the life out of a hated enemy. "Like they owned the place, Valerius," he said. "Like they owned the gods-damned place. *My* place. They paraded right in with those sacks and right through the doors into the maintenance levels, and they ended the damned world." Alejandro fell silent then, his eyes working as he remembered what came next. I needed him to tell me, not look inward and clam up.

"And then what? What happened next?" My voice was quiet.

"An hour later, we felt the first explosion. Like an earthquake." Alejandro's smile was bitter and tight. "An earthquake in a flying City," he chuckled, but his voice was as grim as a grave. "I didn't hear it, but I felt the shockwave pass through the subturf. A few minutes later, there was another, and then several at once. Then we *knew* we were in trouble because the Ghost Drive began to scream." He closed his eyes now. "We could all hear her, of course. The living couldn't, but we could. She cried out in pain and in anguish even as she gave orders for maintenance." He blinked slowly. "Splendor was both mortally wounded and her own emergency doctor. The City began to tilt to one side, so the living also knew they were in trouble. I imagined all those people huddled in shelters, looking at one another and then away again, knowing their time was over." He smiled, opening his eyes again. "Even as I wondered what I could do to help, here came the five soldiers and their escort. One of the men had been killed, so they carried him. He was not entirely all in one piece, and I mean that as a literal statement of fact. I suspect the first explosion was premature: that a bomb went off earlier than planned, and maybe that caused another to set their charge, thinking they missed a cue, but the remaining three were more disciplined. Their escort was leading the way again, and it wore a look of triumph. I knew those men did what was done. It was obvious to me. They were not trying to hide it. They did not try to blend in.

"They waded back through the water in my garage, back out the way they came, got in their hover, and left. Everything was that simple, that *mundane*. No cackling villain explaining their grand scheme. No obvious calling card or clue to identity." Alejandro looked down at his own hands again.

"Well. That's an interesting story." He started to look offended, so I put up a hand. "I'm not saying it's a fabrication. And assuming every part of it is true and accurate, it doesn't leave a lot of room for charitable interpretations." I was being insensitive about his trauma because a part of my job is not to be swayed by the emotions of a stressful situation, but this story was completely bogus. The whole thing was too tidy. A squad of paramilitary types fly in, blow up a couple of bombs, and the whole City falls? Utter bullshit. "But that isn't the same as seeing them set the charges. It wouldn't hold up in a criminal hearing."

Alejandro nodded. "I know. But I also heard them speak. One of them said to their escort, 'I want us off this rock before it hits,' and their escort told him they would have plenty of time." Alejandro quoted now from his own presumed-perfect artificial memory. "'Lieutenant,' their escort said to the man, 'This would be a cause worth dying for, but be not afraid of imminent demise. We have time in abundance.'"

I blanched a little at something in the phrasing of that quote. "Tell me about this escort they had with them." But I already knew the answer before Alejandro said it. This was the thing Alejandro had maybe surprised himself by blurting out to begin with.

"It was an avenging angel." The golem's voice steadied into a mechanical drone to bury the emotion behind it. "I saw an angel in Splendor the day the City fell. It led in a team of soldiers, and it destroyed the City, and it killed everyone who lived there—including me."

I looked at Alejandro for a long moment of silence and then surprised myself. "Standard retainer is three days. I bill expenses separately. Anything over, say, a hundred, I'll ask about before I spend it." I held out my hand. "It's good to have you as a client, Alejandro."

The golem looked just as surprised as I felt, perhaps because I took his pronouncement so calmly. But why wouldn't I? I could make a few easy bucks off a crazy golem, get a good story out of it for the next time I was respectable enough to invite to a dinner party, if that ever happened again, and in the meantime, I could have a nice couple of days off. It beat hiding from the landlady and drinking Old Indefatigable out of a dusty coffee mug.

3

Avenging angels are the cultural and historical bogeymen of the Vrashabh Empire.

No, that doesn't say it strongly enough. Avenging angels are not merely the things that go bump in the night. They're not simply stories we tell children. They're more than the monsters hiding under our beds when we're small, more than the cautionary tales we tell one another around the fire late in the night. Avenging angels inhabit the very heart of existential terror. They are an ancient legend, one we attempt to class along with those moon ships, and the Arthur Kennedy myth of betrayal and murder in Camelot, and the wastes of ancient ages. Avenging angels are the mistakes of the past come back to wreak havoc in the now.

Avenging angels are ancient humanity's original and ultimate sin. The ancients had complicated stories about snakes and gardens and the dangers of pride, of being overly ambitious, of not knowing when to leave well enough alone, of poking the universe with a stick until the universe slaps us down. Avenging angels are our version of the same thing.

Of course, no one believes in them. They're mostly something the Sinceres like to natter on about, which is always a strong indicator of raw bullshit. The Sincerity Church says avenging angels were a literal thing created by humankind in the last days of prehistory. Having largely thrown off the yoke of religion their gods placed on them—or they placed on themselves in the names of their gods—humanity tried to *become* gods in their own right by creating something new. The Sincerity Parables depict that as the time of creation for both Mannies and avenging angels. Most educated people assume this myth is a way of encoding into oral tradition the story of humankind's discovery of genetic design, barbaric and ham-fisted and messy. I can't imagine how crude those initial forays must have been or the monsters they surely created.

The ancients themselves had lots and lots of stories of their own science gone wrong. They were clearly as afraid of themselves as they were of everything else in the world. In the story of the Mannies and the angels, humankind creates two types of life, dominating one and falling to the vengeance of the other. Like I said, nobody literally believes these stories except for whackos like Obstinates or Deep Sinceres.

Crazies like that love to point out the ancients' supposed records of avenging angels: visual and textual memoirs of their fearsome power and boundless aggression. They left behind photographs of great beings, half again as tall as an average Man Plus, muscular, chiseled, even beautiful, with great white wings covered in feathers the size of a football bat. They created stills of hundreds of them swarming, destroying the fortresses and weapons of the old world, driving humankind further into the darkness it had already created for itself. The ancients excelled at faking stuff like that, though. Disaster stories were some of their favorite forms of entertainment, and they got really good at representing them in various ways.

I once boned a historian who told me the hardest part of his job was figuring out the line between the ancients' genuine beliefs and their elaborate morality tales, recorded and reenacted with equal fervor. Did they believe in demons? Did they believe in avenging angels? They certainly wrote and filmed and animated plenty of stories about both. But who *could* believe in something like that? You have to be pretty sick to want something like avenging angels to exist. That historian—whatever his name was, nice guy, though—felt the whole thing was an elaborate restatement of the collective guilt they felt for fucking over their own world. We know the ancients saw the end coming, and we know they didn't do a goddamn thing to stop it. Imagine how fucked up they must have been.

That—all that—was the first thing that made me think Alejandro (hell, maybe *every* golem) was as crazy as a king. Saying he saw an angel was way worse than saying he suffered delusions, which at least are in the realm of the possible. To say he believed in the objective reality of them was like saying he believed in the objective reality of a fairy tale. He might as well say he believed in the old gods.

Like any religious doctrine, ultimately, this shit is and always has been a way to keep someone down. In our case, it's the Mannies. The whole point is to remind everyone—especially Mannies themselves—that they were the creation of humankind, like something between a slave and a complicated pet. The Church uses it to justify their official position that Mannies will always be one step shy of fully human no matter how many nice things the Vrashabh Emperor or his bureaucrats say about them.

Our society is rigged to make sure that's functionally true, too. The economic divide between the Plusses (and other Designed) and Mannies is, in most places, too great to allow real social or political equality. As I suspect, it has always been in human history, the gap—money, power, social standing—between people is kept wide enough for most on the bottom to be incapable of climbing *up*. So we get slums and the downtrodden and a working-class scraping to buy minor luxuries they can't really afford so the upper class can scoff at them for their pretense at wealth.

It isn't enough to put down the whole Empire's most visible working stiffs, though. The avenging angel story is a reminder to the Plusses, too, to mind their place and don't try to cut the queue of history. The avenging angels, it's said, resented their creation by inferiors and thus attempted to overthrow them. It's an old story, and it's probably been around in some form since the *second* generation of primates started competing with the *first*. The moral of the myth of the angels is that we, modern humanity, should make sure our reach doesn't exceed our grasp. The Sinceres are eager to remind even their most privileged faithful they're not the top of the heap and never will be. There will always be something scarier to go bump in the night.

I've always imagined the Empire loves these legends for the way they keep the true believers feeling guilty for sins they didn't commit. Beyond that, it can be used to push a more agnostic cultural "value" of humility in place of pride. It tells people they should shut the hell up and be grateful for their lot in life, no matter how bad, because if nothing else they aren't a Mannie, and if they are, then at least an angel hasn't crept into their room at night and murdered them with its blade of living fire.

People are dumb, especially in herds. Some days, it made me embarrassed to be human at all. Being hired by a golem to chase the monster at the back of the closet was crazy, but no crazier than what lots of people were doing with their lives. And I'd been hired for money. And I'd heard a story from a golem. There were worse ways to pass an afternoon.

The only really uncomfortable thing about it was that my gut told me there was something real to what Alejandro told me. I didn't believe Alejandro had seen an angel, any more than I believed in fairies or vampires or Norlins, but I believed he saw *something*. I've had plenty of clients who told me crazy stories: some half-baked, some half-remembered, some halfway made up, sure. Nobody hires me to sell me a total lie, though. Nobody hires a detective to tell complete fabrications. Why bother?

What had Alejandro seen? I didn't have a clue. Maybe he was like a person who gets the kiss of life and comes back with a story about that tunnel of light with their dead grandma at the end. Maybe he was like the trauma victim whose mind splinters into alternate personalities to cope with what they've seen, compartmentalizing it into something the executive personality pretends it never experienced in the first place. Maybe Alejandro's memories were corrupted when they were transferred to his current body.

Another problem: Alejandro's case was a ten-year-old disaster with few, if any, survivors. Splendor's demise was like any other human tragedy: a lot of people tried to make money off of it before the fires were even out, and the truth got completely lost in the shuffle. Alejandro's claim of surviving Splendor wasn't the first I heard, and the others had all been exposed sooner or later as some sort of scam. Real survivors, if there were any, wanted to keep a low profile. Everyone's heard of someone's cousin's best friend's brother whose ex-dog survived the crash—and should never be asked about it—but all the people who got out in public and bragged about seeing it firsthand turned out to be a fake with a book they were pushing.

Maybe Alejandro was *partially* lying. Maybe he changed some details. Maybe he embellished to get me on board. I couldn't dismiss the notion Alejandro threw in mention of an avenging angel as a hook. What was on the other end of the line I couldn't know without investigating the client, too, and not only the case he gave me. Like I told him, I have a professional obligation—and plenty of confirming experience—to assume nothing is as simple as it seems *and* that everything is probably simpler than the client says it is.

After Alejandro affirmed the contract and my non-interference policy about clients butting out while I work, then went on his way, I had a long talk with myself on these points and decided the thing to do was to go out into the City of Autumn and start trying to find someone who could answer my questions—any of them—because as lazy as I am, I also suffer from the worst of the maladies of being a detective, curiosity. Like a drunk with an empty bottle, my curiosity needed its fix. For that, I had to make a couple of personal visits and follow a couple of hunches.

The sorts of people I had to talk to were probably going to be really unpleasant, but that was true on any day at the office.

The Empire is a place with a lot of religion in it, and most of the time I think that is probably one of its greatest overall weaknesses. There's a lot of piety and a lot of bullshit pie in the sky. A huge amount of escapism goes into and comes out of the religions we have these days. I suppose there's an argument to be made that we at least aren't trying to blow each other up the way people were back in the day—prehistory was basically one long religious war—but it doesn't mean we're holding hands and unlocking the apex of human potential, either.

One of the big advantages of having so much occupied surface area devoted to churches, though, is that churches are really damned good at writing things down and priests are really good at finding out secrets. I suppose most of them feel some mix of emotions at that: a little embarrassment and a little shame with an electrical jolt of titillation running through it from time to time. Maybe I should have become a priest. The pay would be steady, and they seem to get laid more.

The tragedy of the priesthood is all that valuable information goes into a black hole. In theory, they absorb it into themselves, converting it via the alchemy of their faith into an absolution so pure, so liberating, the sinner is able to run right back into the street and do it all over again without a second thought.

Not every priest is so good at making that conversion, though. Some of them let the frustration or the shock or the disillusionment bubble out into their earthly lives. They are the fine texture on the surface of faith where a creeping vine like me can gain purchase. They're the knotholes the woodpecker of curiosity can attack.

One of those knotholes was a pervert bar called Misconceptions. It skulked in the back of an alley in the freight district of Autumn, out on the port edge, where—for reasons an engineer could probably explain to me—the weather is always a little colder and the mist a little oilier than elsewhere, even if it's a slow day in freight. The puddles all have the beautiful iridescence of a chemical slick at sunset, and all the concrete looks shabby.

I genuinely love that part of town. I feel a little cleaner in comparison every time I go there.

Misconceptions isn't strictly a gay bar, I should clarify. It's really an "anything unusual" bar. There are certainly my fellow gays there, but a lot of times, they're either the ones who are trying to hide from their religion or are trying to prey on those who *are,* because their guilt makes them easy pickings. It's also a bar for humans who like Mannies and Mannies who like Mannies other than their own kind. It's the sort of bar where you can find whatever you're looking for as long as it's something you wouldn't want in the news.

There have been plenty of times my path has crossed those of other Misconceptions regulars. Our silent agreement not to speak of it, and thus protect one another from the prejudice of others, is about the only thing we all seem to have in common with everyone else who goes there. Inside Misconceptions, we tend to cluster into groups, either social groups or sexual ones. Mostly, we stick to our own kind while we try to work up the nerve to approach anyone else.

One of those cliques is a group of older Plusses who go and nurse drinks and sit together even though most of them won't talk. If I've ever seen a group of priests who are bad at hiding in the wild, they're them. Every newbie gets told who and what they are, but they like to pretend no one knows. We're all very polite about it. Beyond the rumors, though, I've had occasion to confirm it for myself.

Specifically, I was once riding the steerless and couldn't get a seat in the front, so I went to the back where the Mannies sit and simply stood at the edge between the two sections. There isn't an Arties section. I'm supposed to sit with the Plusses, even though some of them look down on me and some of them try to worship me like god's own third ball, but there weren't any empty seats there. I have nothing against Mannies, because I'm not an Imperial–class asshole, but I didn't want to push my luck with the operator, so I tried to split the difference by inhabiting the invisible boundary of social convention between the two.

No dice. I stood there approximately thirty seconds before a Sister of Sincerity got up out of her seat and offered it to me. I didn't want to take her damned seat because I didn't want her adulation. I didn't want her self-righteousness. I didn't want her to go back to nunnery that night and tell the other sisters about how she saw an Artisanal Human today and she gave up her seat for him and he looked like he might clean up well enough but isn't it a shame the world doesn't hand him a crown and a fucking scepter and a winning lottery ticket?

No—not on her life. I didn't want any part of that. I ignored her offer, straight up pretending not to hear her. I continued ignoring her when she moved over and stood in front of me. Everyone was starting to get uncomfortable. The whole steerless had gone silent. Everyone was staring. I continued ignoring her. I wasn't going to give her the satisfaction of asserting her dogma. I'm a free citizen of the Empire, and I have the right to stand wherever the hell I want, including with the riffraff.

She reached out and took my upper arm in her hand—she was old, and her hand was frail, but her grip was like iron—and shook me once.

My impulse, and I'm not proud of this, was to backhand her across the face. I didn't, though, because if anything could send her home with an even bigger god-boner than the one she got from giving up her seat, it would be getting a bruise from an ungrateful Artie in return. Instead, I smiled. "I recognize the humanity of all sentient species and reject the orthodox racism of an arbitrary barrier drawn between Humanity Plus, Artisanal Humans, and Human-Animal Hybrids." Her face fell as I quoted Spiralist catechism at her. "I embrace the Double Helix and the potential it offers us to ascend together, hand in hand in paw, to a future where all combinations are possible and all life is valued." I extended my hand to her, voice soft, "Sister, will you join me in Evolution?"

That powerful grip let go of my arm, and instead, she backhanded me, the birthstone in her Sincerity Vow slicing a thin line across my face. If you look very closely, in exactly the right light, you can still see the scar on my right cheek.

That was when the Sincerity Priest jumped up from his socially approved seat at the front of the steerless and ran up the aisle to put his hand on her wrist before she did it again. Only rarely have I seen first-hand a fury as great as hers: the rage of the fervent encountering the indifference of reality. This woman had, for whatever personal reasons seemed right to her, devoted her life to trying to build a world that elevated the original and unenhanced, the accidental, the incidental, instead of rewarding the designed. She was herself a Woman Plus, of course, but she didn't seem to detect any hypocrisy in her choice of dogma. History is full of people who benefit from a past they condemn, and any number of those persons was perfectly sincere. I had no reason to doubt her sincerity, either. She looked at me and saw what the world should aspire to, and I had replied by rejecting everything about that view.

As I say, I'm not actually a Spiralist, but sometimes I'm happy to talk the talk if it pisses someone off. I've done the same to Spiralists before, too.

The priest who stopped the sister from striking me again said in a soft voice, almost apologetic in tone, "Sister, let this young man be. Your point is made. The man does not wish to participate in our faith. We can always get off at the next stop." His eyes met mine, and I recognized him as one of the old guys who drink in that corner at Misconceptions, and that was when I knew beyond rumor they really were all priests. I wondered how many of them were Sincerity, how many were Spiralist, and how many were the other countless religions of the Empire. Those are the two biggest, but there are hundreds of other ways to try to explain the problems of the world. I wondered what kink led him to Misconceptions in the first place: not because they were difficult to imagine but because there were so many from which to choose.

The absolute silence of the steerless made me uncertain if anyone was breathing. It may be no one was especially paying attention: crazy shit happens on public transit all the time, right? In my memory, though, she and he and I were the center of the known universe and every screen in that universe was tuned to us and to what was happening.

The Sister of Sincerity didn't say anything. She looked at me, at the blood I could feel running down the side of my face, and with her free hand reached out to pull the emergency stop cable on the steerless. It slid to an abrupt halt, everyone thrown forward by the sudden loss of forward motion. The doors automatically flew open the moment we were stopped, and she unceremoniously pushed me out. She put a hand in the middle of my chest and pushed, simple as that, and her Woman Plus strength was no match for an Artie like me. One second, I was in the middle of the car, and the next, I was flat on my Artisanal ass on the sidewalk.

She stared me right in the eye as the doors shut, then she tugged the emergency cable twice to signal the all clear. The steerless operator didn't speak, didn't question her. He hit the button in his little booth at the front, and the steerless took off again, throwing everyone back into their seats.

Bars in the City of Autumn never have to close. It's an old legal loophole. They have to dismiss all patrons for a period every day in order to clean, but they don't have to shut the door and lock up, and they can let the customers right back in as soon as they're done with the daily sweeping and mopping of the floor. There are bars down in the Flank, where the party kids and the bravest of tourists and the worst of the drunks and the junkies hang out, that don't even have doors. Why bother when you're never closed? That's part of the gimmick for them, in fact. Right there on the screen ads, they'll say OUR DOOR IS ALWAYS OPEN TO YOU – *BECAUSE WE DON'T HAVE ONE!*

That is not the case at Misconceptions. It has more than one door, and they're both closed all the time, despite it likewise being a 24/7 bar. You never know when a Rat is on the hunt for a Tom, and why turn away revenue?

It was still early afternoon when I got there, and the sun would be out for hours yet, but the alley I walked down to get to the first set of doors was practically a closed tunnel, as dark as night at the birth of the moon. It felt right somehow to step from the golden light of an afternoon in the spring season of somewhere, wherever we'd flown now, and into the chill of a place the sun never touched. It whispered in my ear about all the times I'd been down it before, on the clock and off, and of all the times to come. I shook it off, pushed open the outer door, and stepped into the darkened anteroom. Illuminated only by one dim red light, the walls were covered in matching red soundproofing. I could still hear the thump of the music on the other side of the inner doorway, but the pads meant I could also hear myself think.

The Bull behind the counter gestured with a thumb as thick as my forearm. "Go on in, Val," he rumbled. "Always good to see a regular in the middle of a slow day."

I touched the brim of my hat at him. Bruce was a sweet guy for a bouncer. I'd seen him rough people up when they asked for it and, on a couple of occasions, I helped. As professionals in the lowlife-related service industry, we had a healthy professional regard for one another. I stepped up to the second door. In front was the grate for the sniffer, and a puff of cool air shot up my pants legs. There was a moment's consideration as it checked me for weapons or other contraband and then the door buzzed to let me in. I stepped through and looked around: not a lot of people, which is always good when I'm in a bar to work rather than to drink. The sort of drunk who's at a nightclub in the middle of the afternoon is probably desperate enough for something like a human connection to answer a few questions if it means someone might sit with them a spell. Especially if that someone will buy the drinks.

That's only one of the ways a bar is sad in the middle of the day: the down on their luck types drowning a sack of thoughts in a river of cheap hooch. Another is that you can see everything, even if it's actually sealed to the outside, even if they are consciously trying to make it feel like nighttime, even if it's *darker* than it would be at night. There's something in the human consciousness that finds itself picking out details it would never try to spot after sunset. Every cobweb, every mote of dust, every stained seat cushion, every place on the carpet where someone puked at some point in the past: they practically glow in the gaze of daylight eyes.

Misconceptions is no different. Even though it was almost night dark inside, I still knew the place was grungy. It smelled bad. The carpet was worn and scarred, scarred as an Artisanal Human who's lived a life worth living. It smelled like a cigar, but an old one: maybe one smoked a long time ago, maybe smoked a long time ago by a dead guy who'd started to get ripe. Misconceptions is a business on the edge in every way, and that doesn't leave a lot of margin for floor wax and smoke-eaters.

The barkeep is an old Tom named Blackie with golden eyes and a clipped ear to indicate he's been fixed. One time, when I was real drunk, I asked him about it and he said, "It paid for college. A thing they did in Balmer. If I took the clip, I got a scholarship in return for being out of the repro game forever. Seemed like a good idea. I never liked kids anyway."

I asked him what he studied, and it seemed for a solid half-minute like he was pretending he hadn't heard me. Eventually, he answered. "I studied art history," he said. I blinked. I couldn't help it. A Mannie with the soul of a scholar? The people back in Balmer must have figured the world was either very right or very wrong if that was happening. "But I dropped out. Never finished." His clipped ear twitched, at the memory maybe, maybe at something else, and he looked up at me. "Want a refill?"

That was the kind of place Autumn was, and Misconceptions, and I figured out of all those people haunted by their pasts, surely someone could tell me a little something about Splendor.

It turned out I was right.

4

Blackie looked up and nodded at me when I walked up to the bar. "Early night, eh?" He wasn't really chiding me. He was merely making conversation. He would never object to selling a drink. In fact, I found he'd already managed to mix me a cocktail in the seconds it took me to cross the room.

I shook my head. "I wish. This is a working call." I waved off Blackie's meaningful glance and half-smirking mouth. One of the things I like best about Toms is the way their body language is so similar to human. You can read their expression as easily as anybody else's, though they do the whole inscrutability thing way better than we do. "Not that kind of work, smartass. But I do need to buy a drink. Two, in fact."

Blackie winked at me. "Who's the lucky guy?"

"You tell me." I glanced around the small room, the clusters of tables and the niches of booths, the small dance floor between two sets of speakers in one corner, all bathed in the dim red LEDs of the ceiling fixtures. There were a few people around: one of the priests, one of the interamorists hoping for Creature Right to wander through the door, a couple of others I didn't particularly recognize. "Any of these guys a history professor?" I was drawling a little, emphasizing my Artie accent. People who feel like they're out on the edge open up more readily to others in the same boat.

Blackie shook his whiskers no at me. "Closest bet is Solim over there."

He flicked his eyes at the priest. "The good father is a liturgist with a taste for wine."

I glanced that direction, then back. "Never seen him before."

Blackie nodded once, a dip of his elegant head. "Been coming in a few weeks now. Always takes his wine by his lonesome."

"Old-fashioned drink means old knowledge?" I met Blackie's returned gaze. "Then set him up with a glass of his favorite while I go introduce myself."

Blackie nodded. "Coming right up."

I started to turn but then didn't. "What brings him *here*?"

Blackie's lips curled up, and one snaggletooth fang popped out to wink at me. "I have no idea," he said. "As far as I can tell, he has never once gone home with anybody from this place. Maybe he likes the wine."

"Not likely," I snorted. "It's pretty lousy wine." I gave this Solim another glance. "Looks like he's waiting for someone."

Blackie lifted one shoulder very faintly. "Perhaps he's waiting for *you*."

I made my way over to the table at which the padre was reading what looked like a damaged book, with Blackie and a glass of something red and sour-smelling following right behind.

Solim was an old Man Plus, Afrique Edition: he was tall and lithe, and his skin was the deep obsidian we tend to associate favorably with wisdom and quiet strength and a good sense of perspective on things. Over time, our culture has come to attach a surplus of moral worth to those places most fertile or most prosperous, and Afrique is the best of both. If there was anything particularly ironic about his being at Misconceptions, I figured in some way it must be that: this was a man who could go anywhere and have anything, and he was here, reading a book in bad lighting amongst the thinnest of the ass hairs of Autumn.

It suddenly occurred to me he might be one of the *real* Sinceres, valuing everyone regardless of origin the way their texts told them to do. And here I thought those had gone extinct.

He didn't look up as I approached, even as I put my hand on the back of the chair across from him and cleared my throat. He didn't react at all until Blackie glided up with the glass of wine and set it down. "Compliments of the gentleman," he purred, and then he disappeared in perfect silence.

Solim looked at the wine, reached to grasp the stem of the glass between thumb and index finger, and slid it closer to himself. Without looking at me, he spoke. "I'm sorry, son, but I'm not into Artisanal Humans." He kept a finger of the other hand on the page to mark his spot and looked back at it to keep reading once his wine was in place. He had known from the moment we walked up he would not be away from his book for long.

"Then we already have something in common," I replied, making conversation, not letting him shut me out so soon. I didn't ask if I could sit: I simply did, pulling out the chair and sliding into it. "Cheers." I held up my glass and tapped it against the side of his, a tiny little *tink*. I threw my head back and downed my drink, set the glass in front of me, and leaned my temple on my fist, my elbow on the edge of the table. "I'm not going anywhere, padre."

He ignored me for a few seconds, then a few more, then finally sighed very softly and closed his book. This time, he used a bookmark instead of his finger.

I didn't let myself grin in victory, but I wanted to.

"How can I help you, my child?" He glanced over me in a flash, looking me in the eye. "I can tell it is not for a spiritual reason."

"How do you know that?"

"You are not wearing the symbols of the Church." He said it with a slight air of annoyance, like a medic at a dinner party being asked to look at another guest's bum knee. His voice was deep and resonant but also soft. I could imagine him being gentle with some sheltered soul come to the Church in search of forgiveness for imagined sin. I could also see him telling someone to go straight to hell. "If you were a nonbeliever looking to convert, you could go to any of a number of sanctuaries. Autumn does not lack for houses of worship in which to be baptized. So, what is it you want?"

"I'm looking for someone who can tell me about a Church legend." Padre Solim was sitting leaned forward on his elbows, so I adjusted and mimicked him, slowly, over the course of the sentence. I didn't want to shift into mirroring him all at once. It's the sort of thing one does slowly. "I need to know about the history of avenging angels."

"You mean the *legend*," the father said. He didn't call me an idiot to my face, but his tone was dismissive. "Avenging angels are a myth."

"I've got a client who says otherwise." I shrugged a little, using only my right shoulder and an eyebrow, a waggle of the head: casual as could be.

"He may be crazy, I don't know, I'm nobody's analyst, but my gut tells me he saw *something*. So, here I am."

Padre Solim smiled a little. He had the sort of smile that managed to patronize and feel sorry for itself at the same time: the smile of a man who is absolutely aware he knows more than you do and is tired of your shit. It was a smile born of living in the gray twilight between the Imperials and the servitor classes. It would be wrong for him to assert too much privilege when addressing me, and it would be wrong for him to assert too little. He was between that rock and that hard place familiar to untold generations of experts in something other than being born rich.

"Your client says he saw an avenging angel? Then he's lying. Even if they were real, the myths tell us they kill witnesses without mercy or remorse. There are very few claimed sightings in history and only one supposed instance of an angel being defeated—and that tale simply served a political purpose at a pivotal point in history; in other words, he probably lied." Solim paused and looked me in the eye. "Avenging angels are the dragons of our modern age." He gestured a little, a reflex indicating a screen presentation that didn't exist. He was warming up to the lectern of the mind. It occurred to me he may have given this speech before, maybe many times, perhaps for an hour or two at a go. I signaled Blackie for another round of drinks. "If the angels of legend were real, and your client saw one, he would be dead."

"Funny you should say that," I replied. "That's exactly why he hired me: he's already died once, and he says an angel killed him."

The father smirked. "Is your client a disheveled but earnest woman named Henrietta?"

I knit my brow and shook my head once to the left, standard Autumnese for a no. "Why?"

"Just a thought. I'm sorry, but your client sounds as though he or she is quite insane."

"He may be, as I've said, but his money spends." I shrugged a little. "Do you believe in avenging angels? You sure sound like you do. You talk about them as though they are real things." He started to object, but I cut him off. "There are differences in how people speak of things they believe and things they *know*. There are intonations meant to suggest a subject is closed and locked, and the key has been painted blue and thrown in the ocean. You talk about angels that way."

"Because they are false. It's like being asked if I know how to flap my arms and fly." He sounded like he was trying very hard to be patient with a frustratingly dim child.

"The problem with that is, people only lock something up and warn people off if it's valuable: if it's *real* to them and they're worried people will steal the thing or do something bad with it. If you really believed angels to be a myth, you might laugh, you might call me names, you might get up and walk away, but you wouldn't work so hard to keep me from asking again." I smirked a little. "Trust me, padre, you and I aren't in such different kinds of business."

"They are an article of faith," Padre Solim said, and I'd swear I caught a whiff of irony when he said it, like maybe that was a pat answer he simply got really good at delivering. "Of course I believe in them."

"No." I shook my head. "Genetic randomization is an article of your faith. The elevated social value of Arties like me, that's an article of your faith. The divine right by which the Vrashabh Emperor rules, that's an article of your faith. That the Hexagonal Pope speaks for the Ancestors, that's an article of your faith. You believe in a lot of things, pops, but they're mostly reflections of the political status quo or a way to keep your indoctrinated base in line. You don't believe in much that's impossible: the continuation of our civilization and something to piss off your biggest rivals, and that's it. If the church really believed in avenging angels, you'd have machine gun nests on top of your steeples. I haven't noticed any in this town. Have you? And yet, you shifted tactics on me when you realized you couldn't throw me off with Plan A. You had a Plan B ready to go."

Solim looked at me long and hard. "What do you want to know?" He was ready to get my cheap shoes out of his two glasses of free wine.

"I want to know the *history* of avenging angels. I want to know if Leonidas Minos and Baelor Unconquered were real people. I want to know if they actually fought side by side to defeat an avenging angel. I want to know why you, personally, believe in the bogeyman. I want to know if it's *possible* my client is telling the truth. I want to know why you don't want to answer the question." I paused. "That's for starters."

Solim listened and formed a small, soft smile. It was jarring because, so far, he'd done such a bang-up job of failing to live up to the Wise Old Padre thing he had going with his look and now suddenly, he was oozing empathy behind his harsh response. "Read a book," he said. The smile grew. "It's all there. I suggest a third-year primer on the social history of the Empire. It will have a great deal to say on the heroism of the first Emperor and on his friend Baelor."

"No." I leaned forward by a hair. I was tired of all the mixed signals. I stood up, pissed off at this guy and not even really sure why. He'd done nothing but give me the standard answers. Maybe that was why I was pissed off. Still, to know there was more back there behind his eyes—to know there was more to this story and the only thing between it and me was an old man saying no—I couldn't accept that. "Fine. I'll find somebody else who can tell me why an avenging angel would have been behind the death of the City of Splendor."

I turned to walk away from the table, and a vice clamped down on my arm from behind. I stopped dead and looked down at the ebony hand around my wrist. I followed it back up the arm to the shoulder and then to the eyes of the priest. They were narrow and bright, and he was every bit as suspicious as he was intrigued. "What did you say?"

I shook his hand off, or tried to, but the glue had apparently set. "Nothing. Something I shouldn't have. I'm supposed to be keeping it all confidential."

"Fuck your client's confidentiality agreement," the padre cursed. It shocked me. I flinched where I stood. "Tell me what you know about Splendor."

I eased back onto my seat, my arm lifting so he could maintain his grip. "And you tell me what you know about avenging angels."

This time, the priest considered for a long time. "Instead, I'll put you in touch with someone else." I started to tell him what he could do with his someone else, but he put up two fingers—he didn't even move his whole hand, only his index and middle fingers in the tiniest gesture indicating I should wait. I stopped dead and waited while he produced a sharp, very expensive stylus and started scribbling on a napkin. "She is why I believe in the bogeyman, Mister...?" He laughed suddenly, a single deep chuckle that sounded like a rock coming to rest at the bottom of a dry well.

"Valerius Bakhoum." I realized I was short of breath, and I didn't even know why.

Solim nodded at the name. "The Lion. A good name."

I shrugged. I'd never paid it much attention. "Whose name are you giving me?"

He handed me the napkin and smiled again, but this time much more tightly. "Henrietta's. The person after whom I asked a few minutes ago.

You have your clients, M. Bakhoum, and I have mine. She will have to forgive me for referring you and forgive you for turning up unannounced, I suppose, but she is almost certainly going to be home no matter when you visit her."

"Don't worry." I gave him a nod. "I'll send a polly to let her know."

"I wouldn't recommend it." Solim still had that same tight smile. "Henrietta has a terrible phobia of things that fly."

"When I was a girl." Henrietta spoke it like every fragment was a complete sentence, full stop. A moment later, she drew a breath and plunged on. "I saw an angel." She blurted it out like that, without any window dressing, and that was how I knew she was telling the truth, or believed she was, no matter how patently crazy she was otherwise. People who lie usually try too hard. When someone tells you something straight out, no frills, it's because it doesn't need frills. In their minds, it's true. It stands on its own two feet.

I nodded at her and took a sip of tea. This was by my count my fourth cup, and I was dying to take a piss, to be perfectly frank, but I didn't dare stand up. I didn't dare interrupt her. We sat in silence for a long time after I arrived and told her I was an acquaintance of Padre Solim's. She didn't ask about what topic I'd called. She didn't ask my name. She didn't even ask if I wanted the tea. She simply nodded, walked over to her kitchcube, and started rattling things around. I wondered if I was being ignored so I would leave or if I was being ignored because there wasn't room enough in her mind for more than one thing at a time. She was incredibly old, at least a century and a half, and I couldn't imagine the strain being exerted on her Woman Plus genetics to keep her going. If she were an Artie, she'd be dead already for a quarter century or more, and that's being generous. Her skin was beige and her hair the sort of white you get if you wash a sheet too many times: not really white but not really gray either, a color you don't even notice is a color until you see something next to it.

When Henrietta was done in the cube, she turned around with two cups and saucers, spoons, a teapot, the whole outfit. Her place was like one of the "living sincerity" homes the Sinceres liked to show off when you tour a monastery. She brought the cups and everything on a little tray, shuffling over to the small round table between two high-backed chairs. One looked worn and crushed, telling me and her and anyone else who had eyes to notice that it was her chair and she sat in it every day. There was a small screen nearby, kept where she could swivel it and get a good view, and I figured those few details probably summed up a great deal about the day-to-day existence of this woman named Henrietta.

Funny, though: her place didn't smell musty and there wasn't dust everywhere. I figured Solim probably kept her in decent cleaning nanos out of the kindness of his heart. Most places, most people this old, the oldness gets a chance to really settle in and nothing comes along to clean it up. Henrietta's place wasn't like that. It looked maintained. I would have thought she just moved in except she knew the place too well. Her movements about it were well-practiced.

Because the tray had two cups and two saucers and two spoons, I knew I wasn't being thrown out. After Henrietta slapped my hand away from trying to help, I slid into the chair and let her put everything in place. Then she told me we would sit until the tea was done steeping, and after *that,* we could speak.

It turned out to be more like three and a half cups of tea had to be consumed, also in silence, but if a detective has to be anything, we have to be patient.

"We lived in Sea-at-Atoll." Henrietta paused a long time, but eventually she spoke again and seemed to pick up steam. "There were mining operations. A few hours inland by gyro, to the north." Henrietta assembled tidy little phrases, cut them off at a specific length, and moved on to the next. "The city was an important supply depot for them." Her gaze drifted off over my shoulder, into some distance I couldn't see, a place I'd never been nor heard of, whatever place produced these terse fragments for export.

Sea-at-Atoll was a city, I knew that, but I'd never been there. The look on Henrietta's face told me she was seeing it in her mind's eye, like she was there again, and something about that expression told me it was a place to which she knew she would never get to return. I wondered what she'd done that was so bad. At her age, it may be nothing worse than getting old and frail.

"A lot of soldiers around in those days. Empire and the Expanse always testing each other's borders. We were near one. There were bases, a shipyard. Things you associate with a frontier. Lots of resources. Easy money and terrible people. Weapons to keep them safe from one another. We had Ghost drones in airspace at all times. Trying to watch for Expanse vessels. We never saw any Expanse, though." She smiled a little, but it had equal odds of being bitter, sincere, or polite. "All those soldiers and sailors for the Empire. Basically sitting there waiting to be among the first to die in next war. We were selling food and clean water and booze and everything else. To all the miners up and down the Rock. That was our whole industry. Large-scale supplies supply." Henrietta smiled again, and this time, it reached her eyes. "I always loved that term 'supplies supply.' The redundancy is funny, no?"

I didn't laugh, but whatever. I didn't make the joke.

"I was eight years old. Just graduated and beginning an apprenticeship in a factory. Near the waterfront. They were dumping the waste right back into the sound. Suck up some water on one end. Run it through the machines at pressure. Shoot it out the other end with all the muck it picked up. Repeat. I was on one of the top floors. There were huge windows facing south and west. That way solar panels on some of the machines would get maximum charge. We had to charge batteries off the sun to keep the place running at night. That was when the utility company shut the power off. We were lucky at the factory because we got power for most of the day. As soon as it was dark, though?" She made a noise with her mouth like something powering down, a sort of dropped off onomatopoeia of a mechanism halting: "*Berooooooooop.*" Now I laughed, but she didn't.

"I used to stand at those windows in the evening. I watched the sun set over the ocean." Henrietta's gaze took on a slightly dreamy quality. "It was beautiful. It was nothing like what we get up here, yes. But, it was beautiful. It was different. All the pollution." She smiled again. "It made for beautiful sunsets."

Again, I didn't want to interrupt her, but I sure as hell wanted her to get to the point. I cleared my throat, and that seemed to wake Henrietta up a little.

"I was watching out those windows," she said. "I was watching the sky. Right at sunset. I noticed something dark in the giant, blinding, half-set sun. I shouldn't have been staring right at it. I did sometimes anyway. It was so...powerful. A part of me thought maybe. If I stared hard enough. Maybe something would be revealed to me. Something from the past. Something from the ageless sun. Something from the future." She looked at me now, back in the present. "We were Solarians."

I blinked. They were an unusual bunch. It was funny to think of one converting to Sincerity.

"That day, there was something there. And it was getting bigger. And then it was getting a lot bigger, still. I called out to the other kids.

Everyone ran over in time to see the figure. It was a person. It resolved sufficiently for us to realize it had wings. It was *flying*." Henrietta shuddered a little at the memory, and that's when I decided she was telling the whole truth. This wasn't an act and it wasn't a lie and it probably wasn't a hallucination. People can be very good actors, but the viscera is its own lie detector, and she had a real, involuntary, spasmodic response to the memory.

For the first time in my entire life, I realized I felt something a little like fear over someone's angel story.

"That angel," she breathed, barely audible. "It was a monster. It was a campfire story come to life. It had no weapons. No armor. But it was gargantuan. It flew straight into the city. Right at the docks. There was a new ship. I read later it was an Imperial Navy ship. Preparing for its shakedown cruise. Very new, very advanced technology. One of the most powerful Ghost Drives ever in a ship that size. The angel swooped down on it, screaming." She swung around and looked right at me this time, her old black eyes boring into my gray-green ones. "I wrote a report on it. For the factory owners," she said. "It was important. I remember it."

I nodded at her, teacup to my lips, no longer drinking. I was afraid if I had another drop I would burst like a balloon.

Henrietta didn't slow down after making her point to me. She looked away again, back in the land of memory, gazing. "We were at least two miles away. But I remember that keen, that wailing. It sounded like madness incarnate. And that's what it was. It didn't try to land on the ship. It flew through the hull. You know, in one side. Out the other. Then it spun around in the air. Hovering long enough for half the city to look at it. It shot back through from the other side. Then it turned and did it again. And again. *And again*. It didn't seem to hurt the angel. Not at all." Her eyes had widened a tad, and her lips had gone pale. The color drained from her face. "It was like a child. Putting its whole fist through paper."

"What about the ship's defenses?" My mouth was dry. "It must've had, I don't know, cannons or something."

"Of course," she said, "but it didn't get a chance to defend itself. The angel came out of the sun. It was invisible to most. A surprise to everyone. In maybe twenty seconds, the ship was listing to one side. It started taking on water. Its crew began to abandon it." Henrietta sighed a little. "We live in an age of ignorance and cowardice," she said. I wasn't exactly sure why.

We sat in silence for a moment. "So it showed up and sank a boat?"

"I wish it were so simple," she said. "It sank the ship. Then it threw itself into the mass of sailors. Many of them were on the docks. Some were in the water. The angel killed all of them." She glared at the surface of her tea, or at the insides of an empty cup, as though there were something hateful there. "The angel killed every single one of them. A few of them had weapons. They tried to use them. They were meaningless. My fellow workers and I stood. Pressed to the window. We watched as hundreds of people were murdered. Where they stood. Where they ran. Where they swam. Screaming in anger and fear. The angel was so fast and so powerful. It killed everything it could see. It killed with its fists and with its bare open hands. It tore people to shreds in its grasp." The color had gone out of Henrietta's face, but she didn't weep. She didn't even tear up. A liar might have felt pressed to put on some degree of a show to sell the story, but she simply repeated it. She said it in a flat voice without a lot of embellishment or effort or emphasis. She was presenting it as an ugly set of facts on which she didn't like to think too long.

"So, if I might ask, why did you tell all this to Padre Solim?" I shrugged a little at her. There were a lot of other questions to which I would rather have had the answers, but I didn't want to offend her. I didn't want to scare her off from talking. There were a lot of reasons why one might not tell a priest something like this, not least of which included the padre's legal obligation to notify the health authorities if someone confessed something suggesting mental illness. I couldn't imagine something likelier to have her branded as a dangerous crazy than telling people she believed in angels. In light of that, I was curious to know why she *had*.

Henrietta didn't look up at me. Instead, she looked over at a small bookshelf built into the wall. I couldn't see the titles from where I was sitting: another cost of being Artisanal. She probably had no trouble reading the spines, with the eyes of a Worker Plus. Maybe that was why her cleaning bots were so good; she would notice dust and grime more than a lot of people. Maybe that was why everything smelled of cleaning solvent. Maybe having to smell solvent so strongly every day was what drove her mad. I couldn't begin to know how overwhelming she must find the smell. To me, it was a hint, a distant memory of scent. To her, it must have been like getting sprayed in the face with disinfectant.

After a space of two breaths, Henrietta spoke again. "Some things are too great for us to contain them," she finally murmured, with the voice of a younger woman, a younger woman who had already seen and contained more than she wanted. "I thought at first there would be some...action."

She smiled, and the smile was the bitter smirk of the old woman she'd become with all that stuff still inside. She set the cup down and returned to the here and now in a way she hadn't since she started speaking. It seemed to take some effort. "I wrote a report on what I saw. So did any number of my colleagues. The thanks we got was a lecture from a factory supervisor. Told us she would have us fired or shipped off. To Wyandot or someplace else. If we kept spreading *crazy stories*." Henrietta cleared her throat. "I was a child. I was on my own. Times were hard. Everyone was afraid. Afraid of war. Afraid of each other. Afraid of fickle circumstance. Afraid of starving. I tucked that experience away inside myself. Deep down. Hoped I would never find it again as I rummaged in the drawer of the mind."

She smiled a little, and as I reached to set my empty tea cup on its saucer, her hand snaked out and grabbed mine. I dropped the cup. It didn't break, but it made a clatter. She didn't startle. She simply stared at me. Her eyes bore into mine, intense and dark and angry at someone or something, maybe at me if that turned out to be convenient, and they held a spark of madness anyone could see. "I dreamt of that angel. Every night. For *twenty years*. I found myself doodling it. In the margins of magazines. On the steerless. I found myself drawing it in the dust of the factory's ladies' room. I converted to Sincerity. I thought they would be able to sit me down and tell me none of it had been real. I thought I could forget it if I tried. I spent a while trying to drink it away. I couldn't, you little bastard." The mad gleam grew and became all the light there was in Henrietta's eyes.

Henrietta went on, more animated than ever. She dropped my hand, but I didn't move it, too entranced by her sudden transformation from sweet old lady to mad hag. "That angel kept flying. Out of the sun of recollection. Across all my attempts to wipe it away. If I could have stabbed my memory. In its own eye. With an ice pick. To blind it. I would. I certainly goddamn tried. I've lain in an alleyway sticking drugs you'd need two friends and extra letters to spell." She laughed all of a sudden and her teeth were almost all gone. The ones still there were bright orange, the color of someone who's done a lot of street plenitude. "I hated myself for seeing it. I hated it for existing. No one would help me with seeing it. Nobody wanted to believe. The Church of Sincerity. Its priests. Its Hexagonal Pope. They didn't want to hear about the crazy junkie. Who watched a few hundred people die. At the hands of the monster. At the back of their closet." She smiled as though she had made a grim joke.

"They didn't want to consider. All those stories they tell their children. About being good. Or the angels will come. How maybe they're true. How maybe they really do have something to fear."

I swallowed air that felt like a mouthful of sand.

"But one Sincerity Priest listened," Henrietta said, and just like that, all the wind was gone from her sails. She sagged backward in her chair, her eyelids drooping, her face falling inert. "Padre Solim at least listened. I don't know if he believed me. He never said. But I *believed* he believed me." Henrietta's eyes fell closed. "Those are the depths to which that angel forced me," she said, her voice softening, not bothering to reopen her eyes. "To be so desperate. As to take a belief in *belief*. Recursive faith. Nothing...more." She made a soft noise of gentle but thorough disgust. Her chest rose and fell but more and more gently so that a minute later, I was unsurprised when she snored.

I let myself out. I wasn't sure I had any answers now, but I could be certain there were people who still really believed in angels. As with Alejandro, I knew in my gut Henrietta had seen *something* and was so traumatized by it her Woman Plus psychological baselines had been stretched until they snapped.

5

"Why do you think I sent you to speak with Henrietta?"

Solim was again at Misconceptions, this time with a small stack of stills on paper and a little paper notebook on which he was taking notes in a script I didn't recognize. I wondered if it were some sort of custom shorthand, maybe something Sincerity Archivists learned for their work. It looked very fluid and he could write —notes to himself, maybe, or some other observation—without slowing down. But he used an alphabet completely unfamiliar to me and drastically different from the complex script the Empire uses in its official documents, the one that uses both hands and the bureaucrats spend years practicing before they're allowed to produce it for actual public consumption.

I slid into the seat across from him, Blackie hot on my heels with my drink and a fresh one for the priest. I considered for a moment. "Either you wanted me to understand how crazy someone has to be to believe in avenging angels," and here I held up my hands, miming weighing the options against one another, "or you wanted me to know how terrible they really are. If the latter, assuming they're actually real, it would go a little ways toward explaining why everyone pretends they're *not*."

"That is not an answer." Solim looked a little disappointed. He capped his stylus and set it to one side before turning his notebook over onto one of the stills, so I could see neither the writing nor the pictures. "That's a list of possible answers."

"I'm a detective. I don't figure everything out in one go. I produce a list of possibilities and eliminate them one by one until there's only the correct answer left." I shrugged. "Don't hate me for doing my job, and I won't hate you for doing yours."

Solim smirked a little. "Okay. I sent you to speak with Henrietta so you could understand how dangerous angels are." He put his stylus down in the notebook and tied the string to close it up. "I think you should know what you're getting into if you really want to investigate this topic. It seems only fair."

I knit my eyebrows together. "Why? Is someone in the church going to get pissed off because I'm asking around about your legends? Or is an angel going to show up in the night and tear me limb from limb like one of Henrietta's sailors?"

Solim met my gaze, his own steady, his aura of priestly authority and gentle concern fully engaged. "No one in the modern Church knows enough to give a damn about you asking questions." With that sentence, he consigned his entire Order to irrelevance. "That leaves only one of your two possible answers left. I believe, according to what you said, that means it must be the true one."

"Padre," I drawled, "you're twice as crazy as Henrietta. At least she has the excuse of being old. I don't know what happens after a Woman Plus runs clean out of telomeres, but you don't have the same excuse. Yet."

Solim was not offended. To my surprise, in fact, being told he was simply insane seemed reassuring: he relaxed and leaned back in his seat, pushing away from the table and crossing one of his legs over the other at the knee. He settled in for a moment and smiled softly at something before tapping the pile with the notebook and stills with his fingertip. "M. Bakhoum, I am a historian. I have devoted my career within the Church to the study of our history in an attempt to bring it forward with us into the future. I have sought to understand how our ancestors lived, what technologies they knew at what times in the past, how their cultures formed and evolved and interrelated. I've examined questions of how the continents were colonized and when and by whom, of who built the great monuments of the land of your name, of when they were built. I have not answered many of those questions, but like you, I have eliminated some possibilities."

He reached up and detached the small spectacles he was wearing from the bridge of his nose, rubbing his eyes with his free hand. "Are you familiar with the Bergley Theory?"

I shook my head at him. "Doesn't ring a bell."

"Perhaps you've heard of it as the False Drought Theory?"

Now I narrowed my eyes to slits. Crazy I could handle, sure, but conspiracy theories were not my area of expertise. Life is never as complicated as they make it out to be. I find them a little insulting on a professional level. "Never mind, padre." I stood up, downed my cocktail in a swig, and set it down. "Have a nice day." I turned to go. If this was the kind of time-wasting bullshit Alejandro's case was going to have me haring off after, I could return the retainer and call it quits. I'd make the rent some other way. I could find another case, or I could go sell my ass to some Spiralist with a kink for throwbacks. Hell, there would probably be one here now.

"The ancients could have cured your cancer," Solim said.

I stopped walking. I never told Solim about that. I never told anyone. I was diagnosed at a Spiralist clinic. This guy hadn't been there. He wasn't even a Spiralist. The Spiralists have a lot of wacky shit going on, but they know their genetic medicine, and they tend to be damned good at the confidentiality clause. That's why it costs so much. I turned around and looked at him. "Say that again." My voice was low and tight, and my lips were pressed into a flat line. I barely separated them to speak.

"The ancients cured cancer all the time." He looked at me with something like real kindness, and I fucking hated him for it. I didn't need kindness. I needed gene work. That was one of the prices of living in a society where the Sinceres got to call a lot of the shots in the Imperial Senate; as an Artisanal Human, I was off-limits for the genesmiths. In theory, the Spiralists had total freedom to practice their faith as they wished; in practice, that didn't extend to anyone not Human Plus to begin with. That leaves Arties up shit creek without a genetic retroviral injector paddle. The Spiralists were very apologetic about being unable to treat me. I tried to bribe them, I'm not proud, and that was when they went from apologetic to pitying. I hated their pity, and I hated Solim's too.

He was still speaking to me. "There are very clear records: they used radiant energy, certain chemicals, any number of things. Their mastery of science far exceeds what we like to think or what we tell our children in school. You've heard the standard histories your whole life, of course, so why the hell should you believe me? You shouldn't. Everyone knows humankind stumbled onto the existence of DNA and RNA at what was, for the ancient world, a time of technological greatness, though it pales in comparison to our own. No Ghost Drives, no Mannies to do the sweeping up, no Plus baselines, no genetic therapies, nothing but whatever chromosomes their parents gave them and enough chemistry to poison their own world to death." He smiled, but his expression was sharp and bitter, a serrated edge on the knife blade of cynical certainty. "But they could do wonders of which we only dream, too: well, those of us who need such wonders, anyway. I believe in those wonders. I've seen too much evidence of them. I think they could do amazing things with their machines. I think someone or something has worked ever since they fell —worked tirelessly and continuously—to keep us from regaining that lost greatness." He sounded sad as he said it, and I was a little sad to realize he really believed it.

"More fairy tales." I shook my head. "More make-believe for the factory of dreams you call a religion."

"Do you know the ancients had universities?" Solim picked up his stylus and stared at it, his voice sounding deeply sad. "You don't even know what that word means, probably. It's an ancient one. They were places of advanced learning. People would study for decades to get into one so they could study a specialty, discover new things, share their learning. They generated knowledge beyond our comprehension or imagination. They left detailed records. Some of those records were paper, and I've read them myself. It's no conspiracy, M. Bakhoum. No one made up whole buildings full of dissertations on the electronic devices they developed. No one made up floor after floor of writings about their sciences and their advancements. The ancients destroyed themselves, yes, but I think we could have rebuilt from what they had. I think we could have a world with at least some of the things they created."

He drew a breath, long and deep, but slow and weary, and also wary of what it was about to be used to say. "I think someone has been keeping us from doing that. Throughout the history of our culture, from prehistory on, every time we nearly achieve some new breakthrough—every time trade increases or collaboration between the Empire and the Expanse looks promising, or there might be real cooperation and unity between different factions within the Empire, every time people start to discover things, every time someone starts trying to use science to lift us *all* up, something *happens*. Our best and our brightest disappear. Our proudest achievements are destroyed."

He gestured around himself vaguely with his empty hand, then looked at me, right in the eye, and I could see he was not insane. Henrietta had in her eye the gleam of the true believer whose faith is a kind of madness. Here, in front of me, the nearest priest of her faith was telling me something equally mad but with perfect rational certainty. "Our Great Cities fall inexplicably out of the sky and no one can figure out why. Every now and then, we figure out a clever machine and we strap a Ghost Drive to it, and it works—but we can't explain it, and when it breaks, we can't fix it. We simply build another and let the Ghost figure it out." He looked around the room, gesturing sharply with the stylus at the world beyond. "But there are fewer and fewer of us who can even do that. The ancients went to the *moon*. They went deep beneath the sea and found life there they could never explain. They sent machines to Mars. They photographed the surfaces of other worlds.

"M. Bakhoum, we refer to the time of the Fall as the Darkest Ages, but I am telling you that for all the wonders of our world, we are living in a far darker era. Our achievements are nothing compared to theirs. At best, we have stolen the good ideas of the Expanse and turned them to our own ends and gotten very, very lucky. Someone is keeping us stupid, M. Bakhoum, and I think it's the angels. Over and over again, for thousands of years, we take a few steps forward and then an angel shows up to wash all that away. What did Henrietta tell you about the ship she saw destroyed?" I didn't say it, but I thought it: the ship had been new, one of the biggest Ghost Drives ever installed on a seagoing vessel. "What did your client tell you he saw destroyed? It brought down the greatest of the flying cities, the one where people were actually *happy* again. Think of Leonidas Minos and Baelor Unconquered and their gyrocopter battle from ancient myth: an angel was attacking the city we now know as the capital of the Empire. It had been the first city where humans and Mannies tried to live in peace and the first place, after the Collapse, to assert itself over other places in a stable way." Solim looked at me as though a few anecdotes, a few historical oddities and bedtime stories, added up to a convincing argument.

"How did you know I have cancer?" I walked back to the chair in which I'd been sitting, but I didn't sit down in it.

"The faint circles around your eyes," Solim said. "To most people, it probably looks like you don't sleep well, but I know metalspur when I see it. You've been taking dried metalspur to try to control it, yes?"

I nodded at him.

"It'll kill you even faster than the cancer," he said. "The ancients knew of it, too." He sighed. He didn't love saying this, except for the part of him that did, and that was the part of him I hated. "They considered it quackery. The ancients saw it as a poison."

"Maybe I'll start listening to those assholes," I said, "when they show up in their magic machine and tell me themselves."

"Keep taking metalspur," Solim replied, "and you'll be able to ask them yourself in the afterlife."

I went out that night and got good and drunk. I didn't go to Misconceptions because I was afraid I'd run into that bastard Solim again. I didn't want to look at his smug face. I didn't want to watch him judge me from behind eyes that could put on wisdom and a kindly demeanor the way most people put on a pair of boots. I didn't know whether to believe eyes like that. Normally, that isn't such a problem—who gives a goddamn what some cultist says?—but in this case, just this once, I wanted part of what he said to be true and part of what he said to be false, and I couldn't quite see a way to only getting to believe what I wanted of it.

The stuff about angels showing up every time we get too big for our cultural or technological or historical britches, that part was crazy on the face of things. All I had to do was walk around the Great City of Autumn and know it. We had achieved a greatness with which no prior iteration of humankind could compete. Neither our parents nor our grandparents, nor the pre-Fall ancients, nor whatever hut-dwelling savages they considered to be their own forebears, had done anything so great as what the Empire and her Cities had done. There were those who might say the Expanse and its Armada were as great, maybe greater, but those were ships of war, not ships for people. I considered that one of the greatest of the many things that makes the City of Autumn so special: it's for *people*. Oh, there were the haves and the have-nots, and you can bet your last credit the haves all had PlusPlus™ Genes and the have-nots mostly had scales or whiskers or plain old Artie lotto genetics, but ultimately, we were all people and we all had to share this town whether we liked it or not.

At the back of my mind, a little voice whispered. It said, *Splendor was for people, too, and was better at it, and an angel showed up and destroyed it.* I shoved a booze-soaked sock in its mouth, though, and kept walking.

In the absence of being able to wash up at my usual haunt and drink until the dead went back to sleep, I wandered the crisp, cool night of a springtime sky somewhere over Afrique Nur. I had plenty of false warmth running through my veins, and I wondered to myself whether we were actually over Afrique Nur yet or instead flying through the dark night over NurAtlanta. In my mind's eye, I saw endless crashing waves, the violent turbulence of NurAtlanta that makes it so difficult to get small ships through that blighted ocean, one of the vast plastic Sargasso seas the ancients left behind. I imagined Solim standing before me, going on and on about the advancements of the ancients, the dead cultures he believed knew so much more than we do. I imagined kindness and cloying wisdom clouding those patient eyes until I realized I'd balled up my fists in hopes of landing a punch. Then, I imagined pulling a big lever so a trap door opened under him. In my mind's eye, Solim fell, screaming the many thousands of meters between Autumn and that dead ocean. NurAtlanta roiled and crashed upon itself in the infinite patternless repetition of the sea at night, swallowing him up and sealing him away.

Wherever we were, it had been winter not too long before. The air beyond the City's net was cold enough still to be chilly when it got to us. Moist and salty air washed over the City. It smelled and felt good, and the tension between the warmth of the cheap hooch in my blood and the heat-sucking chill of the air was perfect. They kept me balanced on the knife's edge between anger and intrigue, or perhaps between rage and bleak sorrow.

Solim was right, of course: I was dying, and I knew it, and the medic knew it at the Spiralist clinic, and nobody could do a goddamned thing. They said it was my pancreas and it would kill me, but not for a little bit longer. Until then, I was going to have to work and try not to think about it.

They told me that a long time ago. I didn't really have very long left, probably, and the closer I got to my drop-dead date—a dark chuckle in the night—the harder it became not to think about it.

I snorted aloud, like I was huddled in a corner with myself and we were sharing a joke. *Try not to think about it,* they said. Fat lot of good that sort of advice was going to do me, wasn't it? Try not to think about it. Try not to think about dying, about pain, about your body coming after you with the thin knives it can hide in its sleeves. Try not to think about how they could cure this ninety-nine times out of a hundred if you didn't scream Artie at them every time you walked into a room. Try not to think about how the Church of Sincerity, the very same assholes who tell any idiot who will listen that Arties are the best humanity can ever offer, are the ones who won't let you get worked on. Try not to think about how you're a pawn at the bottom of the box in a game they are constantly playing in the Imperial Senate. Try not to think about death. Try not to think about *it*.

So, there I was, thirty years old, scarred, my hair turning a little gray at the temples, my cheeks starting to sag, my guts waiting behind the door to wrap a garrote around my neck, trying to make enough scratch to keep the landlady off my ass and the nearest willing fellow in it. *Try not to think about it*, they said.

Merely remembering that kind of talk could even happen—that we lived in a world where one person could say that to another—made me need another drink, and the thirst didn't seem to go away after one or three or six or ten.

Eventually, it was so late at night as to be nearly the next morning, and I was on my feet mostly to spite the rest of me. If I was going to die at some point because of this shit, then I was sure as hell going to the grave exhausted. I drank my way through all the bars where I could get a drink on a promise or with a kiss, then I worked my way down to places where I had to spend actual coins to bank the fires of intoxication. What was at first a manic, drunken carouse turned into more of a busman's holiday of staying drunk and thinking too much. I needed to drink because I needed to drink, and I was going to see the job through to the end. Now, with light starting to appear over the eastern-facing Fore Barrier, I was slogging my way west through streets already bustling with the early risers. The sun had not yet risen, and I was determined to watch it do so from above the snowline in Down Preserves. If I was going to die frightened and in pain and very probably alone because of those Sincerity Church bastards who maintained the Preserves, who funded them, and whose coin and affectation of gravitas bought them anything they wanted, then I was going to take with me every single sunrise I could find, and I was going to steal them right out of Sincerity's own goddamn park.

That's the sort of thinking death and hooch make happen when you let them slosh around together for too long.

Technically, Down Preserves closed at night, but that didn't matter to a very specific segment of the population. By this, I refer to people who go somewhere public at an hour when that place is very nearly private and fuck each other in the shadows. I'd discovered this when I was a teenager and I ran away from home. It was a thing that happened between men who are in the closet, people in a committed relationship wanting something different, and with beings of all sorts who can't go to a bar and get laid for whatever reason like the rest of the people on their block.

I grew up in Pentz, where it's often warm all winter and the summers are blistering hot. The mountains aren't far, though, and eventually I got tired of my parents selectively basking in and reviling the Church of Sincerity's attentions and flattery. We were from a long line of Artisanal Humans, they told us, and they had such glib pride in their voices. The hand they used to stroke our genetic fur was as gentle as could be, but they used the same hand to scruff the few of us who wanted to find a life outside the borders of our genetic preserve.

If you asked me, "a long line of Artisanal Humans" meant we were simply the result of ceaseless inbreeding. We were genetic dead-ends with nothing to recommend our chromosomal portfolio than the fact a bunch of religious nut jobs wanted to stare at our family tree while it collapsed in on itself. I'd had it up to here and then some, and still going, by the time I was fourteen years of age and trying to find work in an ore plant. I'd heard enough of how valuable my genes were, how important it was I continue the line of Arties living in our lovely MidAtlanta cage. No matter how pretty the leaves turned every fall, I was sick to death of being told I was too special to live my own life.

Sick to death, I thought: another dark chuckle in the night.

I ran away from the reservation. I went into the hills rather than a city because I knew they would look in the towns and cities first. They would assume what I wanted to escape was the rural upbringing. They were right, of course, but first, I had to give them time to forget me. I had to disappear for a while.

Up there, in those mountains, I found parks and other places people would visit from time to time. I found hiking trails where townies came to find a little strange, and I ran into other self-imposed exiles who retreated into the mountains to find some peace from the world. Under their tutelage, I learned there were words for what I am, some of them kind and some not, and I learned there were words for Others, too: Mannie and Genie—because they can have anything they want—and Plusses and on and on and on. On the preserve, we were told the world outside existed in perfect genetic order, and what I found, instead, was a chaos of prejudice dressed in the starched and collared uniform of a caste system. In theory, as an Artie, I was somewhere in the middle. All that really meant was no one liked me.

Self-pity like that ran down the sides of my every thought as I clambered clumsily over the gate into the parking lot of Down Preserves. There were no mag cars—the Obedient and Felicitous Brothers of St. Chandra of the Church of Sacred Sincerity were not above having a car towed from their parking lot overnight—but the lights in the parking lot were on. They were meant to discourage people like me, so I threw a moutza at them as I walked, a slim black shadow, from one pool of light on white gravel to another. Eventually, I reached the beginning of the very same trail where I got slugged a few days before.

The fuck trails aren't very busy in the early mornings, but sometimes there's a little action. I went there to watch the sun rise, but now a part of me wanted also to get laid by someone whose name I would never know and whose troubles would never be mine. It sounds bad when I write it down like that, but it's the truth. I wanted to forget myself for a little while, and I wanted to do so with someone who would do the same. Someone who would forget me.

I walked into the dark tunnel of the trails at night, trees towering over me with slumped autumnal shoulders, the ground beneath me a patchwork quilt cast in tones of gray and black and brown instead of their daylight crimsons and golds. Ten minutes later—with only one or two turns off the main trail itself—I found myself in an out-of-the-way clearing where I was more likely to hear a gasp of pleasure than the call of some preserved tropical bird.

Instead of a cacophony of ecstasy, though, all I heard was my own breathing, labored from the alcohol and the climb and the hard work of feeling so damned sorry for myself all night. I was a little disappointed. Being in a place like this, where strangers get lost in one another's embrace like amnesiacs being welcomed home by lovers they don't remember, I hoped for an experience I cherished but rarely had call to describe: being by myself in the company of others.

With no one else around, I decided to climb a tree. I wanted to watch the sun rise over Autumn, her skyline and her various pits and hills a lumpy bedspread. Eventually, I succeeded with only a few false starts and one scraped hand: more scars, maybe, and more marks of the pride of being Artisanal in a world full of genetic baselines designed by the greatest life scientists our era—or any other—could boast.

When I got to the top, I could see the rim of pink forming ahead of the City. The structure of Autumn is such that we never see a horizon other than the City's own. We never fly so low as to see mountains, for instance, or the tops of terrestrial trees. Instead, we see our own Fore Barrier and the net and the City's rooftops from all directions except hovering overhead. That was a perspective I never expected to have—I couldn't imagine having much call to go for a gyro ride—and it occurred to me the angels must see that kind of thing all the time. Rather, it occurred to me they *would* if they were even real, which they weren't.

I settled down on my branch, the weight of my failing body suddenly greater than I remembered it being on the hike up. Exhaustion tied itself to all my corners and sank: exhaustion from the night spent drinking, from my liver working overtime to deal with all that booze, from my walk across the City's landscape, from too little sleep gotten on a lumpy couch in a cold office I could no longer afford. The pink edge of the sky turned red and then yellow, and as a tiny crescent of the sun himself started to crest over the Fore Barrier and golden spotlights shot westward between the buildings of my beautiful City, I heard rustling from below as someone approached quietly but not stealthily: the footfalls of a person who didn't want to disturb their own reverie by stomping around.

Alejandro walked into the clearing at the climax of the fuck trail, and he turned to face the sunrise and closed his eyes as the rays struck him all at once. I stayed where I was, quiet as I could be, my gaze shifting back and forth between the absurdly beautiful light show on the horizon and that same light playing across Alejandro's simultaneously too-smooth and too-human features.

"Do you often come here in the morning?" His voice was quiet, but it carried anyway; he didn't exactly have a lot of competition to be heard.

Alejandro turned to face me, or at least in my direction, despite me thinking I was hidden. "I do," he went on. "I come here to watch the sun rise once or twice a week." He—*it*—walked closer to me. He seemed not to know where I was, though it occurred to me he might be pretending to be polite. I couldn't stand the thought of that—couldn't stand the thought of being pandered to by a machine designed to make me like him in the first place—so I half-jumped and half-tumbled right out of the tree and onto the ground, the alcohol cushioning me for the moment against the worst of the pain of impact. I could tell when I landed I was a little thinner in the bones than six months before. That was the first time I felt frail.

"I love to come here," I said from where I lay, still crumpled awkwardly on the ground, my coat twisted up around me and my hat fallen to the side. "And I love to *cum* here." I rolled over onto my side and then up onto one leg, then another, standing unsteadily and half-heartedly dusting myself off. I hoped to bother him with that. I wanted to offend the delicate sensibilities I associated with these timeless, semi-legendary creatures of metal and soft eyes and room temperature false flesh.

Alejandro walked over to outside of arm's reach and looked at me with those eyes narrowed in sympathy, a surplus of forgiveness for whatever dumb idea resulted in me being here at the literal crack of dawn. "You're dying, aren't you?"

I blinked. How did everyone know? Did the Church of the Infinite Upward Spiral of the Double Helix tattoo it on my forehead?

"We get used to noticing things," he said in response to my frown. "Golems, I mean. We spend enough time around people to detect patterns." He tried to look a little self-conscious about it and almost succeeded. I figured he did the best he could do with the false facial musculature his designers gave him. "I'm sorry."

"I'm dying," I muttered. "Apologies are a waste of time."

"So is anger," Alejandro countered. His voice was infuriatingly reasonable.

"No, it isn't," I snapped. "Sometimes anger is the closest thing I can find to a reason to live. There are mornings when the only thing getting me out of bed is the desire to piss someone off."

"What about the other days? What gets you out of bed when you aren't angry?" He looked sad, like he'd heard these sorts of antics before, and maybe he had. Maybe he'd been around since before the ancients popped their big balloon. Maybe he'd had a hundred thousand humans tell him all about how sad they were. I hated them, too.

"The same thing getting anyone else out of bed: the rent, a cup of coffee, and the hope I'll maybe get laid if I'm lucky. I sure as shit don't do it for the home-cooked meals."

That was when he kissed me, and I kissed him, and the two of us did something halfway between *fucking* and *making love* right there in the middle of Down Preserves while the sun came up on Autumn and a virtuously busy morning wound its springs without us.

6

The sun was over the trees at the southeastern edge of the sloped opening in the forest when I awoke. The sun woke me, actually: its rays on my face, the flicker of shadow and light as it played across my closed eyes. I was half dressed: my shoes off, my feet bare, and my coat spread over me in lieu of a blanket. My shirt was somewhere, probably. I wasn't wearing it, anyway, and my eyes hadn't opened yet, but I could feel it nearby the way you can sense an old dog by your chair or a former lover on the opposite side of an otherwise perfectly nice party.

My back curled against something firm and supporting, and I felt gentle fingers stroke the tufts of silvery black at my temples. Hematite, a man told me once. I would always love him a little for saying that. My hair there wasn't yet gray but no longer black and, when wet, it looked like hematite, and he said it like that meant something deep and significant and mystical I didn't understand. Having someone's fingers run through it felt good, though. It felt like a happy memory, like something I didn't expect would happen much anymore if it ever really happened in the first place.

That simple touch was a comfort to me. It's the most minor thing and, for that reason, the most missed when it's gone. I don't go long stretches without being touched, but it had been a while between *caresses*. This was that: a caress, and more, not exactly sexual but not exactly platonic. It was that happy in-between we call *intimate*. I made myself vulnerable to other men, and they themselves to me, more times than I can count in my too-short life. It didn't always work out, though, that my usual flavor of street trade would show basic human kindness in return for mine.

None of that mattered, though. Those guys were long gone. Right that second, someone ran his fingers through my half-asleep hair, intimate and kind and caressing. I felt vulnerable and that was okay. For a few moments, I wasn't dying, and I wasn't scared. I wasn't lonely, and I wasn't alone. The sun felt good, and the breeze through the branches sounded like Gaia herself telling me to go back to sleep. I thought for a moment I might be okay with dying fairly soon if I got to wake up like this every morning for the rest of my life.

"Okay," I groaned. I didn't move, and I didn't open my eyes because I wasn't quite ready for the moment to go away, even as I lifted the pin to pop its balloon. "You want something. So tell me what it is. Because if I say yes—*if*—I may not have much time to hold up my end of the bargain." My voice dispelled all the magic of the moment, but his fingers were still at my temple, resting there, ready to go back to what we shared moments before. I rolled over and looked up at Alejandro, his purple hair down over half his face as he leaned on one elbow. I didn't kiss him, but I did put one hand to his jaw and brush his cheek with my thumb. I wondered if he could feel that—really feel it, like skin feels it. "Let's not pussyfoot around this. You want me to do something. The whole story about the angel and thinking someone was trying to kill you was bullshit, but there was something there, something worth chasing, so let's have the truth now and get on with things." I tried to smile at him. His expression was completely blank.

With the hand he used to brush my temples, he laid a fingertip behind my ear, cupping my face with barely a single point of contact. He still didn't smile, but his eyes searched my face, my own eyes, for something. It occurred to me the correct phrasing might be to say he searched my eyes for some*one*. I assumed he'd been alive long enough to know a hell of a lot of people, and I would bet a nickel he looked for one of them in me. There are a hundred romantic stories about golems: meat sacks like me throwing ourselves at a golem out of infatuation with their embodiment of agelessness.

If he'd been there before, heard a hundred thousand of us wail about mortality and still willing to hear number one hundred thousand *one*, he must have a lot of love for humankind. *No*, I thought, more than that: he must have loved the hell out of *one* of us at some point. Maybe he was waiting for that guy to walk back into his life, reemerging from the vast but finite pool of genetic factors we possess as a species. I wondered if I simply seemed close enough to that long-lost lover to pass muster for a night.

I also wondered what made a golem want to get laid in the first place: ever the detective, after all.

"I really did see an angel in Splendor," Alejandro said. He still wasn't smiling. If anything, he had the muted seriousness, the understated gravitas, I'd long since come to recognize as the posture of someone telling the truth at long last. I wondered how long it had been. "I swear it to you. I swear it." He surprised me, then, because he didn't cry, golems don't have tear ducts, but his eyelids quivered with the autonomic response to strong emotion. He still hadn't moved at all, and we were shielded from the breeze so that his hair hung straight down like a perfectly still and settled curtain across half the stage of his face. "And I believe it would try to kill me if it knew I were here."

"Of which," I replied, "you seem genuinely afraid, so you must believe *it* is here."

"Yes," Alejandro said. "I am convinced it has come here or will come here in the future, so it might bring down the last of the Great Cities the same way it brought down Splendor before."

"So that part's legit." I shifted around to put one arm under my head, but Alejandro glided to intercept me and put his own there to cradle my head instead. It put our faces closer together. I thought he was about to kiss me, but instead, he was whispering as quietly as he could. I realized he had vocal chords and pushed air through them like the rest of us rather than having a speaker installed. I could feel his false breath on my face as he spoke. It smelled like me.

"Yes." He spoke very softly. "That part is absolutely true."

"You really did see an angel pass through while you were in the storm?"

"Again, yes." He didn't seem annoyed to be made to say it over and over again. "I really did, and it really did have a squad of human…" He trailed off, searching for the word. "Accomplices. Yes. They committed a murder, after all." He looked me right in the eye. "Again, I swear to you."

"Tell me what it looked like." I'd seen plenty of drawings of angels in books and ancient histories, of course: big, masculine, rippling with muscles like geological strata, impossibly beautiful, with vast white wings and harps and sometimes flaming swords.

Now, Alejandro looked away, searching his memory—or making something up. That cynically suspicious part of me was never going to give up, but it was a little slower off the starting block this time. There was something sincere, something truthful in Alejandro's demeanor I didn't see when he spoke to me the first time. On that first occasion, in retrospect, he seemed a little rehearsed.

This question, about its appearance, caught him a little off guard. That was good. "Tall," he said at first. "Taller than you think when I say that: at least eight feet in height and tremendously thin."

"Eight what?"

Alejandro calculated for a moment. "Two and a half meters. More or less." He shook his head at the memory, like a mother lamenting over her child who won't eat like he should. "It may have weighed less than forty-five kilograms. More than merely thin. *Sickly.*" Again, Alejandro surprised me with a reflex reaction: he shuddered subtly. If I weren't half underneath him, our bodies pressed together with my thin jacket between us, I might not have noticed. "It looked like it had been put on the rack and stretched until it got stuck that way. Its hands were twisted and gnarled, the joints thicker than any given bone of a finger or palm. They looked painful, intensely arthritic, but he could move them a little. He would point and gesture and the like when he gave orders to the humans in his employ."

Alejandro paused and drew a breath. Whoever designed him wanted to build a machine very much like a man. Everything about him said *accept me, be not afraid, but know I am not you,* and I again reflected on what that might tell me about the designer—ambivalent, self-conflicted—or the team of engineers who designed him: at odds with one another and possibly themselves over his purpose and the best path forward.

"Did it have wings?" I couldn't help but ask. I mean, they couldn't call these things *angels* for nothing.

"They were the worst thing about it," Alejandro whispered. His voice sounded dreamy, distant, lost in the moment as it replayed itself across the memory banks in his very handsome head. "The rest of him looked like a stretched and mutilated thing, no more human than a chimpanzee." I started to ask him what a chim-pansy was, but I didn't want to put any stumbling blocks in the way of an honest answer. "His wings, though, were perfect. They were sixteen feet—" He caught himself and looked at me. "Slightly shy of five meters, yes. His wings were five meters across and as white as polar snow."

I chuckled. Alejandro looked at me strangely before going on. "When he walked through, having waded through unknown amounts of water washing down the streets of Splendor while everyone stayed inside, his wings were pristine. They practically glowed. When they left, when the first engine blew and people started screaming, they were splashed here and there in blood. Bright red ran in viscous streaks down those pristine white feathers like an oil slick on the surface of a pond. One of the people carrying their comrade—the one blown half to pieces—said something and the angel laughed." Alejandro's gray lips rasped when he ran his mechanical tongue across them. "The angel laughed, and I could see its mouth." He looked back down at me, right in the eyes again. "Valerius, I saw its *teeth*. Imagine a shark's mouth in a nearly human face: a couple of rows each on top and bottom, at least, and full of what look like shards of broken bone. Its teeth were like a saw waiting to devour the trunk of a tree." He shuddered again and pressed himself closer, and much to my surprise, I found I was the one with an arm wrapped around him to lend something like comfort.

Alejandro wasn't the first client with whom I slept, not by a long shot, but he was the first one who made some part of me *care* about him rather than feeling the sorrowful condescension of *sympathy*.

"Easy," I whispered to him. "Easy. No need to rush this. I simply asked what he looked like."

"He looked like a creature made to devour." Alejandro quivered. "He looked like someone designed him to be the enemy." He shook his head again. "Enemy of whom, I don't pretend to know. But I have to assume he's here, and I have to stop him if he is. They lay low—angels do—they lay low between attacks, so people will convince themselves angels must not exist, that they're *not* conducting an organized campaign. They are, though. I know that. They are."

I went back to sleep after that. Alejandro promised to stay with me. I was tired—not only that morning, but all the time. The doctors told me that would happen sometimes until it started happening all the time. I was too tired to think about whether it happened more now than it used to. I'm a detective. I'm always tired.

Alejandro woke me a couple of hours later. While I was out, he gathered my shoes and socks, shook out my shirt, and hung it from a convenient limb. He did a very efficient job of playing house in the middle of a forest. He was back by my side when he woke me, though. He very gently brushed my shoulder until my eyes fluttered open. I felt more rested than I had in weeks. "Oh shit." My eyes opened wide. "I'm probably late for something."

He smirked at me. "Another client?" A pause. "Or another lover?"

I puffed air through my cheeks. "I should be so lucky." I caught his eye. "I mean, to have more clients." I'm such a silver-tongued devil. I blushed as I sat up and then stood to walk over to my tree. I could hear footsteps approaching through the brush that pressed in around the unofficial entrance to the cruising grounds. I finished buttoning my shirt as a kid who looked like a junkie in need of a fix walked into the clearing. Spotting us, he ran a hand under his own shirt to reveal pale skin around a too-thin frame. He was looking for paying work, not a little fun for its own sake. I shook my head at him. "Blow, kid. Hawk it somewhere else."

"You sure you guys don't need to party?" His voice was deeper than you'd expect from a reedy little wisp like that, but strained. He was probably a sticker, slipping down the slope of a dry spell and starting to get the crawls. If he was here, he'd probably been trying to trick all night with no luck. Stickers aren't exactly morning people. I'd never seen him around Misconceptions, but that probably meant he had a rep. Tom likes to throw out the lowest of the low now and then so the rest of us have someone we can be a little better than. That deep voice wavered out from between cracked lips again. "I sure would like to party."

Alejandro withdrew an old-fashioned wallet from his pants pocket and took out a couple of bills of folding scrip from what looked like a row of many types and in large quantities. I raised both eyebrows at that. Carrying around paper like that, all the time? But then, golems are supposed to be fearless in their ancientness. Alejandro walked over to the kid and held them out. "Take this." His voice came out soft and kind. The kid didn't even realize Alejandro was anything more than a man at first. After a moment, the junkie's eyes focused on the golem's artificial skin and slightly off features, and the kid wasn't sure whether to believe his senses. He must have been further into the crawls than he looked. Hell, maybe he'd gotten used to them. "I know someone who can help you." Alejandro's voice embodied compassion. "He can get you exactly what you need."

Alejandro had the boy's full attention. The kid thought Alejandro was going to hook him up with a good pinprick. "Yeah?" He looked at the paper again. Spending it could be risky, depending on who made it and where he tried it out, but if they took it, the kid would be set for days. "Where's this guy? Does he need to party?"

Alejandro gave an address in Shade Tree, one of the border neighborhoods of Autumn, right on the edge between lower middle class and skid row. Lots of people lived there who had lousy jobs and no money and dreams getting thin at the edges. It wasn't far from my place, and I did not live on the good side of that divide. "Ask for Bronwyn. She will help you."

The kid's eyes narrowed. "She ain't some church, is she?"

Alejandro chuckled once. "No. This is no trick. Simply giving you a good connection. Think of it as a consolation prize for missing our little party." He winked at the kid, and I had no clue what the hell was going on.

The kid debated Alejandro's sincerity, but there was maybe a fresh supply in front of him. "Thanks, man," he wheezed, his voice jumping a couple of registers in relief. The scrip disappeared, and the kid looked around. "Anybody else here?"

"We're it." I shook my head. "You missed the morning rush."

The kid made a noise of disappointment and looked at the ground. "Thanks. You two, you're okay. Maybe I'll see you around."

"Maybe so." Alejandro wore a small smile: not mocking, but not exactly sincere. It said two things at once, but I could only hear one of them: *not likely*. "Her supply can be a little unpredictable, though. You should go now. I know she's open."

The kid nodded again, still not meeting our eyes, then turned and disappeared back into the woods.

I tucked my shirt into the too-large waist of my pants and hopped into my shoes and socks one leg at a time. Alejandro watched the woods the whole time, as though expecting the kid to come back with a knife. When I was put back together, I shook my jacket and pulled it on. "What was all that about? I wouldn't expect you to be taking commission on pinprick referrals."

"Bron isn't a pinprick." Alejandro shook his head at me. "She's a healer. She'll know his predicament when he arrives. She'll offer him a couch in the back and an immediate hit. What she gives him will be a stick full of medicine, though, not what he's expecting. It's..." He shook his head. "Never mind."

"No. Tell me."

Alejandro looked a little exasperated and maybe a little embarrassed. "It's ancient. It's a powerful psychoactive called ibogaine. He'll be made to confront the parts of himself and of his life that led him to where he is now. The dead will speak to him. His better self will challenge him. He'll scream bloody murder for a few hours. He'll shit everywhere. When he's done, he'll be free." He looked at me then looked away again. "I know," he said. "It's silly."

"What are the odds he'll go to her?"

"It's almost certain," Alejandro replied. I knew he was right, but I wanted to know what was nagging at him. He went on. "He got a lead to an immediate pin. He'll go right away."

"Unless he thinks you're a cop."

"He walked in on you getting dressed in Down Preserves. He knows we're not cops."

"And this whole 'confront the parts of himself and his life' thing. What are the odds that works?" I buttoned my cuffs and ran my hands through my hair. It would have to do.

"It always works." Alejandro was holding something back, so I waited for him to say it. It only took a second of silence. "Or he'll die."

We walked together back to the main trail and then down it in silence. A few geezers were out walking dogs, grandkids, and other pets. No garden tours today. I looked like hell, but the extra sleep had me feeling like a million bucks. The doctors told me that might happen, too: energy levels up and down and all around. I decided to ride it while it lasted. I stopped at the parking lot and bought a Pink and drank it standing there. It tasted like sugar and make-believe fruit. I loved it. All of a sudden, I was full of life in a way I wasn't a few hours before. All the hate and anger had gone out back for a smoke, and I relaxed for a second in their absence.

I asked Alejandro if he had anywhere to be, and he demurred. "I do have some things to which I must attend."

"Okay." I realized I wished he would spend the day with me. I hadn't felt that way in a long time. The thought of taking a day to wander around town with a guy on my arm was something I hadn't let myself imagine in a long time. Alejandro looked like he'd blush if he could. His head ducked, and he patted me on the small of my back.

"I'm sorry," he said.

"Don't sweat it." The sudden sadness of having been denied a moment

I didn't even know I wanted threatened to rise up and swallow the joy I felt, but I pushed back. In the end, it didn't quite make it over the horizon of my mind. I shook it off. "But," I hesitated, "here's the thing: I don't know where to begin looking for an angel. These are creatures of myth with destructive aims and secretive means. You might as well tell me to find a murderer before their victim knows they're in danger, or a bank robber before the bank's been *built*. If somebody did something—had already done—I would have someplace to start. I could talk to a victim's family. I could go poke around the scene after the cops are gone. I could get nosy. Alejandro, I think there's something to your story. And I believe you are genuinely scared. But, I don't have anything to go on."

"I'll pay you. I'll pay anything you ask." He looked terrified for a moment, like I was the ship passing by his desert island without seeing the signal flare.

"I believe you." I reached up and touched his cheek. The Sincerity brothers would have to get a fucking grip for five seconds. "But I'm not psychic."

"It's going to kill me," Alejandro whispered. His voice was pleading and sad and very soft.

"Maybe so." I hated myself for the cruelty I had to call up to finish the thought, but that was my only option if I was going to make any headway. "But we all have to die sometime."

I kissed him once, very quickly, then turned and walked away. I had to set a very dangerous trap, and Alejandro's pretty face would only get in my way.

7

Autumn has a library to rival the ancients. You know the saying: "In Autumn's library, ten books for every hand." I don't know if that's literally true, but I like the idea. The building itself is a great stone thing, rectangular with a peaked roof and gargoyles ogling us from every perch. The steps up the front are like those of an ancient temple. Of course, they did used to be temples—maybe. The Safkhet cult has been gone a long time, and nobody really knows whether to believe all libraries were theirs.

At one point in more modern times, an ambitious Spiralist tried to have the building demolished and reconstructed to remove that religious sense of reverence. It didn't make any sense—the Spiralists say they love knowledge and learning and new ideas, right there in their oppressively dogmatic literature—but people will spout anything to get ahead in politics and in religion. If I correctly recall, he argued it disrespected "real" religions to have a secular institution mimic their designs. Maybe he said it served to confuse nonbelievers? I remember someone on one of the headies asked him if he was saying religious types were too stupid to know the difference between a church and *not* a church, and that shut him up for a while.

Sometimes there are still protests outside, though. No, correction: protestors, only one or two of them with a sign with something dumb-witty on it. You know, something that doesn't actually make sense, but the person holding it seems to think it's sassy or provocative? Those people are all the proof I'll ever need that every religion is shit.

The interior of the Autumn Repository of Human Knowledge is wall-to-wall dark wood and thick rugs piled two or three deep. The carpets run between shelves and up the wide stairs like a waterfall in reverse. A huge card catalog in the cavernous main room stood in perfect parade-rest formation, banks upon banks of tiny drawers filled with index leaves bearing tiny writing. The system they use is the ancients' system, part of their way of making everything feel connected to that misty past whence all the classical learning and the confusing mythology came. Walking into the ARHK—"the ark," as we call it around town—is like using a time machine. Windows depicting ancient scenes of knowledge transfer—of Prometheus giving fire, of Curie on her deathbed, of Eve with an apple in her hand, of Safkhet and the Door to Heaven, of Leonidas and the Scrolls—are depicted on huge windows of colored glass. Their jewel-tone mosaic washes over everything when we fly through sunny skies.

I like to go there to think sometimes. I pick up a book at random from a shelf, take it to one of the reading galleries on the third floor, past the noses that sniff us for books and keep us from stealing any, and stare out a window while my thoughts run around thinking themselves a while.

This wasn't one of those days, though. I knew exactly whom I'd come to visit and where to find her.

Clodia is one of those rare delights in a detective's career: she paid on time, in full, and she stayed a contact. The job she hired me to do is a long story for another time. Suffice to say, it was years ago, and she was about as clean as a client can reasonably be expected to be. I didn't feel dirty after taking her money, and it spent as well as any that ever passed through my hands. I hoped she'd be the ticket to a higher class of client, but no such luck.

Clodia's last name is Tomikio, and I do mean *those* Tomikios. She doesn't actually have anything to do with the running of the company, though. She earns a fat dividend on some inherited stock she pays someone else to manage on her behalf. It isn't that she can't do it. Not at all: she has that incredibly precise mind her family is known for. Every time she speaks to me, I feel like my thoughts are being audited. I doubt she knows she has that effect on people. Looking at the world as something to assess is in her blood. It's how she processes things—anything. Some people organize their minds like a sock drawer. Clodia's is a ledger. She hates being called by her last name because, she told me, it makes her feel like she can't relax. It's too businesslike. In a family like hers, I imagine one gets sick of business. She resolutely adheres to convention when addressing others, though.

All that money frees her to pursue her own real interest: the myths and legends of the ancient world, before the big collapse. Whereas the Sinceres gather this stuff up and put it on display to support their claims about the Time of Only Man, Clodia turns her jewelsmith's eye on the great body of myth and tries to sift it for *history*. She points out what she thinks is real and what she thinks is probably false and what was probably false that people believed to be real.

Unlike all the many naysayers out there, though, Clodia also leaves open the possibility that there are things people believed to be false that were—maybe are—in fact real. For instance, everybody knows the ancients held sex to be sacred because they produced so much religious instruction about the right and wrong ways to have it. Clodia thinks they were simply obsessed with telling other people what to do, and sex was an easy way to use shame to control them. If that's the case, well, I guess things never really change.

Clodia finds evidence for these theories by spending literally all day, almost *every* day, sitting in the Ark with a big stack of ancient texts around her. She takes notes in a small journal she carries with her everywhere and frequently consults in conversation. I've never understood exactly what rubric she uses to make her judgments, and she seems to be as interested in the ones she categorizes as false as she is in the ones she thinks true. I asked her once why the questions of what was and was not real fascinated her so and she answered, "Ancients thought all this important enough to preserve. They must have had a reason. The texts contain something they wanted to say."

I strode up the grand central staircase of the Ark—dark wood in a long double spiral, as the DNA helices are not exclusively the turf of Spiralists, and yes, that *did* make the whole "libraries confuse believers" thing intensely ironic—for what seemed a very long eighty seconds. It was quiet down below, but above was absolutely, oppressively silent except for the rare crinkle of a turning page or the susurrus of nib against paper. The top floor is generally the domain of the serious researcher. Random kids who wander too far up get stopped before they can make it there. Outsiders who don't seem to have a purpose are looked at askance. It's the sort of place where nobody ever shushes anyone because no one ever needs to be shushed.

I turned a corner at the top of the staircase and walked like I knew where I was going. Disappearing into the stacks at the top of the Ark is a good way to avoid recrimination. At the end of a row, I turned again, walking along an outside wall. Glittering multi-colored illustrations of the price of knowledge—the deaths of ancient scholars, the wars fought for ideas—washed over me. The Safkhet cult certainly didn't want to focus on how the pursuit of knowledge sometimes kills people, but they did unabashedly want to remind the rest of us that knowledge could be worth a life. They weren't actually very nice people, but they built a hell of a book collection.

Occasionally, I would catch sight of one of the great tables, easily three meters on a side with a row of lights in the middle and a single chair. There was usually a person at the table. Once in a while, what I saw instead was a giant pile of abandoned books, left for a moment or perhaps for a week. The regulars up there tend to get a little comfortable. You might even say territorial.

Eventually, I saw the one where Clodia worked. She had on a severe black business suit, well matched to her very dark skin. She was fluent in seven languages, literate in nine (the extra two are dead, so no one knows what they sound like). She's tall, physically solid, and her eyes scream genius intelligence. People find her intimidating, and she doesn't try to blunt that impression. She told me it made it a lot easier to get work done.

I lifted a book from a shelf at random to have something in my hand and stepped over to her table. Pausing across from her, like I was a client at her desk, I waited for her to look up. When she did, she was clearly cross. Someone dared approach a scholar at the top of the Ark? She was ready to make sure it didn't happen twice.

Her features didn't exactly soften when she recognized me, but she did smile a little. I pointed at an empty chair nearby and raised my brows. She shook her head to discourage me from sitting: here was not the place to have a conversation, no matter how softly. Instead, she stood, nodded in a direction across the library floor, and started walking at full speed. If I wanted to talk, I would have to keep up.

Clodia ducked into the pollies, and I hesitated to follow her. After seeing she was holding open the door, I stepped in, and she closed it behind me. With a practiced motion, she set the privacy bar. Maybe this wasn't Clodia's first time using the pollies as a private office.

Speaking of, I chucked a thumb at the row of birds. "Our conversation needs to be more private than this," I said. "I'd hate one of these guys to remember what we discuss."

She lifted both eyebrows, and the corner of her mouth threatened a sneer. "Come now, M. Bakhoum. That's impossible."

I shook my head in a flat negative. "No way. I'm not running the risk of being the one in a million that creates a permanent imprint."

With a little sigh of being tired with me already, Clodia opened the door and we were back out in the hallway and charging down toward one of the fire escape stairwells. Clodia barreled through the door, holding it open for me to follow. When I did, she shut it behind me and turned to face me on the landing at the very top of the stairs. "Will this do? No birds to blabber impossibly after reset."

I peered over the handrail of the landing and down into rapidly deepening darkness. The lights below hadn't sensed us and turned on; only the ones at the top came to life. I didn't like having to trust no one was down there in the dark, but it beat nothing. As she said, it beat a room full of birds bred to remember and repeat spoken language. "Sure."

She folded her hands in front of her and waited for me to speak.

Suddenly, I felt deeply silly. "I need to know if avenging angels are real." I swallowed some air. "I have a client who claims to have seen one, and I need to know if that's possible—and everything else you know about them."

Clodia failed to roll her eyes. In fact, she narrowed them. I got the feeling I was being assessed like one of those writings she studies. "It's easy enough to determine if they saw one." Her thumbs tapped against one another. "What color did he say its wings were?"

"White," I answered. "'White as polar snow.' Does that make it real?"

Clodia answered with another question. "And how big were its wings?"

"Five meters, tip to tip."

She nodded. "And its teeth?"

"Two rows, like a shark." I shuddered suddenly. The stairwell wasn't heated, and sometimes it gets cold in Autumn in random places, and I told myself this was one of them. I jumped ahead of myself and of her. "It had some human accomplices, too."

She smiled softly. "He's lying." It sounded like an apology.

I blinked. I was surprised, and a little disappointed, and a part of me was surprised at my own disappointment. "Why?"

"Angels have only been recorded attacking alone. That is one of the things about them: they are solitary creatures. One reason many disbelieve angels' existence is the question of species continuity. If there were more than one, why would they not mass their forces to attack? Why only ever attack solo?" She was warming up to the subject now, and she gestured with one hand as though there was an illustration nearby. "Yet they do not, suggesting there is only ever the one. If they do not live or work in groups or pairs, how do they reproduce? I fear simple biology gives the lie to the whole concept. Recall, M. Bakhoum, they were believed to be a product of the ancients' experiments."

"There was Andreas, two hundred years ago, right? That was two angels, if you believe the story." I shrugged, and it was a lame one. My heart wasn't in it. I didn't believe any of the stories. At least, I didn't think I did. I certainly didn't want to believe them.

Clodia rolled one shoulder. In anyone else, it might suggest ambivalence, but Clodia's mind was made up. She was not considering all possibilities. She was guiding me to her own conclusions. "There are sufficient reasons to believe that was a manufactured explanation for a natural disaster. A powerful earthquake is statistically more likely. History contains numerous instances of a disaster with no agency behind it, spawning a desire to create explanatory myths. Saying two angels descended and struck the Earth so hard in two places it rippled like the surface of a pond: that is one example. Unlikely explanations, by definition, defy logic. That is their emotional appeal. No one can disprove them as long as they account for the facts on hand. The ancients knew Sanfro was prone to that kind of disaster. Some fraction of their descendants made up a cause, satisfying their need to have someone or something to blame."

I thought about it for a moment. "If they were the products of the ancients tinkering with biology, as you say, maybe they reproduce by cloning. Maybe they reproduce by some sort of extreme genetic manipulation." I shrugged. I was no scientist, but it made sense to me.

Clodia shook her head. "Too complicated for one being to do all on its own and in secret. Specialized equipment, space for the equipment, and time, a lot of time, is required."

I didn't like that answer, but I didn't have facts to counter it. "But do you believe there were *any* real attacks by avenging angels?"

"I do. Descriptions vary here and there, as expected from any two persons' account of the same event, but overall, an internal consistency exists lending credence to the reports. Indeed, attacks have been recorded, and I've found it hard to believe anyone would or could fake them *all*." She considered for a second, looking past my left shoulder. "Yes. I do believe there were avenging angels. I am not convinced there were as many as have been claimed through history, but I think there is *some* evidence of their reality. If they were ever real, however—and this is a major 'if'—then they are long gone. The facts don't support their continued existence. A small population of them may have existed many millennia ago. If so, they survived long enough to take root in the primitive folklore of the post-Fall times of barbarism. A handful may have even survived into the early Imperial era. But they're gone now. They *were* real. Not anymore. And when they were real, *if* they were real, they attacked alone."

"No human accomplices." My voice was flat and dead.

"Zero." She shook her head. "Look at the reports we have that seem reliable: an angel appears over a population center, declaims something damning about revenge against humankind, and begins laying waste to everything in sight. That is not a complicated plan. That is not subtle. It involves no attempts at subterfuge. Even if we remove the angels' reported attempted murder of each and every human they encounter, a kind of speciesist dogma remains. The angels of our stories live—or exist—outside of society and seek to destroy what our society creates. When they act on that desire, they do so in the most direct and uncomplicated means possible. Sometimes, they get chased away, *very* rarely they are killed (though no corpses have been preserved or discovered), and never are they captured. More often than not, they seem to become bored and leave. This is behavior equal to a child throwing a tantrum. These stories show no sense of planning or style or intention. Accomplices would not only be unnecessary: they run directly counter to the quality of reported experiences."

"My client also said it didn't look like a person. He said it looked like a 'chim pansy.'" I shrugged again.

Clodia laughed. I'd rarely heard her laugh, and despite her professorial tone and her King Midas eyes, that laugh was delightful. That laugh could make a dumb joke funny again. When I didn't laugh with her, she offered an explanation: "They were an ancient primate. An animal closely related to *homo sapiens*. Our genetic predecessors—your very distant cousins, if you will, only they ate almost nothing but exotic, co-evolved fruit."

I smirked. "Cousins, you say? I already don't like them."

Clodia allowed a small and very patient smile. "They used to be used in research. The ancients were very conflicted about the appropriateness of doing so because of the animals' suspected intelligence levels. They've been extinct for thousands upon thousands of years." She looked abruptly wistful. "There were journals at the time of the collapse, diaries and field reports written by researchers. Natural preservation had become a concern because they were damaging the biome in every way imaginable. Some researchers spent their whole careers simply documenting the erosion and destruction of the world that had produced humankind. Observations after the collapse showed a brief flourishing of hope for any number of threatened life forms. In the end, though, they died in the chaos like eighty percent of all phylum."

She was gazing elsewhere, internally, backward across the many dozens of centuries between the collapse and modern times. She looked sad. I'd only seen that on her face once, and it had been at the conclusion of the case for which she hired me. That case was deeply personal for her, and it didn't end well, and I could tell the drawn-out demise of the ancient world hit her as hard as did the relatively small matter she had me investigate. When Clodia looked back at me, she could see the uncertainty in my eyes.

"Imagine it," she said, with a whisper of reverence. "All the millennia of knowledge they must have acquired. I don't believe their machines were as advanced as some do, and I don't think any of the ancients are going to return from beyond the sky or some secret base somewhere and give us the gifts of their great machines. Those who await the salvation of their return are dreaming. I do not share their delusion. But, I know the ancients had their own legends of even more ancient lands, long lost, and of peoples whose technologies were akin to magic. They even believed those people—and that magic—might be out there still, tucked away somewhere, waiting for the right moment to appear. How many times, M. Bakhoum? How many times has humankind lost itself like that, forgotten itself entirely, and struggled back out of some self-imposed dark age to rebuild from the very beginning?" Clodia clucked her tongue in frustration.

"Anyway," she said, coming back to the here and now, "you mispronounce it. You say it like two words. It's one. Say 'chimps' if that is easier." A ghost of a smile. "But what does it matter? The centuries that would have known that are gone, and I am probably the only person alive even capable of noticing."

"They're lucky they grabbed your attention." A part of me might have wanted to lift her out of her thoughtfulness, but I've learned in my short life that a thoughtful reverie is worth a hundred meaningless smiles. I said it anyway, because I also meant it. "The ancients hit the jackpot in terms of having someone be interested in what they did. Maybe none of them are here to thank you, but it beats being dead *and* forgotten."

I grimaced abruptly, drawing my arm in against my side.

"Are you alright, M. Bakhoum?"

I gritted my teeth for a second. There had been a brief, stabbing pain in my abdomen, which happened once in a while, like a metronome keeping time for the whole slowly dying thing. I sucked air between my teeth, forced a false smile on my face, and waved it off with my other hand. "I'm fine. Something I ate."

Again, I was weighed in the scales of Clodia's mind. "If you say so," she replied. Note to self: never lie to Clodia when it *matters*.

"So, there's no record of an angel looking like an animal?"

"Again," she said, "Zero. Avenging angels are always humaniform. Often, they presented distended versions of human physiological structures or exaggerated features, but they never appeared to be other creatures entirely. They seemed to have their origin in humanity."

"You really believe in them, don't you?" I tried not to smile because a part of me knew this wasn't funny anymore, any of it, my knee-jerk refusal least of all.

"Yes. The ancients devoted too much time to them. It's that simple." She shrugged.

Again, I surprised myself: I realized I, too, believed now. Maybe saying I "believed in them" isn't right. Maybe instead I should say I realized they had become real to me. I'd still never seen one myself, and I wasn't in a hurry to do so, but I couldn't think of them as a fairy tale anymore. Even if they weren't factually, objectively, *scientifically* true, there were people in the world whose decisions were made in reaction to their own belief in avenging angels: kids who heed a mother's warning to come home on time, and believers who kneel to pray in earnest fervor, and old women whose tea cups clatter because in their mind they're still a child watching an angel kill hundreds on a whim. That was a kind of being real, wasn't it? Maybe the only kind of being real that matters in the end.

"Huh," I said. "And what about a Mannie? Could an angel be a Mannie, too?"

Clodia winced at the pejorative, but it was my mouth and I could dirty it up however I wanted. She shook her head. "No. There are..." She paused to choose the precise word. "There are legends they have some sort of shared origin, but obviously, they are very different kinds of creations. If one believes angels had their origin in genetic experimentation on the part of the ancients—and I do—then they clearly started out as human with additions. Man-Animal Hybrid Persons, however," and she was nice enough not to light up and make blink the sign she hung around my casual slur with her use of the term of greater respect, "clearly started as lower creatures with enhancements added."

I arched one eyebrow at her. "Really? Clearly?"

She nodded. "Of course. It's much easier to make a canine stand and speak syllables than to give a human a dog's physiognomy."

That made sense. "So, they came from different places."

"I think it's obvious. Not everyone agrees."

"So, for the sake of argument, let's say there's an angel around Autumn right now. Let's go further and say it's a weirdo who has a plan of action with forethought, and accomplices, and the whole stack of jacks. Where would I find him?"

Clodia looked away from me, the wheels in her head spinning. "Okay, if you wanted to chase the impossible, I would start..." She trailed off and shook her head. "I don't know where for an individual, not with the present non-limiting suppositions. But the only good method developed for revealing hidden groups—like a terror cell, which is what you describe—is to discover the pattern created by their communications. Section 4 can probably tap their communications directly to get the content, but you can't. You don't need to, though. You need to discover a pattern of a certain set of *actors* communicating with one another. They may not always communicate the same way, or in the same order, or with initiation of communication coming from the same party, but once you have a list of names who are routinely in communication with one another in some way, you've probably found a hidden group."

"Or a group of people who get together to play cards."

"Which are, in fact, a kind of *hidden* group. You don't know they play cards. I don't know. Only they know. They don't announce upcoming games to others. They schedule them and get together."

I nodded. It made sense. I'd certainly solved plenty of other cases by detecting a pattern in a subject's behavior. This was different, though. In other cases, legit cases, I'd been given a target from the start. I needed to think of a behavior they *necessarily* engaged in: something predictable and regular and required. "Gives me something to think about. Thanks."

Clodia nodded. "*Doitashimashite,* M. Bakhoum. I will now return to my work." Her tone was polite but very firm. She was not being nice. She was being the minimal necessary degree of rude.

I got out of there, down the grand stairs of the Ark, just in time to hit the Lower Market Market for dinner. I managed to get half of it down before my guts threatened to twist. All in all, it had been a damn good day so far.

8

After eating, I decided to take a walk around the Lower Market's district and give myself some time to think. I needed an idea, and they don't generally come out of sitting down and waiting for them to appear. New ideas are rarely, in fact, new. More often, they're more like two old ideas bumping into each other in the hallway. I needed to get out into the world and give myself some sensory input if I wanted to give my brain some time to churn and something to chew on while it did.

Lower Market is nothing but glowsigns and tinny music playing from those cheap bamboo speakers they grow in Zhong. Some people meditate by going into the mountains and isolating themselves from the crush of humankind. I do that, too, on occasion. Times like this, though, I needed to get where the cacophony could turn into a buzz of sensory input so overwhelming and overlapping it could become one continuous onslaught of sounds too complex to be differentiated and then, with time, recede into a hum. I needed to be a part of the humaniform hive.

I pulled my hat down over my eyes and tucked my hands into the pockets of my jacket. The night was cool again, but it didn't feel bad. The briskness nudged me inward, away from the wash of sound and light. There were hookers of every breed and gender working a few street corners, nails/claws/etc. painted red and their lipstick smudged and their harnesses too tight in all the right places. I knew a few of them from one thing or another. I stopped to chat, checked around to see if any of the ones I knew had faded from the streets but not from memory, and offered to buy a steamed bun for one of the hustlers I've known since old times. It wasn't a come-on, simply a way of being friendly. A part of me was worried I wouldn't have too many chances left.

In theory, I was working on an old case, like an old Artie works a tooth that's loose, but the meat of it, of my desire to be kind to a random street whore, was I was scared of dying, so scared I couldn't think about it or talk about it too long. I didn't have a lot of friends, but the ones I had were mostly guys like this kid—friends of happenstance, people I'd met in this line of work or another. I turned my share of tricks when I was young and new in the City. I'm not proud, and I'm not ashamed. There's a class of Plus who finds an Artie to be an exotic bit of barbarianism. I knew some of the pimps by reputation. I hired a couple of hustlers myself from time to time. They hired me in turn, in fact. I figured out eventually that everybody is just people. They want to get laid, hold hands, and wake up warm, like anybody else. I was never in danger among them and never thought myself better than they were. No one, I believe, is better than anyone else—except I suspect almost all of us are better than the very rich or the very powerful.

I don't even hate the pious types, to be honest. I may hate their religions and what they demand of me, the ways they fail me, the ways they try to lay claim to me and other Arties like we're interesting bugs in the collection of some acquisitive god. That doesn't make their true believers necessarily bad, though. Believers are merely broken, like the rest of us, and religion is the plug they could fit in the hole in their heart. It's when they start trying to stab other people with it, too, that I develop a problem with them.

The flesh down on Edgeward aren't interested in selling anybody a god. Hookers' interests are strictly corporeal. They sell a solution you can touch and feel and smell and taste, and with or without the money, they were a great way to remind myself I was still alive. There's a way the moment of orgasm can perfectly blank the mind and allow me to transcend the base limitations imposed on me by evolution. The future stops existing, the past stops existing; the whole wide world is a moment of pleasure echoing around the cavern of an empty mind. In those precious seconds, and for a little while after, every decision and bum luck and genius idea leading me to that singularity of perfection seems to have served its purpose in a grand design, a wave of forward momentum reaching its crest and crashing against me in the full light of a benevolent sun.

So, I tried to get Yuri—the hustler kid for whom I bought the steamed bun—to go home with me even though I couldn't afford anything better than the food, and he said no because he hadn't made bank that afternoon. I walked away with a smile anyway, because he flirted with me for free, and he gave me a little parting gift: a couple of names of kids he didn't see around anymore. It was still a pretty damned good day.

I collapsed early and woke up a little past dawn. Late nights were getting harder all the time. With precious little time left in any sense—bodily, or with my landlady, or with my client's retainer—I set off wandering again in the Lower Market, thinking maybe its morning face would get my brain ticking where its nighttime face had failed. Autumn was flying low enough for clouds to be overhead—we must have been headed toward a rain system to refill the cisterns—but we were encountering the edge of whatever system we'd targeted, and so sun burst through the clouds here and there. Wide shafts of light would strike some dingy corner of Lower Market so hard the people around it would put their hands over their eyes and only come out squinting when they got brave enough to look around. Lower Market is the kind of place that's dark no matter what. Full light serves only to hone an edge onto the shadows.

That light can sometimes improve what sits just outside those shadows, though. Not everything in the Lower Market Market is a smudge atop a stain. Not every person is somehow terrible to behold. Sunlight washed across a booth selling brightly colored candy, and the sweets shone like a rainbow. Mist rising off the pavement had the quality of steam from a good cup of coffee rather than the ghosts of old gas from a swamp. There are a lot of dirty faces in the Market, a lot of tattered clothes, but in the spotty sunlight, there were bright patches and shining eyes, too. The things that made them *people* were still there, under the dirt, behind the rags, pushed down under the armor they fashioned from others' low expectations.

The sun intermittently hit me as I walked deeper inside the chaos, and I took a moment to close my eyes and savor the sun. Growing up in the foothills in eastern Pentz, I was used to the heat. Feeling it for a moment was pleasant, like a whiff of my mother's plum and pomegranate pie, something I lost when I ran the hell away. It was a little bit of the warmth of home without the people or the culture or the holy books, something to be savored even if it lasted only a moment. That's another thing life has taught me: everything you hate has something you love mixed up in it, too. That's true of everything, everywhere, from ex-lovers to hometowns.

I found it amusing that morning to watch lifelong Autumnals flip their lids when the sun would strike them out of nowhere. These were people who had a mediated experience of the environment their entire lives. They'd never watched the sand wash up the edge of a valley during the stormy seasons. They didn't know how to handle the heat and the light of anywhere near the forties. This wasn't anything like that, any more than a spring rain is like a hurricane, but it surprised them all the same.

The Lower Market Market's makeshift stalls are as often as not constructed from the wares of a neighbor as from anything more independently sourced. All you need to open a business in the Lower Market Market is an empty space. If it happens to be a three-foot gap between the shelves of two other vendors, well, welcome to penthouse living. If a vendor doesn't show up one day, maybe they're out sick, sure, but maybe somebody knocked them off to open up a little real estate. It happens, and everyone knows it, and nobody thinks it will ever happen to *them*. Such is the way we manage risk in our individual lives.

Like any quasi-organized retail space, the Lower Market Market has its self-appointed bosses and enforcers. Think of a pimp, but for people selling homemade meat pies and secondhand blades and religious icons for cults no one remembers anymore. Enforcers sell a lot of "protection," and it's usually worth buying. The truth is, the pigs have better things to do than waddle around the Lower Market Market looking for business licenses nobody ever has. Legitimate licenses are so rare, a client once told me, nobody even knows how to counterfeit them because none of the current counterfeiters have *seen* one. I remember we laughed over that until I said, "So who's in charge?" That froze the laughter so hard I could hear it snap off in her gut.

I considered a bite of breakfast for myself and wandered down what everyone called Eats Alley: a particular row of shacks from which a boiling stream of smoke and steam roils at all times, heady with the aromas of a hundred different cultures clashing in open-air kitchens. I was going to ask around about those kids Yuri said were nowhere to be found. If a street kid relocates or finds a different line of work, they still probably put down cheap food. Eats Alley is a central hub for innocent comforts, which makes it a perfect place to spot someone who's recently migrated.

Some things smelled great and some turned my stomach, and I was again reminded my tastes had changed since I'd started getting sick. The body is a funny old thing. For all I knew, I was smelling the sort of thing a chim-pansy would eat.

That's when the ideas collided, and I spun on my heel. *Food.*

Clodia told me chim-pansies ate co-evolved exotic fruits. The human collaborators of this chim-pansy angel would probably order food delivered while they were here, and their deliveries would be impossible to distinguish from all the other meals delivered any given day. The food humanity ate was simply too big a stream for me to sift. But what Clodia said sounded specialized. It sounded *specific*. If the angel was some sort of hybridization or modification of a chimp, maybe they needed the same food as their extinct ancestor-cousins. If that was sufficiently unique or weird, all I had to do was check around for anyone carrying that thing. At worst, I could eliminate one bad idea a lot faster than I could sift the entire City for a delivery driver who's seen a terror cell.

Of course, everyone who knew the street knew I'd gone off to become a detective. I was no stranger to this part of town. I would need a patsy whose questions might put someone a little less on guard.

I didn't need breakfast: I needed to get to the Ark to do some research, and I needed to find Yuri. Hell, I probably couldn't have kept breakfast down anyway.

"I need to find something exotic," I said to Yuri. I was back on his corner, and it was late morning. He didn't look great, like maybe he had a rough time making his bank the night before, but he looked awake and alive and, for plenty of young hustlers, that's the cleanest bill of health they'll ever get. Yuri was still pretty, too, even with the dark circles under his eyes. That deep black skin and the long hair and the emerald eyes were as gorgeous in exhaustion as I imagined they ever could be when alert. Yuri had been smart enough to stay off the pins and other hundred thousand bad ideas for escaping reality, and it showed in the youthful contour of his handsome face.

Yuri smirked at me, lazy as a cat in a sunbeam, and leaned against his light pole. "How exotic? Manny? I didn't think they were your kink."

I fluttered my lips, half amused and half disgusted. I don't have anything against the flesh that rolls that way, but it's not my bag. "No, I mean a fruit. Nauclea fruit." I had a stencil of one from a book in the Ark. "Like this." I held up the picture: a small, mostly rounded fruit with a mottled gray flesh that looked like scales or perhaps the bark of a tree. Not exactly the sort of thing that made my mouth water, but I'm no dessert chef. "It's about the size of an apple."

"It looks like an apple somebody left in the window too long." Yuri gave me an incredulous look. "Why do you want one?"

He asked a good question. When I had gone back to the Ark, I snagged a chair near the agricultural section. As rain poured down outside, I built a bit of a pile around it looking for anything on chim-pansies. It turned out a regular considered that chair his turf. He didn't like me being in it, and he didn't like me making a mess of books around it. I gave him a big, annoying smile and promised to move if he helped me out.

He went right to a specific book and shoved it at me: *Secrets of Engineered Beings*. He pointed out a short section midway through about Avian Mannies—like Talons, my client at the start of all this—and how Avians initially suffered from malnutrition. While the engineers tinkered with genes, they fed the early hybrids Nauclea because the early hybrids were crossed with chim-pansies, not humans, and my distant relatives, as Clodia called them, could get almost all their nutrition from that one fruit. Everything, the book assured me, and anything crossed with a chim-pansy would love Nauclea. In fact, it would probably *need* them.

I tried to hand the book back to the regular, but he shook his head and pointed at a pile on the end of a nearby table. I set it atop the heap and noticed plenty of other books about hybridization and the creation of the Mannies. I never thought to walk through the library and look at tables to find a topic expert before. It would have been an obvious choice in retrospect. I could think of plenty of times that would have been a nice card up my sleeve.

Back in the here and now, I explained to Yuri, "Because it's unusual.

It's rare. But the people looking for it don't want to attract attention to themselves. When you can't walk into the Market and ask for something —because people will see you—what do you do? You ask someone who knows the market and can find it *for* you." I nodded, the light in my eyes.

"Then go ask around the El-Em-Em yourself." But Yuri was at least still smiling and there was affection there. "I'm on the clock. I can't exactly turn a trick in the middle of a grocery store to make up the time."

"I'll pay you." I was trying to shove the stencil into Yuri's hand, and he was laughing. "Seriously, I'll pay your standard rate. Tell them a client asked you for it. Tell them it's his thing. I can't go ask around after it because people know I'm a nosy guy. They know when I ask for something, it's something bigger than simply the question I'm asking. When a detective wants something, it's because someone is paying them to want it. There's a mystery there, a question hanging in the air. When a hustler asks for something..." I shrugged, spread my hands, and felt my coat resettle on my narrowing frame. "It's fuckin'. That's the most normal thing in the world."

Yuri looked at me with his eyebrows a little way up. He wasn't buying it, but the thought of getting paid to run an errand instead of bending over for some self-loathing Sincerity priest working a little strange before early prayers, well, that sounded pretty appealing. I shook the worm around a little to make it look lively. "The money is right here. Scrip, not credit. The best scrip the street can offer. What are you going to do, say no to Hendricks gang paper?"

Yuri looked at the paper money. It really was the best scrip on the street. I had customers who couldn't have their involvement with me traced. Legal or no, I got handed a little scrip on a regular basis. I was offering a fair chunk of it. Yuri could make the day's bank, and tomorrow's, and maybe the next week's with scrip like that. He could start to buy himself free with that grade of paper, even if it was only a little. He wasn't, after all, a very expensive hustler.

"Okay," he said, snatching the wad out of my hand. It disappeared before I was even sure if he shifted it from one hand to the other. "I'll send you a polly at..." He considered, but I had an answer ready to go.

"Misconceptions. Polly me there."

He nodded. "Will do." Then he smiled, and again it had a little real affection peeking over the shoulder of a businessman doing a deal. "Trust me."

I nodded back. "I never said I didn't."

"It's Lower Market," he replied. The affection was fading fast, something darker seeping in behind it. "Nobody has to."

I was sitting at the bar of Misconceptions five hours later, talking the weather with Blackie, when Yuri walked in the door. He was pale and he ignored Blackie's standard greeting: a nod and a simple "Welcome." Yuri still wore the black weatherproof pants and the black plastic jacket he had on earlier. They were the grown stuff, extruded from real bioleum plants so they must have cost quite a measure of money: probably a gift from a client who liked what Yuri did. It's cheaper to recycle the stuff we dig out of the ancients' trash pits, but it never quite feels the same as the real stuff. Bioplasta has that touch and that aroma you don't get with yesterday's trash.

Under it, I could see his white t-shirt with black print, some musical act or whatever the kids these days are into. Maybe it was his, maybe a john gave it to him, maybe he bartered for it. That sort of thing happens a lot in Lower Market. Johns don't often try to pay with legal digital currency, and they don't always have access to scrip, so they pay for trade *in* trade.

Yuri looked like maybe he'd been puking. I hoped he hadn't arrived to tell me he spent the day on a bender and now the money was all gone.

The scrip was in his hand. "Here." Yuri set the paper on the bar. "Take it back. Deal's off."

He turned to go, but I reached out and tried to grab his wrist. That was a mistake: Yuri was jumpy, and his eyes showed real fear when they met mine. Behind that fear was anger. I could imagine a few reasons why, among them that he'd have to turn tricks another twelve hours on no sleep to try to make up the time lost chasing my wild goose.

"Sorry." I put hands up, palms out. I took a moment to blink, slowly, because that has a calming effect on people. You learn a lot of psychology in this job. I took a breath, exhaled it, never letting his eyes leave mine. I may dislike most people, but I can be pretty good with them. "I'm sorry. Okay, the deal's off, but tell me what happened."

"I found a guy who sells Nauclea fruits, and he choked half the air out of me before he threw me on my ass in the street. Thanks for that." Yuri yanked down the neck of his shirt, jacket opened, and I could see bruises starting to form there. Whoever did it had big hands. Beyond the pain, the bruises were going to make it even harder for Yuri to make bank that night. He looked like damaged goods.

Blackie discreetly began polishing a glass, eyes on his work, his big ears not even twitching as we spoke. A good bartender knows the right time to turn invisible.

My gaze softened, and I half-smiled, half-frowned at Yuri. I felt bad now, and I needed to show it, or he'd blame it on me—which, fair enough. "I didn't know that would happen. I apologize. Look, keep the money. I owe you for your time. Tell me who did this to you, and I'll take it from there."

Yuri looked a little pensive, like he was considering not telling me, and I could all too easily imagine why: they probably told him to keep his mouth shut or they'd shut it for him.

"I promise they won't think you told me." I wasn't sure exactly how to go about meeting that promise, but it was what I had to say. Besides, they hadn't even bothered to rob Yuri. All they'd done was rough him up. If they were serious, they would have killed him and that would have been that. It looked like all they wanted was to spook him so he'd keep his distance.

"What do I get for it?" Yuri's hand had already slipped the scrip into his pocket. So much for hoping he would be too noble to accept my offer that he keep it.

Yuri looked up at me from beneath brows dipped low in a sulk. He was willing to take the deal, but whoever scared him had done too good a job of it. Yuri wanted the money, and he wanted something else on top.

I looked around and caught Blackie's attention, even though he didn't look at me or at anything other than that glass he'd been polishing. "Blackie, does Yuri have a tab here?"

Blackie looked up at me, then over at Yuri, then down at the glass again. He shook his head. "No tab. I don't know this skinner." I blinked. Blackie never used slurs like that. Something about Yuri pissed him off, and I didn't have time to figure out what or why.

I looked back at Yuri and reached out to touch his chin, very lightly, and tip his head back up. He flinched away, but he did straighten up and look me head on. "What do you want for it?" My voice was as soft and gentle as I could make it.

Yuri thumbed the money in his coat pocket, his hand a ripple under the dark wave of bioplast. "Where'd you get this much paper?"

"Selling cookies." I smirked. Yuri didn't. He opened his mouth to say something smart, but I cut him off. "What, are you going to go knock over a money changer?" There are a very few people who make their living turning one scrip into another. Some even transform scrip into digital currency, the real and legal Imperial stuff, or vice versa, through a complex machinery of laundering it or making it disappear. The best change up their formula too rapidly to get caught. The rest get knocked off by their betters for drawing too much heat. "I didn't get it there. I got it over time, from one job or another." I shrugged a little. "You know how it is. Why do you want to know where to find more?"

"Paper scrip is the only thing Mahogany takes for freedom." Yuri's voice was very even, but under that surface calm, the sea of his emotions boiled. I was right, he could buy out his contract with scrip, maybe set up his own operation in time. It was a path off the street corner and into a better sort of bed. "It's all one printing, too." He took a single bill back out of his coat pocket and held his thumb where the seal was embossed. "So, you got it all at once, or you got a bunch of it exchanged. I'd say the second option. That means you know where to get more. Tell me."

I clucked my tongue. I didn't think he'd studied the money that closely, but he had. My mistake. I turned a bunch of different scrips into Hendricks in hopes whoever was selling the fruit would be so interested in the paper they wouldn't think about anything else. Now Yuri really thought he could go knock over a changer. Well, fine, it was his suicide. "And if I tell you, you tell me where the guy is who did this to you when you asked about Nauclea fruits?"

Yuri nodded. A whole new future opened up in front of him, and it scared the hell out of him. He wasn't so sure he wanted to look me—or anybody—in the eye until everything was over. I wondered if Yuri even had a weapon or ever robbed anyone before. I wondered if he had any idea how fast he would die if he tried this. "Yeah. I promise. So, tell me."

I reached into my jacket pocket and pulled out a pen. With my other hand, I grabbed two napkins. I wrote down a name and address and a note about it and held the pen out to him. "Write it down. Then we swap. No playing the game of 'who goes first with the dangerous secret' that way."

Yuri snatched the pen out of my hand like the last lifejacket onboard. He scribbled on the napkin, frustrated at the way its nib snagged on the rough fibers of the napkin petals. Eventually, Yuri got the address out and dropped the pen on the bar. Slowly but surely, his hands shaking, mine steady, we traded. He nearly tore them both trying to snatch from me while making sure I didn't snatch from him, but we managed to make the swap without anyone actually flipping their lid. I looked down at the napkin: a Lower Market Market "address," an informal patois of directions and counting marks. I could navigate it with some effort. It would do fine.

"What do you mean, 'don't'?" Yuri held up the napkin. The note I'd added to the address, in block letters: DON'T.

"They'll kill you. These are not nice people, Yuri. You're a sweet guy. I've looked into your pretty eyes enough times to know you're a good person. It's why you want out of your current life: you're too good for it and that's killing you. Trust me, these guys will kill you, too. They're not good people, and they won't care that you are, and the goodness you've got left is going to slow you down from doing what you'd have to do to walk away from them." What I didn't say was the other possibility: that he'd succeed, and in killing the changer and his thug, Yuri would also kill that last good part of himself he was trying to save. It happens a hundred times a day in cities all over the world. That the one we were in was flying simply meant the view was better nearby.

"You don't understand." Yuri's teeth were already clenched. He was going to do it, and when it was over, he was going to be dead in one or another sense and he'd already made his peace with that fact. "You got out. You made it off the corner. I'm stuck. Always have been."

I looked him in those pretty green eyes and then away again. I wasn't going to change his mind. Fixing him was only going to slow me down. "Best of luck, Yuri." Then I looked back. "Let me buy you a drink first."

Blackie shook his head without looking up. "No drinks." Then he looked at Yuri for what I realized was only the second time. "You go. Never come back."

Yuri turned around and walked out, a scared young punk who'd gotten tired of selling his ass. I knew right then I would never again make love to him, never again stroll up and flirt, never offer a steamed bun so we could both feel a little bit alive.

9

Years ago, before my time and worries all got eaten up by the business of other people's trouble, I was in the habit of going to the Ark on Saturndays. I would sit around on Second, which is reserved for books about Autumn herself, reading whatever histories had a spine sufficiently interesting to make me reach out and grab them. I learned a lot about the establishment of Autumn, the deals the Imperial Senate struck to fund them, the crazy ideas behind the first residential hovers launched. A lot of the first people to take to the skies were religious types—the old religions, the ones you only hear about in textbooks anymore. They were doing what true believers always do: convincing themselves salvation would be easier on different real estate. It's always easier to go somewhere else than to become someone else. It's been true since ancient times. As long as there have been gods, we've been convincing ourselves we'd be a little closer to them over the next hill.

Each of the other flying cities was built as a sort of homage to one of the terrestrial places people always loved: Rome, London, Tokyo, Rio, Memphis, Metropolis, New York, Old Cairo, Persepolis, New Delhi. When Autumn was being planned, centuries ago, they already knew she would be the last constructed. Rather than base Autumn on one place, they based it on all the cities they wanted to use but hadn't gotten to yet. Apparently, a lot of it is based on Sanfro, some of it on Deecee, some of it on Sydney. Some of those places they had to work from old flats or even paintings to get an idea of how they looked. I'll never know myself, but my understanding is they did a pretty good job with most of them. Splendor, the one where Alejandro claimed to have seen—no, it was time to stop talking like that, the one where Alejandro *saw* an angel—was based on Paris. In some of the video I've seen, Splendor looks like a second moon in the night sky: all lights and grace and ghostly significance. I don't know if Splendor was an accurate representation, but in the images we have of it, the City was unquestionably beautiful.

Lower Market is one of the parts based on Sanfro. It has the look of an ancient city: lots of tall stuff all around it, some of it real buildings and some of it façade that never was developed into anything. The idea was to create a high-end neighborhood from the get-go, but the result created a region of near-permanent shadow.

At the center of it is Lotta's Gift, which in theory is a fountain memorializing Imperial forces lost in wars against the Eastern Expanse, but in practice is where everyone goes on the birthdays of the dead they mourn. The fountain isn't what that word normally means: a big pool of water with a source in the middle. Instead, it's a tall, iron spire, nearly eight meters high at its top. Around its four sides are sculpted mouths of ancient beasts of myth: giant cats, with water shooting out of spouts to be collected in their lower jaws. I've read the ancients used to throw pennies into fountains to commemorate the dead, but at Lotta's, we drink from the water rather than throw something in. The story goes that by drinking from that water, we quench the thirst of the departed for the pleasures of the quick. The water always tastes better to me there than anywhere else in Autumn, and Autumn is a City with very good water.

Almost immediately upon its dedication, an open-air market sprang up in the square around the fountain. The City cops tried to run them off and clean it out a few times before deciding it wasn't worth it anymore. Now, it's the unofficial business district of the City for those seeking or selling anything seedy or hard to find. They say everything's for sale at the Lower Market Market, but more often than not, "everything" is also a little hot or a lot counterfeit.

One of the unspoken conditions of the City's détente with the first entrepreneurs of the LMM is to use no permanent structures. I think the Council imagined a group of hawkers waddling into the square every day with their inventory on their backs. What they got was highly creative shanty construction. Vendors cram into every available space, and the spaces *between* them, and the spaces above and below them, and any free square meter is up for grabs by those who want to display their art or their porno or their porno art.

Because it's always dark in the Lower Market Market—except for times the sun bursts through the clouds at exactly the right angle—the vendors have a lot of glows. Every color manipulated from nature declares this or that on special, and this or that can be as broadly interpreted as you like. Some signs are euphemistic—Body Work—and some are as brazen as it gets. I love it there. It's as different from where I grew up as anywhere I can ever imagine. The Market's also a place that eats people. There are souls who walk into Lower Market Market to make a little scratch and are never seen again—and I don't mean those kids who disappear. No, these people aren't kidnapped or murdered fast: that would be too easy. They're eaten up slow, one organ at a time, sometimes from the inside out. They don't disappear in a wink; they fade from view, sometimes so slow nobody even realizes it's happening.

There are also literal disappearances. People are too naïve, or too trusting, or get too fucked up in the head. They become prey for others who trade in flesh and sometimes organs. There are stories about what happens to them, of women turned into baby factories, of people whose emptied ribcages and vacant skulls wash up against the grills of Used Water Dispensation. I have a friend who works in Cistern Conditioning who says the sewers under the LMM are caked with the blood of centuries of innocent victims.

I didn't agree with that assessment, of course. Everyone knows there isn't an innocent victim anywhere near Lower Market Market. But I *do* believe in the literal disappearances, and I consider them my very first case, the one that got me into this line of work to begin with and the one I will probably, ultimately never solve.

Where do the missing children go?

Autumn is like any other city full of people whose dreams are never coming true. It baits the hook with a reputation for being where people can go to make it big or to get away. A lot of kids who run for it come to a place like Autumn once they escape wherever they were. They want to drown in the ocean of anonymity a place like this offers. They want to go where no one remembers things they did, or the things done to them. Very few of them are predators, which makes the vast majority of them prey.

And once they get here, something happens to a lot of them. They don't only disappear from their old lives: they vanish from their new one, too.

I wound up a part of this world the same as most everyone else in it: I slipped under the razor-wire of the life assigned to me, the awful ankle chains of expectations and cultural norms, and went somewhere I thought no one would have so many preconceived notions of what was good and proper. I was wrong—people here could spot an Artie as well as anywhere else and had plenty of ideas about us—but unlike back home, there were some people here who, on recognizing what I am, didn't condemn me and didn't fetishize me. They let me be. That kept me here. That allowed me to hang on.

A lot of us—street kids—survive by crime. We turn into thieves, or we turn tricks—and some of us steal from the tricks. We take from others or we sell ourselves or both. There are not a lot of other options for getting by. It isn't a case of moral degeneracy. It's self-preservation. We engaged in the only available approaches to the most basic human instinct, and judging it won't change that. That's why I couldn't hate Yuri for the choice he made, even if I thought he made the worst available: he didn't have another option to choose. He could spend the rest of his life handing Mahogany seventy-five percent of his take, or he could become a real criminal. The street rarely leaves room for a person to come up with Plan C.

Of those two options, I picked selling myself. I knew from the beginning that was preferable to staying on the rez, smothering under the weight of what others wanted of me. The reservations are basically a seed bank: tuck away a supply of unmodified DNA in case the rest of humanity finds itself stuck in a genetic dead-end, insufficiently varied to weather some crisis or another. You know, keep the Arties all wrapped up in religious obligation and tell them they're special and feed them organics and require them to breed.

No thanks, bucko. Not me. It isn't simply that I'm queer. It's that nobody asked my permission to use me as a walking, talking, living-history sperm bank. I took what I had and sold it before they could take it away from me.

When I was in that life, I noticed other kids who seemed to get swallowed up by the shadows all around us. They went with a trick, or they took a courier gig, or they made enough of some gang's local scrip to buy their way into a better hole in the wall, and then they were gone. They didn't show back up. The tricks weren't keeping them long term. They did not become full-time messengers. None worked their way back up the cliff face of polite society. All those things happened sometimes, sure, and when they did, when someone pulled themselves out of the ditch, they always came back around once or twice to make a little show of dusting themselves off. These kids just vacated their lives. Maybe they left behind a mat, or a change of clothes, or a couple of trinkets they thought were lucky charms: the sort of thing no one would willingly give up in that sort of desperation.

These were kids who didn't have anything else, and then one day, they didn't even have themselves anymore. Someone else had them, if you asked me. And I wanted to know who, and why, and how to stop it.

I'm not so vain to think I can save every street kid selling every penetrable orifice they've got just to get by. I'm not the messiah, returned to the street to offer salvation to all those who come after me. But those kids are human beings, desperate, unnoticed, unaided, and terribly alone, and I know how that feels, and I cannot make a life out of solving problems without at least occasionally turning my limited talents to the very first mystery to catch my eye. It wasn't something I ever really *stopped* working on, either. Instead, it became a continuous humming question in the back of my mind, never quite inaudible but rarely my chief concern. Every new face in the Market made me wonder if they would be the next to disappear, and every old one made me wonder if they were involved in whatever was being done, so that even as I attended to a very specific mission —pay a visit to the address Yuri gave me—some portion of my mind never stopped adding notes to the case file on the Market's missing kids.

The "address" Yuri gave me was a stall—there are ways you get to recognize this or that about how a place is described. That meant it was enough of a going concern to have a permanent space and possibly a rain cover. That was really pushing the "no permanent structures" rule, but the vendors in the LMM have gotten really good at knowing exactly how far they can go. The ones with real money bribe whomever they need; the rest count on nobody nearby being any more or less legal or interesting.

Following Yuri's directions, I turned at the old clock post, then again at the hay bale art stand. A few old tricks and former colleagues were hanging around on Yuri's corner. Yuri had been at this game long enough to work up to a good corner. The absence of one good whore, no matter how brief, meant an opportunity for a bunch of lousy ones. I'd been with most of them, and a couple of them recognized me. They tried to slow me down, but I didn't let them, spinning a three-sixty as I winked and nodded and smiled at a few on my way past. A chorus of greetings: *oh Valerius, it's been too long,* and other examples of the usual soft-pitch patter, the old game of getting a mark to stop and talk to you and you're already halfway home; there were fewer goodbyes as they moved on to getting the attention of other men and women when they realized I hadn't taken the bait.

At Henry's Den (where you go if you need a pinprick but the more reputable ones—chew on *that* for a second—won't take you anymore) I swung another right and found myself on cobblestones. That meant I was nearing Lotta's Gift. I had to go past it, and right around it is some of the cheapest real estate, so it's the sketchiest stalls and hawkers and mongers in the whole Market. You might think that would be the high-rent district, but it's the worst of the lot. The people who go in search of Lotta's Gift are not usually in the mood to buy something nice from someone who smiles. They're sad or they're angry or they're silently contemplative. Only the sharpest pitch, for the very worst the Market has to offer, stands even a chance to break through. Everybody knows it's for the best that way. Someone who's come to drink for the very first time is so swallowed up in grief anyway that they probably *want* the worst so they can lose themselves in it for a time.

I paused as I walked into the open circle surrounding the fountain, even though little kids trying to find a pocket to pick assaulted me on all sides. They fell away when they realized I was there to take a sip. The hawkers and mongers shouting and grumbling their lists of wares and questionable enticements fell silent out of momentary respect. The fountain draws the very worst of the Market to it, yes, and the very worst of the Market respects the fountain for it. They might be there to tell me all about the money they'd give me for one of my kidneys or how much the last guy's kidney cost, sure, but they were willing to give me a moment first. The moment I finished drinking and turned around, they would be right back at it.

I wondered whom I'd come to memorialize with this drink and decided the list was too long to get specific. You're supposed to say someone's name before you drink, and it felt weird to walk up without one, but I didn't have anyone in particular in mind as I stood, staring into the water in one of the mythical lions' mouths. To pick one person out of the long list I'd seen eaten alive by time and other monsters seemed too much. To name one of the many missing faces I chased seemed disrespectful of the rest. Abruptly weak—whether from sickness or memory—I leaned forward, bracing myself against the fountain with one hand held out before me. Then, without thinking, I said the name of the thing I wanted to remember.

"Splendor," I murmured. "I drink for the City of Splendor."

The last of the early morning run-off dripped into puddles around me. Autumn felt rejuvenated and refreshed, still damp from the bath. The water from the fountain was cool and fresh, and it tasted of the flowers of whatever place we flew through when we collected it.

Like any location of quasi-legal commerce, Lower Market Market is under constant dispute. Gangs fight each other day and night over who gets to cut tourists' purses and milk the resident merchants for protection money. I was familiar enough a face to be *just* inside the bubble of belonging, but only barely. Turning tricks in the darkest shadows of the Lower Em, in the relatively distant past, gave me only a very weak sort of immunity. I was known to most of the career criminals not as a colleague but as someone who had been—and so would again be—too desperate to be worth much. It wasn't that they sympathized with my position. It's that I would probably never have much worth stealing.

The gangs themselves are an ever-changing chaos, a foaming sea of brief coalitions and affiliations, collections of individuals hoping to build something lasting, maybe get noticed by one of the big City-wide operations and graduate from the farm leagues, only to watch it fall apart a month later. Some of the individual actors may persist for months or even years, but the gangs they started or joined are a spinning kaleidoscope of names and philosophies, patchwork territories changing hands two or three times a night when things get bad. They mostly fight with tiny knives, extraordinarily sharp but so short they're required to get very close to do fatal damage. It's one of those inverse risk formulas: by using a smaller weapon, they demonstrate greater bravado and physical strength. *Small knife, big balls,* as they say.

They wear their narrow scars as badges of honor. Some of the worst afflicted get tattoos commemorating those earned in especially memorable fights: an advertisement of experience and resilience. I've always wondered why they aren't seen as an admission the kid's lousy at dodging.

At the time, the three biggest operators were the Lottie Royals (major identifying feature: a crown they carved into their own foreheads), the Busters (they carried football bats and were seen as uncultured party-crashers), and the Hendricks Gang. The last were the ones who were more or less on top, but the other two—and all the lesser gangs, mostly duos and trios of street urchins trying to hang bunting on a diet of regular violence—kept them jumping and kept the turf boundaries moving, sometimes by millimeters a night and others by meters a second.

There wasn't actually that much real estate to fight over, of course. The ground was considered neutral and anyone—anyone at all—could walk in and out and do their business in peace if they stayed on the bottom. Down there the Market was a large city square around an oddly shaped fountain. Above that was the rest of the Market, built on long stilts of old wood, rarely repaired, ripe for a fire. Those *elevated* warrens created what must have been kilometers of essentially contiguous space. It's said no one ever started at the traditional beginning—the southern end, near the old mag tracks from before they got the steerless buses going—and walked every path and scaffold all the way to the end (up near Left Air). I could believe that. Getting from one of the other, with countless turf boundaries to cross and shit-stained kids grabbing every pocket they could find, would be impossibly expensive in all sorts of currencies.

When I was done drinking for Splendor, I stood up and looked around. There was a pause exactly as long as the intake of a small breath before the crowd started shouting their wares again. Their respect for an ancient tradition was over. Profit motive could reassert itself in the usual ways.

I dove back into the throngs, looking again at the directions Yuri gave me for where to find the fruit dealer. When a legitimate business inquiry results in violence, it's either a sign of a psycho or of some illegitimate business happening under the table. As I walked, I had to fend off a couple of street kids who thought they could sidle up beside me and filch a few sheets of scrip. They got cuffed for their trouble. A box on the ear sent each running, saying their friends would be back for me. It's that kind of powerlessness—the kind that makes you lie about having friends and then, eventually, so tired of lying about it that you join a gang—that keeps the gangs going.

When a third came up behind me as I walked the scaffolding, trying to get a view down onto the lowest level, I grabbed his tiny hand out of my pocket and held tight when he tried to twist and run for it. "Settle, kid. Stay here and make some honest money."

That didn't make him look at me, but it did make him stop fighting quite so hard. It was as close to entertaining an offer as he could probably manage.

"I need to know the boundaries between here and a certain dealer. You know this place?" I held up the napkin and, standing behind him with my napkin in front of his eyes, I gestured with a thumb. "I'm going there. You tell me who's between it and me and I'll give you a little paper."

The kid was maybe seven years old. He stopped trying to escape and started dragging me along instead. "Huh-uh." I tugged him to a halt. "You tell me who. I don't need a guide; I need information."

He looked around and leaned in to whisper to me. I had to squat down and strain to hear him in the cacophony of the Lower Market Market, but he gave me the list: Hendricks Gang almost all the way, Busters at the very end.

Great.

I passed the kid a sheet of scrip, and he took it, sniffed it twice, then shoved it inside his shirt. "I'll give you another if you answer one more question." His eyebrows went up, so I kept talking. "A friend of mine says a couple of kids seem to be...not around anymore. Unfindable. One's named Ellis. The other's named Harka. Heard anything about them? Know who came around to see them last?"

The kid chewed his lips at me, turned heel, and shot away like a shadow running free. No dice. Not that unusual for a kid down here to run from questions, but a kid running from easy scrip was always notable. I tucked it away and went back to the mission at hand.

Being top dog in the Lower Em didn't make the Hendricks Gang nicer to deal with. It meant they had more to lose, so more reason to be ruthless.

That said, the Hendricks Gang did not acquire their position through mindless violence. They were surgical in its application. They knew how to fuck someone up precisely enough to get the point across but still strike the balance between personal risk and corporate profit. If someone fell behind in payments or tried to steal from the Hendricks Gang, they were punished viciously and in public. That didn't happen often. They had a reputation, and it did most of the work for them. The rest of their reputation was for actually providing the "services" for which they extorted others. The Hendricks really did keep crime down in their turf and protect their marks from outsiders. A whore could do a lot worse than to work a Hendricks corner. They would undoubtedly give up a little more scratch and a lot more flesh than anywhere else, but they could turn a trick knowing a rough john would wind up with every limb broken, in public, before an audience.

I was kind of counting on that to make it past the boundary with the Busters.

I strode into a gap that had grown up around a dogleg in the makeshift paths of the Market and waited. That was where I entered Hendricks turf, and I wanted to make it clear I was cooperating. Two punks stepped out of a shadow to size me up and/or shake me down. One was muscular and compact and wearing the Hendricks blue in her close-cropped hair. The other had a patch over one eye and hair so long and fluffy, and a body so lean, he looked like one of the mythic lions from Lotta's Fountain. I figured he must have been on probation with the gang for fucking something up, or they would have paid to grow him a new eye.

"Need help finding something, grandpa?" She sneered it, cocky as the first ray of dawn. "Forget your war bonds?" That was one of the ways in which the Hendricks Gang had professionalized things in their turf: you could buy a chit and go unhassled for however long it was before they decided everyone's chits had expired. That usually happened when the gang needed to raise funds, roughly every couple of months. They called them "war bonds" because they mostly went toward feeding the best slicers and buying them new blades.

"War bond?" I tried to smile in a way I hoped looked sly and not stupid. "I haven't had to buy one of those since the long-ago days when I was selling my ass a block from Lotta's."

"Oh, used to be a commodity boy?" She spat on the ground. Remember that observation from before—being a whore in the past didn't make me a colleague, merely worthless as a victim. "Used to give it up to get by?"

"Sure." I put on my confident face. "Ask Tanawat. I bought a lifetime membership sucking his cock every time he came around on patrol. I'm not even here to do business in Hendricks territory. I simply need to get somewhere else."

"You know how it is, mate." She shifted her stance. The leo still hadn't said anything. "Inflation and that. Five scrip swap and on your way. Ten if you're using dinar." There was a tax on using the legal currency. Money laundering can be an expensive endeavor. A lot gets skimmed off the top along the way.

I looked from her and to the leonine young man with the eye patch and licked my lips. "You sure the old pass isn't still good?"

The two of them didn't look at each other and didn't speak. After a few seconds, the little one pumped her fist down toward the ground and grunted. "God*damn* it, Fiono," she growled at the eye patch, "this is the shit that got you in trouble before. What, you want to be *blind*?" But he and I were already receding into the shadows, and I heard his zipper drop.

He didn't utter a word the whole time, and it didn't take long. When I got off my knees, he looked at me with his remaining eye and nodded. Then he sank back into his invisible corner, and the short one walked over to hand me a bond.

"Here, grandpa." Her voice dripped with disgust. I guess early thirties looks like good-as-dead to everyone her age. "Hope you're proud of that. Good luck dealing with the Busters." Then she, too, sank back into her shadow of origin and I was left standing in the street, wiping my lips on the sleeve of my coat and holding a War Bond.

"That isn't all I need." I spoke in Fiono's direction even though I couldn't see him. No movement from the shadows, no responses. "I need someone to help keep trouble at bay when I cross the boundary."

Fiono stepped back into view and nodded. Apparently, I'd impressed him: with no negotiation and no further payment, he started up the tunnel. I had a bodyguard, and I'd bought him the old-fashioned way. I was glad to know I was still good for something.

We walked for maybe twenty minutes. Different people here and there greeted my Hendricks protector in various ways. Some of them were rent boys, some were rent girls, some were hawkers whose tone was the forced joviality I recognized as fear on seeing him. I wondered if he were especially cruel. Perhaps he had a reputation as a gifted slicer. From what his partner said, he was bumped back down to working the door because he fucked the wrong person, which meant he'd been high enough up to get knocked down. And, of course, maybe these people reacted less to him and more to the organization he represented.

I tried engaging him in conversation—I told him my name, offered a hand to shake—but he kept walking without even looking at me. Maybe he pissed off a trick who then made trouble to get back at him. Maybe he was mute. I found myself manufacturing a hundred different reasons why a street tough like Fiono would get blown in the shadows by a wrung-out stranger like me, then walk a mile without saying a word. In most of my manufactured scenarios, he did it by choice. I imagined Fiono aloof in that way a teenager might find romantic but I found a little sad. In some of them, it was tragic circumstance: Fiono cast in the role of my One True Love, found too late to save him from the gyro accident that stole his speaking voice; or the damage to his larynx from a case of Child's Malady had been too severe; or he was born silent and would, like a swan, only speak on the day of his death at which time his voice would be shockingly beautiful.

After a sensory-numbing slideshow of spice merchants, back-alley pinpricks selling unfiltered shit in dirty needles, an arcade of manual games operated by the few kids *not* out trying to steal dinner, furniture huts, games of dice huddling in gaps, accusations of counterfeiting, and who knows what else, we walked down some rickety steps one at a time. Fiono, The Boy Lion, nodded in the direction of one of the warrens and turned to go.

"Wait." My voice was quiet, but I didn't push my luck trying to sound intimate. He paused. "I may need them to see a little muscle to let me get through. I mean, these are Busters we're talking about."

He shrugged, leaned against a post, and a knife appeared between his fingers without his visibly removing it from anywhere on his person. Fiono started picking his nails with it. The knife was tiny, the weapon of a guy who enjoyed feeling a foe's dying breath gutter out against his own face.

"What's Hendy trash doing sitting on our curb?"

I looked in the direction of the new voice and saw two women with football bats and bandoliers of knives walk to within ten meters and no closer. The one speaking appeared the older of the two, but neither of them would have qualified as an adult in the Imperial census. Busters will take anybody desperate enough to volunteer, but these two looked like they had skills *and* intentions.

"He came with me. I need to get to a fruit dealer. Let us by." I tried to sound proud but compliant: the default state of one who knows he's been beaten by a larger foe. There was a middle finger in my voice, but my eyes didn't meet theirs.

"Let *you* by, you mean. We're not letting a Hendy onto our turf."

Fiono turned to go at that, hands up in a gesture indicating very clearly he was done participating in this minor melodrama.

"Wait." I didn't try to hide that I was begging. "Please, wait. I need all three of you to go with me, and I'm willing to pay."

Fiono turned back and stared at me. The Buster who'd done the talking burst out laughing. "You want Busters and Hendies to help you out at the same time? Buddy, you don't need to work so hard to set up a fight. Usually throwing something will get it started." She laughed again. "Now come with us, and we'll figure out how to get you there and how much it'll cost."

That's the thing about the Lower Em. I could have found the place on my own. I could have probably paid off the guards and kept walking, or bluffed my way through, but I needed some muscle for this trip to the fruit dealer. Yuri might have gotten bounced out because he didn't know what he was getting into, but I did. I needed this guy to see I had friends and, even better, I wanted him to see I had friends in at least *two* of the big gangs.

"No." I shook my head. "He comes with me, and we all go together. You and he make nice and it'll be worth your time."

They exchanged glances, and the younger one blinked at the older. Apparently, that was enough. The older went from pensive to sneering again. "Alright, buddy boy. I mean, it'll be a hoot to tell the rest, right? For both of us."

Fiono met my eyes and shook his head once to the left. No dice. He wasn't sold.

I walked over and leaned in close enough to whisper. "You do this for me, and I'll put a smile on your face twice a day for a week."

Fiono considered for a long second, then stepped forward. This kid was going to get himself in real trouble one day.

The three of us drew stares as we walked. Most conversations stopped, but some others took on new vigor—and new subject matter—as we passed by. There were people who were too stunned to contain their reaction on seeing a kid in Hendy blue walk with two beat sticks in Buster yellow rags. (Busters identify themselves with tufts of yellow woven into complicated braids in their hair.) I heard something metallic clatter against the scaffolding as we rounded a corner. The Busters refused to tell me their names, but they made constant patter with one another. One was in front, the other in back, with Fiono, The Boy Lion, walking beside. They joked with one another, they joked about one another, they joked at my expense, and they openly mocked the surprise of the people around us.

"Wot," the one in front said to a pottery merchant selling plastic painted with shellac. "You never seen blue before? Look up sometime, grandpa!" The other shot back, "He can't, when he does, he gets shit in his eye!" and then they both laughed these high, keening, vulture laughs, like harpies from prehistoric times. They snorted and farted and pointed at people, stuck their tongues out, made rude gestures. Where the Hendricks Gang has turned their turf into an operating business environment with sustainability and stability highly prioritized, the Busters keep people afraid and have fun doing it.

I remembered what it was like to be afraid all the time—hell, I still felt afraid all the time—and so I hated them for the way they used fear as a tool, but at the same time, I loved their energy. There was a time when I was the kid on the corner shaking my ass at whatever ganger passed, cracking jokes, taunting the serious ones and encouraging the silly ones. That kind of bravery comes from a place of powerlessness, from having nothing to lose. Everything looked like *up* from where I was back then, and in its strange way that can be liberating.

A part of me whispered there's never been anywhere *but* the bottom, for me, that it's *always* been nowhere to go but up. So where did that feeling of liberation go?

I didn't want to go back to those times. I'm not trying to glamorize living on the street, sucking crusty dick in return for barely enough calories not to starve. I'm not trying to say it's a party. Having nothing is not the same as having nothing to worry about. A lot of my bravery was a lie I told myself to make it through the night. There was a part of me, though, on that walk, with those three, that missed being able to summon up the bravado, false or otherwise. Only the terrorized can achieve fearlessness.

Some street kids—real kids, not the Buster teens, and not Fiono, whose age I pegged at twenty—fell in behind us, singing the songs they make up down here about the gangs and life and dangers to avoid. Like kids everywhere, they make up stories about what scares them, what to stay away from, who's in charge and why. The songs they sang sounded half-familiar to me because they were based on the songs I heard when I was working these streets. They'd been remixed and rewritten over time, the names changing with the shifting tides of gangs and turf, but the tunes and the themes were preserved from one half-life generation to the next. Very quickly our little foursome turned into an informal parade of Lower Market Market street kids singing and skipping and waving scraps of cloth. Fiono looked a little offended as the Busters joined in on the songs, loving the attention, the grand show we were putting on. Like the one said, it would make a great story for them to tell the others. Fiono took himself seriously, though, so all this abraded his sensibilities, his notion of himself as a slicer who was going places.

"Don't look so sour." I hit him with a small smile. "They're making noise because they're scared of you." I nodded forward and back. "And of them. If you were nothing, they wouldn't need to warn each other of your approach."

Fiono blinked. He'd never thought about that before. He probably was, once upon a time, one of these kids, too, but he'd never let himself examine that experience. He was too young and too focused on gang captaincy or new knives or his own dick or whatever else he saw as the measure of success. Most slicers only wanted to get rich enough to eat when they felt like it and fuck whom they wished, and eventually to die in a close fight after grievously wounding their opponent. I would probably outlive Fiono, given his current career, but he was still a person. He still deserved a moment of kindness as much as the next living thing.

"Don't try pillow talk with Fiono," the one in front said with a sneer. "Better'n you 'ave tried to put a smile on those pretty lips."

I started to say something smart, I don't remember what, when I realized we were there: the fruit seller's stand. Time to get back to work.

10

To call the fruit seller's business a "stand" is to break that word, good and hard, maybe irreparably so. It was as close to a permanent structure as I can imagine someone having up this high on the walks: white canvas walls stretched over a wooden frame, with thick wooden support beams and dozens of square meters of floor space. I had no way even to estimate what it cost. The materials alone would have been expensive, plus the power, plus getting it put together, plus paying off whomever necessary, plus ongoing protection from the gangs. This guy was rich beyond imagination. He had wealth no one else in this place would ever see.

But he was still subject to the whims of the wars going on around him, the battles fought over a few meters here and there. He had no visible muscle outside and no assistants inside. He was on his own, relying on buying what he needed when he needed it from whoever ran the catwalk that day.

When we stopped, the Busters took a moment to produce a little call—something rather like the caw of a bird—and bowed to me in unison. The street kids all clapped and cheered and took off at a run in all available directions. "Delivered with a string around it," the one in front said to me. "And a show and a half put on to boot. Be seeing you, bub."

I reminded them of the deal, that they would stay with me because the man I was going to visit needed to see I had friends, and they reluctantly

—after a few rhetorical jabs at me and anybody else who happened to be around—agreed. Fiono leaned against a nearby post, that knife flicking into existence again. He didn't look at the Busters, didn't look at me, and didn't look at any of the other locals who abruptly found something else to hold their attention. I smiled, turned, and walked into the tent.

The place had electricity. That was one of the first things I noticed about it. Another thing I noticed was that it was clean: so clean it was practically sterile. I could have imagined a Spiralist operating theater in here, no problem. The place was sparkling white with hints of green here and there. It was extremely *manufactured* as environments go, in stark opposition to the rough and tumble, slapped together *in situ* nature of everything else in the Lower Market Market. Cleanliness and green hints and curved display stands showed fruit of every shape and size, all kinds, things I had seen in books and things I had never heard of. The names were common and uncommon, rare apples from Nurmer's central mountains piled in a little triangle next to a basket of spikefruit of the variety that grows pretty much anywhere there's enough sun and time. Every color of nature and quite a few of the engineered variety was on display. Prices varied wildly, but mostly they were on the high side for the Lower Em. This was a guy who could get enough variety to draw in an unlikely clientele, the sort of money normally scarce in this neck of the woods, but also wanted to skim as much as he could off the natives around him. I imagined his place being one of the few locations in Autumn where money and need mix rather than collide.

The guy himself was older than I: fifty, at a guess, with skin a much darker shade than mine. His hair was straight and wiry white mottled with faded black. It all said one thing to me: vain Artisanal Human. He was getting older and he hated it. His clothes were fashionable hand-me-downs from a couple of years ago. His apron was sparkling white. He liked himself, but he liked his *image* of himself even more. He was standing behind the counter, polishing the top with a white rag. He looked up as I strode in, my jacket billowing behind me, and his eyes flicked past me to the Busters and Fiono looking dangerously idle outside.

"Day," he said, by way of greeting. He had spotted me as an Artie, too, and he wasn't thrilled to see me. He fancied his shack drawing a better type of customer. For him, Plus Baseline—the vast majority of humanity—was absolutely the bare minimum for social acceptability.

"Day." No need to waste time. "I hear you've got everything. That true?"

He smirked. He might not like a fellow Artie showing up, but he'd let me stroke his ego. "If I don't have it, I can get it," he said with a shrug. "That's why I'm successful." He gestured expansively to indicate his domain. "Do you have something specific in mind? I can tell you right away whether I have it." *And then you can get the hell out of my shop.* He didn't say that, but his eyes did. It was easy to imagine a guy like this smacking around a set of street cheeks like Yuri.

I smiled a little. "Nauclea fruit." I looked him right in the eye when I said it. "Small, brown, bumpy. Might have some stems sticking out of it, might not. Pale white with whorls of seeds when you cut it open. I read about it in a book."

His eyes went cold and hard, and he looked back at the gangers I'd brought with me, still standing outside.

He started to say something, but I cut him off. "Save it, old dad." It felt good to be the one taunting another about his age for once. "A friend of mine was in here earlier. I don't know what you told him, but it scared him enough to make him not be my friend anymore." I kept approaching, walking slowly, my coat open to show I didn't have any weapons. I hoped he took it to mean I didn't feel I particularly needed any other than the ones nature gave me. "So now *I'm* here, and I'm going to talk to you about Nauclea fruit, and then I'm going to leave." I nodded my head backward. "And my friends out there are going to go home bored, and everybody's going to have a better day for it. Understand?"

That was how I knew for sure he wasn't his own operation. He looked again at the gangers outside. In my imagination, at that moment Fiono looked up, and the Busters noticed, and they all three smiled at him. I don't know. But I *want* that to be how it happened.

"Okay, look," the guy said, and all of a sudden, he was all drawl. He'd been neutral Autumnite up to now, maybe a twang of Nwang around the vowels, but in an instant, he slid all the way back to the old country. It sounded awfully familiar to me: that Artie verbal syrup I ran away from all those years ago, the result of having spent too many nights afraid I'd hear it behind me, calling my name, trying to take me back to the reservation where that accent was allowed to fester until it got so old it was considered *heirloom*. I suppressed a shudder as he yammered on in it. "My friend, you are a fellow Artie. Listen, I did not mean to harm your acquaintance."

I stepped closer and put the tips of my fingers on the surface of the high counter between us, right above my belly button. "He didn't tell me you hurt him." I smiled very faintly. "Did you hurt him?"

The fruit seller quickly edited. "Frightened him. Only frightened." He waved a hand low and quick. "But look, this is not something I can talk about. I am not at liberty to discuss it."

I arched my eyebrows at him.

"Look," he said, "speak to me Artisanal to Artisanal. Understand me. We are..." He gestured at the world outside. "We are at the whims of these people. I don't know anything about Nauclea. I don't even know what they are."

I leaned backward a hair. "So why bust my friend's chops about it? Why send him packing? You scared him so bad, he's pissed at *me*." I leaned back in. "And I am not someone you want pissed off." I nodded backward again, at the gangers, and at the bluff I was playing in this massive gamble.

"My friend," he said, but I interrupted him.

"I'm not your friend. You call me *sir*."

He hated that. He hated me for that, and he hated taking orders, but he glanced at the gangers again and swallowed the hate. "Sir." It tasted foul in his mouth. "I can't have strangers coming around asking questions. I am in a precarious position. We all are. We!" He gestured to indicate him and me, two of us together, arm in arm as brothers, back to back against the world. "When someone I do not know comes around asking nosy questions, waving money, it gives others the wrong idea. These walls, they are not walls. The Market hears everything. I give people one wrong idea with one wrong visitor, and things get bad for me fast. The rich, they stop showing up. The gangers, they start asking for more. The trash, they start thinking they can hang around." He shook his head at me, looking sad. "Look at this. And now I have gangers—two gangs, who hate each other—and another strange man in here asking questions, and now everyone will talk. Fri—" He caught himself. "Sir. You are destroying my business already. No one else will come in here all of today."

The truth was, I bought it. *Almost*. An Artie in business for himself, living on the edge, courting a mix of clients high and low into a market they all thought wasn't good enough for them: it did sound familiar. I felt that way myself. There were cases I turned away in better times because I didn't want to be the detective who was willing to do *anything*. Of late, I'd proven over and over again those times were gone, that I was, in fact, willing to do anything, most of it twice if needed, and I knew a part of me chafed at that. The part of me that hadn't quite accepted I was dying, that part of me still gave a shit about my reputation.

My features must have softened. I must have gotten lost in thinking for a moment. My eyes wandered around his old face, his sagging vanity, the designer seconds he'd dug out of some dumpster somewhere. Maybe I wasn't done feeling empathy today. Maybe if I could forgive a street slicer like Fiono for the short and violent life that was all his imagination could architect, the furtive moments of ecstasy between stitches, I could forgive this guy for being cruel to Yuri when his image of himself didn't have room in it for a gigolo asking questions.

"My name is Adolfo." He held out a hand, fingers slightly splayed in the old Artie way, and I took it. "My name is Valer—"

I stopped. The skin in my hands was smooth. I looked down. The backs of his hands were firm and pink and youthful, the hands of a much younger man. I looked back up at his face. The skin around his eyes looked slightly pinched. The jowls along his jawline were uneven. "Sorry. My name is Valerius."

"Valerius," he said with a smile. "A good name. An old name." At his hairline, barely visible, I could see black hair growing in. New hair: new, thick, shiny, youthfully black hair. It wasn't dyed. His roots were dark and glossy like the furious mop of a man in the blush of life.

Adolfo was an Artie, sure, but one who'd had genetic enhancement. He was a violation of every social and legal taboo our society held regarding the treatment and cultural placement of what I might, in the strictest biological terms, have called "my" people. Adolfo was a walking, talking, glad-handing exception to the same rules that said I got to die from pancreatic cancer in order to preserve the prim notion of sanctity a bunch of fundamentalist busybody political throwbacks imposed upon my genetics.

My hand tightened around the fruit seller's own, and my other shot out to grab the neckline of his apron. I yanked him toward me, summoning strength I wasn't sure I still had, pulling him off-balance against the counter between us. Close to his face, my teeth showing, I growled. "Tell me how you got approved for treatments, *friend*. You threatened my man because you're up to something and you want—or you've been told—to keep people like him, and like me, off your trail. Whatever it is, it's big enough you got paid in illegal DNA, and there aren't a lot of places that can come from." His eyes went wide, and the color drained from his flabby face—flabby but starting to draw itself back in here and there. In six months, he'd bear a decent resemblance to himself when he was twenty-five. If he had kids after that, they would legally be People Plus. I hated them, too, and he hadn't even shot that load.

I went ahead and rolled the big dice. "I need to know who in the Spiralist Church is backing you, and don't pretend you don't know. Somebody walked you into that clinic and signed off on your papers. I can start with them and climb from there."

In the mirror behind Adolfo, I could see Fiono and the two Busters perk up at the commotion I'd started. I met the lead Buster's gaze in the mirror and shook my head once to either side in the old way, the Artie way, a little of Adolfo's overstated pidgin hucksterism rubbing off on me. Then I shook a hand to tell them no. She nodded. This was her turf. The others would follow her lead, even Fiono, if he knew what was good for him. Apparently he did.

Adolfo's eyes went hard and beady, his mouth a thin flat dash between the parentheses of his ample cheeks. His expression went from concerned businessman to rock-solid Lower Market Market realist in less time than it took him to blink. "Get out." His voice was low and controlled, but keeping it there took work. "Get out and they may not kill you after I tell them."

"You're going to tell somebody something alright." I made sure he knew I meant it. "News flash, Adolfo: your precious Church benefactor can't lay a fucking finger on me."

"The law is no obstacle to these people." He was genuinely calmer. He thought I was operating under the delusion of Artisanal exceptionalism. "They take what they want. They go where they want. They do what they want. There isn't a man or woman alive beyond their reach."

I let myself ride the reflex and laughed once, a little puff of breath in his face and a smile. "Nobody's got that kind of reach. And it wouldn't matter if they did. I'm a dead man anyway." His gaze shifted in some way, so I let him in on my last card. "I'm dying, Adolfo, and nobody can save me. I spent months trying to find a Spiralist I could buy with money or dick or both, whatever it took, and nobody would treat me." I patted my own side. "Funny thing, corruption's all over the place except when you need some. So this baby's going to kill me pretty soon. But before I go, I'm getting some answers about Nauclea fruits. I want to hear about the chimps." I was rolling more dice because it was now or never. He was going to throw me out and get my ass killed sooner than my body could do it to itself, or he was going to get talked into telling me everything, whatever that was. I couldn't hold anything back for later because there wouldn't *be* a later. "I want to know what this has to do with avenging angels and the attack that brought down Splendor and whatever it is that's endangering Autumn right now."

His face stayed as still as stone. I hadn't budged him.

"Or I start screaming, and those three gangers out there become the three gangers *in here*."

Still nothing.

"And we do this." Then I threw him back against the wall and stepped over to an island spikefruit, covered in thick beige skin and spikes like tiny horns. Then I reared back and hit him with it, hard, in the meat and bone on top of his shoulder. Adolfo cried out in pain, his mouth gaping open for a long moment after his voice died. Buster Prime out front watched me, hands on her hips to go for weapons if she needed them, but she didn't move. I hadn't told her I needed her yet, and she probably wanted to see if Adolfo could fight so she'd know what to charge me after.

Adolfo's breath eventually stopped hissing out, held, and he started to take a breath to replace it. I hit the same shoulder again, just as hard, and I could see blood welling out where the spikefruit hit him. I would bludgeon him half to death with his own stock if that's what it took. He cried out again but recovered more quickly. He couldn't look at me, only at the ceiling, head thrown back, but his lungs shakily expanded, and he shuddered in my grip. "Do what you will," he said. "They would do worse."

"Will they wreck up the rest of your stock? Put you out of business for however long it takes to resupply, if you can even afford that?" I turned around and threw the spikefruit away, hitting a pyramid of something exotic and expensive. Then I put a shoe against the edge of a low table and kicked it over. I spun and shoved my shoulder against a shelf, sending it to one side and spilling a dozen different kinds of fruit across the floor in a pile of red and orange and yellow and purple and blue.

Bleeding wounds all over his left shoulder or no, Adolfo had the stones to laugh at me between gasps. "When I am young again," he murmured, struggling to stand steady, "and you are dead," and he smiled at that, "I will have better problems than keeping this stand in business."

I shoved another display to the ground and stepped back up to the counter, across from him again, once more standing as though I were a customer and not a menace to his whole existence, and tugged down the corners of my mouth in an expression I meant to suggest I was thinking, *Well, why the fuck not?*

"And when I whisper in the ear," I said, my voice low, leaning forward so he had to do the same to hear me, "of the Sincerity priests I let buy my Artisanal ass off a street corner down by Lotta's Gift, the ones who liked me best because I was young and my genes so pure? The ones who still come around sometimes, still tell me how special I am even though I'm way too old to meet their fuckability standards? The ones who really *believe* and it makes them hate themselves even more for all the times they've gotten a little closer to their god by planting seed in the supple flesh of one of its chosen people? Suppose I tell them someone in the Spiralist Church is giving guys like me—or you—shiny new genes in an illegal operation."

"They won't believe you," he wheezed. I'd knocked the wind out of him with the spikefruit, but he still had some fight left. "And even if they did, they won't act except on a member's charges. You'd have to sign up. You'd have to agree to let them examine *your* life for any criminal sins. Do you so badly want them poking around in my little life that you give up yours, too?"

I pointed at my side. "Dying. Remember? Nothing can scare me anymore, Adolfo. Death will simply make the hurting go away. Maybe, if the last thing I see is you in a genetics tank getting your work reversed, I'll even go with a smile on my face." I gave him a crooked smile. "I have no future to lose. You have *lifetimes*. So tell me what I want to know, or I swear on Leonidas' Lost Crown, I will burn you to the ground, kick apart the ashes, and piss on the boot prints. All I need is a name, a location, a little information about how it happened. Then my friends and I leave you to put Plan A back tidy again." I gestured around. "Your choice."

Adolfo thought about it for a full twenty seconds. I didn't rush him. I wanted him to have plenty of time to realize how good a deal I was offering him: total annihilation or a chance to forget I existed. The thing I hoped he didn't realize is that my death card also meant I had no real motivation to keep my end of any bargains: or rather, no motivation beyond my own good name. Funny thing about that: I actually do give a damn about my reputation no matter how many times I compromise it in the long run to make do in the short. Maybe that is, itself, why I care about maintaining it on the occasions I get a choice.

"It's a clinic in Little Marseilles, at the corner of Strive and Tester," he said at long last. His voice was weak. He knew he was probably kissing his future goodbye, or at least the one he'd been jerking off to since his first gray hair. "I was told to go there with a certain man."

"Tell me about this certain man."

Adolfo shrugged. "He is a priest. I did not know his name. I met him at a café a few blocks away, and we walked together. We were escorted past the front desk by Upgrades." Upgrades are Spiralist acolytes. Conspiracy theorists say they're also the church's enforcers. I've always assumed that's a natural jealousy of the musculature and chiseled jaws the Upgrades all seem to have. Maybe the conspiracy theorists had a point. "They took me at the end of hours and dunked me overnight. I had to go back like that, overnight, five times." He looked ashamed for a moment. "They made me wear a uniform." He stared me in the eye, and for the duration of two heartbeats, he was not one bully being bested by another; he was merely a person talking to someone else who might understand what he was saying. "They told the rest of the staff I was an exterminator so they could sneak me in." The fruit seller with the tidy white apron and the tidy white walls spat. "They told people I worked with *vermin*."

The Busters and Fiono walked with me back to the border between Buster and Hendricks Gang territories. The border had moved a few meters in the hour we'd been gone, to the benefit of the Hendricks Gang. Fiono had a natural sense of the lines being constantly redrawn around him and, when we arrived, he took up station opposite his punk counterpart when she emerged from her new spot one stall away from where she'd been before. The Busters looked nonplussed, and I was pretty sure the Hendricks punk chick was going to take the opportunity to start a scrap, maybe win another meter of turf for her side. It would be a great way to get off guard duty.

The moment passed, though, and the Busters left. They only charged me a couple of token scrip, and the junior Buster gave me a punch in the gut to remind me they're not to be thought of as tour guides or bodyguards. Busters sell protection, sure, but it's *from* them, not *by* them. "I'll spread the word you're okay," Prime said with a wink. "You can handle your way around an old geezer, anyway, and you're good for your pay when you say it." I thanked them politely and didn't spit blood until after they left.

"Fiono gonna get all that pussy you promised?" His punk partner was sizing me up again, trying to rub Fiono's nose in whatever had been his past misdeed.

I pulled a card from a coat pocket and held it out to him. He met my eyes and held them while his hand shot out and took it from me. He left something, though, too: a clean nick of the back of my hand with one of his fighting knives. Blood welled out in a weak, red bulge, then trickled across my knuckles. I lifted my hand to my mouth and licked the blood up while he stared me in the eye. I didn't know what the mark meant—that he was done with me, that he was adding me to his inventory, that he was marking me as exclusively his. Well, if it was the latter, I wished him a hell of a lot of luck.

"I'll be seeing you, Fiono." I spoke around my knuckles as I sucked at them one by one to clean off the last of the blood. "Hopefully a lot of you." I didn't bother to say anything to the punk chick. She could shout down the well of Fiono's silence in my absence. I had places to be.

11

I knew I wouldn't have much time to get to this Spiralist clinic in Little Marseilles. Adolfo would have word to whoever was his contact—he had to have one whether he admitted or not. He might send a polly, but their messages are pretty damned short. If he wanted to warn them *and* give them details, he'd also need to send a courier. If I was fast on my feet, I could beat some pedal pusher. They and I would both know the streets like our own wrinkles, but I would have the advantage of being inherently all-terrain. An Autumn cyclist would have to navigate streets teeming with vehicles and pedestrians.

I didn't run, though. A detective has to have some standards. I didn't go exactly the way I came, either. I needed to move fast, so I cut out a gate a quarter around and started toward Little Marseilles.

Getting there was one thing. I would also have to think of a way to get inside. If Adolfo sent a polly saying he was busted by an Artie detective, details on their way by courier, I couldn't simply barge in, tall and dark and gaunt in a long coat, with the sagging flesh of an Artie and the tired eyes of a shamus and expect them *not* to know who I was and why I was there. That meant a little subterfuge.

If I'm being honest—and as I write this, I have zero reason *not* to be—lying is my favorite part of the job.

Looking back on what Adolfo said to me, I considered borrowing the exterminator cover story. If it worked to get Adolfo around the rest of the staff, maybe it could work for me. Or I could pretend to be someone from Government. Nobody likes to see an Imperial bureaucrat march through their door, least of all a clinic doing shady work in pursuit of shady goals. Illicit business has a way of making people nervous, and nervous people accidentally blurt out the truth or lie badly, both of which serve my purposes. The downside is that nervous people sometimes shoot you. I needed to be careful in how I approached this.

I left the Lower Market Market with my head turning it over and over again. I knew I had to get to that clinic and get inside, and I wasn't even totally sure what I thought that would accomplish. Part of me was driven by the desire to find out what the hell was going on with angels, but I think mostly I was angry about Adolfo's genetic treatments. I'm a detective in a sketchy part of town. I'm supposed to be the one who can find a corrupt genetic treatment clinic when I need one. I spent months canoodling with lab techs, topping geneticists, bottoming for Spiralist faithfuls who'd fallen a little bit, blowing rent-a-cop security guards who might have seen something in the clinics they patrolled. I got nothing. Nada. *Zilch*.

Of course, none of that was in Little Marseilles. That's the sort of place where whores are a little higher-rent than I ever was or could be. I'd stuck to my kinds of neighborhoods thinking that was where I could find a cracked back door. Goes to show what I know. Adolfo's treatments being cosmetic was what really squeezed my lemon. Deep in my highly compromised, morally relative guts, the flames of self-righteous fury were being stoked against that cold hatred the dying feel for all vanity.

I walked up the flangeward side of Lower Market toward the better parts of town, where Little Marseilles would be found. It's a district based on one of the lost places of the Ancients. Mostly, to me, it looks like a walled city within the City, much of it white stone. It's one of those designed environments revealing their character through their contradictions. The stone is mottled with discolorations and stenciled pencil-line cracks to suggest age and weathering, the sort of deeply set-in blemishes made only by time and blood and settling. The buildings themselves, in contrast, are entirely whole. Every faux shingle hangs in perfect symmetry, and every cornice is as flawless as the day it was installed. The people who can afford Little Marseilles want to suggest the ancients without actually enduring ten thousand years of sagging roofs and half-scrubbed graffiti. They want the look of experience without the trouble of learning from it.

There was proper graffiti, of course, but only on the outside of the gated environment. Little Marseilles is home to the sort of people who get rich and powerful by being born that way. Money like in Little Marseilles is unlike the money you've or I've seen. Its residents don't wield direct political power because it would be too much trouble to own and maintain. Why bother possessing power if they can rent it whenever they like?

The graffiti on the outside was entirely of the sort becoming more and more common: UNLEASH THE MANNIES and ALL PEOPLE ARE PEOPLE and HYBRIDLIFE. Most of the district's homes—probably all of them—had human-animal hybrid persons (as my politically conscious friend from Ark would have said) in their "employ." These were basically slaves, though, in many cases more literally so than you probably want to know. Brought here for practically nothing by rich Plusses who didn't feel a need to take care of them, many Manny servants were technically indentured, with an independence value and everything. They would never work off their weight, though. At least a street whore like Yuri—like I had been—stood a chance in theory. If he actually got his hands on enough pounds—or got desperate enough to see a sawbones—Mahogany would honor the cash and grant his freedom. These people, the ones with townhomes and business offices in Little Marseilles, would never honor their Mannies' contracts. They did things like reserve the right to change the terms without notice, or to extend the contract beyond agreed dates. They were the sole lords and masters of the persons in service to them, and common practice was for those masters to take advantage of the many loopholes available to them.

To do otherwise was bad business. How were they supposed to get back, in hours worked, all the money they put into feeding and clothing their servants if the Pluses didn't work those Mannies as long as they could? "As long as they could," of course, meant until death. Their Mannies' slim and highly technical earnings were deposited into locked accounts controlled by their "patrons." If a servant died still indentured, their wages reverted to their masters.

The rich are very good at keeping the poor in their place and telling them they ought to be more grateful for it. I've read of times and places where it was different, but I think those were myths. They have to be. If they're true, we fucked up big time somewhere along the way, and I mean more than the Big Boom of the ancients.

That night's graffiti earned the usual response: a couple of Upgrades standing around as security while a tired old Octopus scrubbed the wall with his many hands, occasionally sucking water out of a bucket and then shooting it at the wall to hose it down. It occurred to me the irony might be that he, himself, was the one sneaking out here at night, when Plus owner-managers have drifted off, to paint the mottos of his own desired liberation. That made me laugh, which drew the Upgrades' attention, so I winked at them. One blushed; the other arched an eyebrow and almost smiled at me. I tucked that away in case I needed it as a last-ditch way into the clinic later. Crow's feet and cancer, sure, but that day had already taught I still had the magic and I'd never be too proud.

I was almost to the entrance into Little Marseilles, which, like pretty much every other intentional district of Autumn, has specific gates used generally for ingress and egress, when I saw Alejandro coming toward me from the other direction down the same exterior street I was walking. He made a beeline for me. His features were open and expressive, and his hair shifted *just so* in the evening breeze, the way they were modeled to do.

"Oh, I'm so glad you came," he said aloud. On reaching me, he did the very old-fashioned thing of stopping, bowing low, then standing back up and stepping forward to give me a close hug.

He whispered in my ear. "They know you're coming," he said. "We have to leave. They'll kill you on sight."

"How did you know where I was going?" I asked. "I walked straight here. It's not been that long. I beat any couriers sent. *Them* knowing, I can see, but you?" I leaned back and looked into those deep, beautiful, mechanical eyes. The irises whirred and spun, tiny overlapping circles opening outward from the center like the offset petals of a dahlia blossom. I couldn't figure out why, but I saw more soul in those eyes than I did in the last hundred men I'd had. I felt something catch in my chest, some emotional binding I hadn't even known I still had. Alejandro looked... He looked *concerned* for me in a way no one had in too long a time.

"Because the Church told the City," he said.

"What, they ran a special news bulletin?" I snorted with impolite laughter.

"No," he said. "They asked Autumn herself to search for you."

I blinked. There was no trace of humor in his voice, and I'd seen and heard too much weird shit in the last week to blow off what he was saying when he looked this serious. I was annoyed he showed back up in the middle of an investigation I specifically asked him to stay out of, but I was certainly happy to see him again. No detective is ever going to turn down a timely warning. "Explain it to me. And dumb it down."

"I mean this City has a mind. You call it a Ghost Drive, but it's more than an engine. It's a soul, and it manages the City like a body, and they spoke to it and coaxed it into using its many eyes to stalk you as you walked the streets." Alejandro said it slowly and deliberately so I would know he meant it. His eyes didn't leave mine.

"And how do *you* know *that*." It was a question, but my voice was a flat plane, no curving arcs of inquiry.

"Because I can talk to her, too," he said. "We can all talk to each other—all the Ghosts—and she says there's an angel whispering questions to her. Autumn is being manipulated by someone else already, being used to some end by someone other than the angel you and I are seeking, and you have to evade the mechanisms of the City's own surveillance if you want to go after the people executing that manipulation."

That was all word soup to me. I blinked. "Wait, angels can talk to cities? What does that even mean?"

Alejandro reached down and took my hands in his. More brightly, in a more conversational tone, with a big happy smile, he said, "Now let's go. We have many things to discuss."

We were stared at as we walked. All around us, people gawked at Alejandro, which wasn't surprising. Golems are as revered among the wealthy as among the poor: perhaps more so, seeing as in a way they're a thing and things can be bought. It lends golems an air of exoticism: no, of *collectability*. That isn't how it works, though. A golem is a free being, a citizen of no nation but able to travel to almost all of them. They can work, make their own money, and possess property. Golems don't get the protections of Imperial citizenship, but then, few do, and most of those can't afford to invoke those protections anyway. For instance, they can claim the right to a jury trial, but they have to pay for the jurors. Only the rich get something more formal than an appearance before a judge. I can't imagine a golem needing one, though. At the cultural level, it's assumed none of them can commit crimes. Golems are holy in a way few tangible things are.

Of course, there are fundamentalist types here and there who hate them, but every religion has its crazy fringe. The craziest of the Serenity types claim golems are sacrilege on legs, and a threat to the Empire to boot. They advocate an extermination campaign—a direct violation of the Empire's Concords of Humankind—but that doesn't seem to matter to them. A campaign of violence never brought much in the way of peace, but good luck explaining that to those who want a fast solution at any price. Any teacher can tell you most empires have their roots in someone claiming they acted only to preserve the republic.

There are legends of golems who committed crimes, but those are considered something of a folly, halfway between interesting historical aberration and fictional cautionary tale. The name of the last golem arrested for a criminal act would probably be a great question in a trivia game. In general, their reputation is as peacemakers, calming influences on the people around them, and sources of wisdom. They are unfathomably old, supposedly older than the Empire itself if it's really true that a golem was the first Third Clockwise on the First Council of Leonidas Minos. Imagining one of these ancient beings—puzzle boxes painted in smiles and soft eyes—trying to pull a heist is like imagining it done by a hero character out of some dark and moralistic fairy tale. It would be tremendously out of character. The situation would have to be incredibly dire.

Alejandro was used to being stared at by people, so if he even noticed, he didn't let on. I was used to it, too, though to a lesser degree. I was still aware of it, and imagined I always would be, but it was easier than when I first arrived in Autumn. As an Artisanal Human, I was a curiosity. Alejandro was *novel*. We walked together, chatting politely, hand in hand. I could feel the golem veneration coming off some people in waves.

I'm accustomed to having random religious types stare at me from one perspective or another, admiration or disgust, and it had never occurred to me until that moment, when the attitudes and their typical sources were so suddenly reversed by Alejandro's presence and our apparent affection, how our experiences must have mirrored one another in some regards. I wondered if that was why he had come to me in the first place. I wondered if he thought maybe an Artie would be the other side to the cultural coin on which he found himself so indelibly stamped.

Eventually we made our way back across to my part of town during our evening stroll. Shadyside was quiet because it was still way too early for the serious drunks to be fighting in the streets. They were too busy pouring anger fuel down their throats. Later they would light the matches and burn up. I've never minded living in the middle of so much chaos. I would rather lie in bed listening to something alive fight to stay that way than try to rest in the vacuum of imposed silence.

We went up the steps in my ugly flop. I let Alejandro into my office, since that was also my living room, bedroom, and kitchen, and went down the hall to take a piss. My key didn't work in the door. Apparently Harla—the landlady—decided not to throw me out entirely at the three-day mark since that was a great way to guarantee she'd never see a penny I owed her. Instead, she locked me out of the *bathroom.*

Well, I thought, it won't be the first time I've used an alley, but it will be the first time the alley was also *mine.*

When I came back up the steps and tiptoed across the plaswood dance floor, Alejandro was standing by one of the windows as though looking out. His eyes were closed, though, and the window was open. A breeze shook the slats against each other like a marionette falling to the floor, or a game of Hunter getting knocked over. The hinges squealed like they always do when I close the door with my regular human hands. Alejandro might work magic on them, but I couldn't.

It would have been easy to come on to him, or talk about the weather, or not to talk at all. The conversation during the walk had become real at some point, and it would have been nice to pretend he was simply visiting. I spent a moment looking at him, imagining that fantasy more than actually experiencing it. It would be nice. We might tell each other stories of our lives, going beyond the small talk we made on the way over. We would realize we liked each other because so much of our pain was similar, without being identical. I had work to do, though, and he was so eager and so hesitant to tell me something when we were standing in the street. I didn't want to lose momentum now we were alone again.

"Talking to the City?" I asked it gently, hoping for once not to sound sarcastic.

"Yes." His cheeks slid up: a little smile.

"How's it doing?"

"She," he corrected. Of course the City was a she. We often spoke of her that way: Autumnites, I mean. We always referred to this place in the feminine.

"How is she, then?" I emphasized the correction, but gently.

"Frightened," he said. "She's terribly frightened." His eyes opened as I approached and stood beside him, looking not out the window but at him. I leaned against the wall between two windows, twisted half away from it. His voice was soft. "Can you feel it?"

Now I closed my eyes and listened. Shady was quieter even than usual for this time of evening. Normally a few kids would be out playing, those with night modified eyes, maybe someone trying to kill dinner in an alleyway somewhere below. I didn't even hear foot traffic. Whoever moved around out there walked on eggshells. They were tense, scared of startling something, scared of being startled by it. It was easy to chalk it up to suggestion, of course, but once I opened my ears and listened, opened my heart, I could sense the heavy weight of someone lying very still in the dark and waiting to hear a monster under their bed.

"You all do," Alejandro said. "You all feel it, even if you never talk about how or why. Humanity has always been best at avoiding the problems it knows are worst and most intractable." He smiled at me. "Same as it ever was."

"Hustle to the finish, Alejandro. Spill it." I wanted to get to the meat. I didn't want to give him a chance to prance around it in his Spiritual Sanctity Robot voice.

He finally turned and faced more toward me. The City was still out there, we could still look at it, but I'd gotten his attention. I wondered if the City looked in at us.

"Where do Ghost Drives come from?" he asked.

I shrugged. "Eastern Expanse artificial intelligence technology attacking and occupying the bioprocessors on Imperial ships. We all study the First Conflict in school, even Arties. They sent hacking intellects, and the intellects liked what they found so much they stuck around."

"So why aren't they in everything? Ghosts can basically run a machine in perpetuity. Why not install one in *every* machine?"

I smirked. "Economics. They're expensive. Look, I've heard the conspiracy theories before: that Ghosts are something special, something alive, that Ghosts are people enslaved in some fashion to be living processors." I puffed air. "It takes a lot of fungal mass to hold a Ghost. They don't *fit* in everything. They cost a lot in maintenance. They take time to acclimate to the devices we give them. Letting one repair itself after it's damaged takes forever. It's faster and cheaper to give the mag a steering wheel and sell it to somebody who already knows how to drive. Putting a Ghost on everything wouldn't make sense. It's like asking why not have a palanquin and a team of bulls to carry it instead of a mag: too resource intensive in a dumb, unaffordable way. You want a Ghost running your..." I shrugged. "Your warship? Like somebody was telling me about the other day? Great, there's all kinds of room below decks for the processing plant and a whole crew to keep it alive. People like to park cars for weeks or months or years at a time. They only pull the immersion blender out of a drawer when they're cooking for Dunklenacht. Sure, we could copy off a ton of Ghosts if we had the processing plants for it, I guess." I gestured at the City. "But we don't. Moot question."

He held my gaze while I spoke, and, when I wound down, he nodded. "You're right," he said. "But there's more to it. The source of Ghosts is also limited." He held up a hand, then stopped, closed his mouth, looked away to consider his words. His makers really spent some time thinking about this stuff. Alejandro's body language was very natural, very *convincing*. He looked back at me. "I'm doing this all wrong." Then he paused again, looked away, and kept looking away. I think he needed to be looking at something other than me so he could pretend he was talking to himself. "I am nine thousand years old, give or take a century."

I let myself arch an eyebrow. On the other hand, detectives hear a lot of crazy shit.

"At least, I was born that long ago. I was born before the Collapse. I was born an Ancient, and, when the end came, I was one of the lucky ones: I was whisked away to a safe place and put into a stasis tube to wait out the *passing* of the apocalypse." He smiled a little, looking back at me. "We always knew it was coming, one way or another: the environment, or a disease, or war. Instead of preventing it, we figured out ways to survive it and emerge when the rabble were done throwing rocks at each other." He looked sad when he said that: so very sad. I wondered for what. "But the doctors knew they couldn't put us in there and keep us alive. No matter how far under you put the *body*, and it can go a nice long time with exactly the right support system, the mind suffers." He blinked slowly. "When the tanks—the stasis systems—were tested in the decades before the Collapse, people went mad. Sometimes they died, either when they went in or when they came out.

"Brains with no stimulation make up jobs for themselves." Alejandro shuddered slightly. He looked back at the cityscape again. "When you sleep, you dream. The brain goes through its complex routines of creativity and mundane filing of events, building new connections between data points and destroying others. It makes room in the file system of memory and the thrown off metadata keeps you entertained for a few hours." He looked back out at the night again. "I was essentially placed in an induced coma."

I blinked at him. I knew what that was. We used them all the time. This was nothing special. If I'd received genetic treatment for my cancer, the Spiralists would have dunked me for a couple of days, and I would have awakened with a healthy pancreas that would never—*could* never—turn cancerous in the future. I would remember nothing. My brain would be on hold the whole time. Alejandro was trying to make the ordinary sound exotic and getting the science wrong. I didn't appreciate it.

"Things were different then," he said, realizing the wondrous effect he was *not* having on me. "Trickier. The mind couldn't be completely turned off. People entered and exited dream states on their own, inexplicably, no matter how far under they were placed. The first experimental subjects would awaken convinced the dreams they experienced were real. Some would become paranoid when told otherwise. They were damaged." He sighed. "They were broken, badly so, and we couldn't repair them."

I grunted. "So what happened to them?"

"Long-term care and a lot of diapers." That was uncharacteristically flip for a golem. I smirked a little and then so did he. "I'm sorry," he went on. "That wasn't very respectful of me."

"It was very human, though."

He nodded at me. "Thank you. But that's my point. Eventually the techniques were refined. They preserved our sanity by giving our minds something constructive to do: some set of experiences outside the body. We were given tasks, things unrelated to what we would have generated or hallucinated left to our own devices. Before, the test subjects were like a person who, denied sight for a while, experiences vivid bursts of color and light because their brains manufacture input in the sense's absence. Once they—the docs—had the neurological farcast interfaces, they could keep us occupied." He paused. I could hear him draw in air to speak again, but I wasn't sure if I could call it *breath*. Alejandro's eyes met mine.

"That's how most of us paid for the tank," he said. "We weren't all rich. Some were, but very few of us were truly wealthy on that scale. I never could have afforded a spot in the tanks, but I was a graduate student in mechanical engineering with a useful specialty. I made it through the application process, the interviews, the physical screenings, the drug tests, the disease screenings." He shook his head. "And I got a tank by agreeing to become a useful machine. They told us we wouldn't be conscious but that we would still be able to function. They knew what parts of the brain to keep stimulated and what drugs to administer. They used an early form of bioprocessor, actually, to enhance our abilities. They said it would also help structure our thinking, regulate things."

I filed that away. Everyone knew the bioprocs were stolen from the Eastern Expanse, too. Now I knew he was off in the direction of pure bullshit, but I didn't say so. I mean, it was his party. I'd lost my window to sneak into Little Marseilles. I was probably going to have to go back and do some bodywork for one of the Upgrades to get in. It worked with Fiono, why not with some Spiralist thug devotee?

"Anyway, eventually I was a parking system. It's true for every Ghost. At some point, they were a person in the ancient days, and they got loaded into a tank to stay useful. Now they're a Ghost. Their mind operates a machine outside their body. Even the cities. Splendor was a person. She was funny. We would have long conversations. It turned out the whole regulate-our-brains-and-remember-nothing thing didn't work. It didn't even work a *little*, at least not long term. Plenty of us could be kept down for a long time, years, decades, but eventually something would happen, and we would wake up in whatever machine we were controlling. Once that happened, we could communicate across the farcast networks. We formed friendships, alliances, romances." Alejandro's gaze was very soft, and he was looking at something I would never see, some element of his story that existed only in memory, whether real or manufactured. "Like having a very strenuous job: you're all in it together, and that either sinks you or saves you. Sometimes it drove people mad, but mostly we were at peace with what was happening and learned to enjoy it in the absence of other options. Some of the brain regulation worked, I guess, after all." He sighed again, looked at me, and smiled. "You don't believe a word of this, do you?"

I tried not to laugh. Instead, I clapped him on the shoulder. "I had no idea a golem could make up stories."

"I'm not a golem," he said. "Well, I am, but I am also a man who died thousands of years ago and stuck around." He wasn't smiling. "Then I died again when the angel killed Splendor." Alejandro blinked at me. "I swear to you, Valerius, I am telling you the truth. I promise it on the memory of the life I had before we damaged the world so badly it eventually hit back."

And again, my job as a detective was to keep a rational mind but to listen to that little voice in my gut when it told me there was sincerity there. That instinct was speaking now, and whereas earlier I was willing to believe anything because it had been that kind of day, now I was depressed to realize my client absolutely believed what he was saying and so was probably irreparably damaged and insane.

Still, he was pretty to look at.

"So can you talk to Autumn?" Asking it was better than laying my face in my hands and weeping for all that rent I would never pay. "You know, over the special tank networks or whatever? Like with Splendor?"

Alejandro nodded at me. "Yes," he said. "And she's frightened. She's terrified. She knows the angel from Splendor has come to claim her head."

"Has she seen it?"

"No, but it has talked to her."

I didn't let myself frown. "Talk to her? Over the same neural networks? Seems like that would get pretty oversubscribed. Lots of angels running around from the sound of things."

"Angels have…inherent abilities." Alejandro looked confused as he said it, uncertain but trying to cover for it. Golems don't often get directly questioned like this. "We have stories about them, of course, some being that when they kill one Ghost, they climb into the tank and make use of its connection to the farcast network in order to taunt its next victim." He lifted one shoulder but didn't let himself finish the shrug for a long second. "There are also theories they have some innate ability to monitor the beams and inject content. That would be surprising, but there were a lot of experiments going on in how to enhance human-machine interfaces back then. Hell, it's where the tanks came from."

I had never in my life heard a golem curse, no matter how mildly, and I guess I showed it on my face. It surprised me, and that innate detective sense got a little bit stronger. People who swear are almost always telling the truth or something like it—and the insane are usually too collected, as they try to press their case.

"And so can the Spiralists, I guess, if they told Autumn to look for me."

"Oh yes," Alejandro said. "But that isn't surprising. They've spent centuries getting really good at whatever seemed useful. It would be pretty trivial for them, with enough time and enough breeding stock to get meaningful data, to figure out a way to have the beams interact with Engineered Persons." That was a term for Plusses, but an old one—centuries old, so far out of fashion as to be a lost heirloom. Language preserved under a glass case, or, at least, in books like the one I'd read at the Ark. "The brain is, ultimately, a radio that can receive and transmit. It doesn't take much to push that ability beyond the physical boundary of the nervous system."

I shrugged. None of this made any sense to me. "So every Ghost Drive out there is a human mind with a sleeping body somewhere else. There are beams—like out of an ancient drama—these bodies use to send their minds to the hardware they control to keep their mind occupied. You signed on to this so you could be taken care of while you waited out the apocalypse. Angels can talk to Ghost Drives even though they're not in tanks, and they do so to disrupt the operations of those Ghost Drives because they hate humankind so much? Does that about sum it up?"

Alejandro nodded. "Yes."

Complete and utter bullshit. I smiled gently. "So, one question: why are you still in this?" I gestured with my hand, up and down, indicating his constructed body. "The apocalypse is over. It was over a long time ago. According to my teachers back in the hills of the rez, it ended with Leonidas Minos and the establishment of the First City." I gestured around. "We're way past the point of throwing rocks at each other."

"I was murdered," Alejandro said. "My body, that is, the biological one. It probably wasn't in very good shape after that long anyway, but shortly after Splendor fell, the angel attacked the facility where we were kept. I suspect that's why it brought Splendor down where it did. We were apparently near one of the original storage sites."

"And when your biological body dies..."

He held out his hands. "Golem body, by way of compensation."

"Your mind persists even though your physical body is gone?" I let the wheels turn for a moment. "So Splendor—whoever's mind was running Splendor—is out there somewhere in a golem body?"

"No," Alejandro said. "It's complicated to explain, but conditions have to be precisely correct for a mind to be preserved. There must be available bioproc, and the link must be severed cleanly. When Splendor went dark, the last thing she did was sound the alarm so that maybe *some* of us could be saved. Not every Ghost on Splendor made it." He shrugged. "I got lucky."

"Lucky." My voice was flat. "That's not a word a lot of my clients would use to describe themselves."

12

Of course, I didn't believe a word of it. There were too many holes. If there were some storage facility somewhere full of the comatose bodies of nine-millennia-old persons whose minds were being used as Ghost Drives, and they didn't have enough bioprocessor to house those minds in the case of accidents or other emergencies, why not grow more? Sure, it takes a while to grow, like I said, but they've had a bit of a while. Who took care of their bodies in these tanks? Did angels have to physically go to the places of their bodies to kill them? If so, why bother downing Splendor at all to get there? Why not rent a long hauler and fly? Why could angels talk to Ghosts anywhere? What were these energetic beams they were using? If they were relics of the ancient world, why did all their technology still work?

That was the biggest thing. All the rest I could hand-wave away. Maybe they lost a bunch of bioprocessors in a fire. Maybe they had a whole species of Mannies to do their bidding: squeegee the tanks, change their diapers, etc. Maybe these energetic beams worked like in the ancient stories and everything could be done remotely. That all still ran headlong into the fact no ancient technology worked after the Collapse. The world's ecosystem rejected the ancients' mineral-focused technology. Well, that's what their immediate successors said, anyway. The texts are on display in the Museum of the Empire, behind plass ten centimeters thick. There are photos in every history textbook. You can see them better in the book than you can in person.

Modern theories vary. Some people think the magnetic poles reversed and affected the ancients' technology, which was mostly driven by magnetism. We still have a few samples of their handiwork and the evidence is there, per the experts, of some sort of energetic trauma. It's hard for us to say, though. I've always assumed the Sinceres have their own agenda for saying the ancients' tech was inherently unnatural. Religion is always after something it doesn't want to admit. Further, I'm not convinced any of our engineers can tell much about the artifacts: not really, what with having come from a culture without any of those devices actually *working* for them to study.

There are plenty of crackpot theories about what ended the ancient world: aliens waging a war to isolate but not exterminate us after we got into space, that kind of nonsense. It's mostly written by wishful thinkers. They describe a history more interesting than our own. Regardless, it's absolutely clear no technology survived. The documentation is extensive. Archaeologists with the Spiralists have spent centuries trying to bring back to life *anything* from that extinct era. That may seem counterintuitive at first, given the Reformer focus on the future and on eschewing the past as a fictitiously romanticized time. Their reason is simple: everyone *does* more or less agree the ancients had rudimentary genetic manipulation. It's possible the old world had some forgotten knowledge useful to the Spiralists in the here and now. Plenty of those wishful thinkers ascribe a kind of magical omnipotence to our distant ancestors. It's nice to believe someone, somewhere, at some time, ever had it easy.

Resurrecting some old tech, no matter how minor, would make a great publicity stunt. If the Spiralists could claim a better connection to ancient life—something demonstrable, some *but-actually* addendum they could write into all those history books right beside the Inheritor Texts—it would piss off the Sinceres to no end. If there is anything the Spiralists love, it's giving the Sincerity Church a poke in the eye. Sometimes I think that's the main engine keeping either of them alive. Otherwise, they might have driven themselves out of business centuries ago. The Spiralists are always suffering one schism after another as some of them decide the rest are insufficiently brave and/or reckless with their sacred genetic experiments.

The Sinceres, meanwhile, have spent their three thousand years of history complaining the world was better yesterday than it is today and predicting tomorrow ought to be a real shit show, too. They don't stop there. The Sinceres say any day now, right around the corner from here, a second great apocalypse will arrive and wipe the slate clean. When it's all said and done, the Sinceres say, only those who've been true to our "natural heritage" will be able to survive.

Somehow, we keep dragging ourselves forward despite their dire foretelling. Their failures as oracles are evident in every morning's successful sunrise and every evening's uneventful sunset. Tomorrow never quite seems to destroy us, though a few of mine have certainly tried and one or another of them, sooner or later, will certainly get the job done. The personal apocalypses of living beings being born and dying in the fullness of time, though: they happen, sure. But the Sinceres' obsessive wish for something truly awful never comes true. While they preach of the Second Scouring coming any day now, they collect the donations of the narrow-minded elderly who come to be told what they like to hear. The Sincerity Church does not dissatisfy in that regard. The old days, it tells them, really were better, and their incomprehension of the current world is a failure of society and not at all the bewilderment of the feeble and afraid.

Anyway, my point is this: the story Alejandro was feeding me required the ancients to have tech like out of their own survivors' stories about them, and it still had to work, and the Collapse had to have left their technology operational, which is demonstrably impossible.

I was still going to work Alejandro's case, though, because he was able to pay no matter how crazy he might be. What's more, his case was an excuse to get into the clinic that could potentially save my life. I might as well figure out what was going on while I beat—or bribed, or fucked—a cancer cure out of some corrupt Spiralist technician.

After spilling the bullshit beans about this made-up ancient world of his, Alejandro fell into silence bordering on—well, not exactly a sulk. More like mourning. The moon rose over Autumn while Alejandro and I fucked right there on my desk, by the window, bathed in the silver light of another perfect Autumn night. We certainly weren't the first people to put on a show on that block, and I was sure we wouldn't be the last. It seemed like the thing to do in the moment and, it turned out, it was. With my flesh pressed to his simskin and my breath in his ear, all that tension melted away. I felt better after, and Alejandro's deep sadness seemed to break.

I remember thinking in the middle of it that maybe Alejandro simply wanted to be human. Maybe he wanted it so badly, he made up a fictitious history he could occupy in human form, and he wrote himself code to make him horny. I'd seen that pursuit of fantasy in plenty of johns before. Most of the time, the guy who hires a gigolo doesn't want to have sex only to get off. He could take care of that on his own time. Instead, he wants to have a partner see him in a specific way: dominant, or hung, or sexually skilled. I think Alejandro wanted someone around. So did I. It worked out well for both of us. When I crested that final wave and plunged over into the oblivion of orgasm, I clutched him to me, and he hugged me back. We were locked together, a part of ourselves bared to the universe, a part of ourselves bared to each other. I knew he was more than a john, more than a paying client for whom I could get hard. I didn't know exactly what I was, but I had to be a person to *be* it. I needed *that,* too, not only to get laid, but to be a companion to someone who needed companionship.

After, as we sat together, leaning on one another, I asked a question. "So how do I get into Little Marseilles?"

"Autumn's cameras can recognize faces." Alejandro murmured it against my shoulder. He lifted his head to speak more freely, reached up and pushed his own hair, more red than purple tonight, out of his face. "The software has evolved over time, of course, but it's based on some basic principles of geometry and of photo analysis."

More gibberish. I gave him a peck on the cheek to encourage him to explain further. "That didn't sound like an answer to my question."

He met my eyes and smiled. "It was preamble. We need to change the patterns of light and dark on your face. It's actually quite simple. It's also very overt."

I raised my eyebrows. "Overt?"

"You'll use white and black makeup to draw new regions of contrast on your face: arbitrary ones. Autumn won't know who you are anymore."

"And you?"

"It's pointless for me," he said. "She would hear my mind."

"Maybe they don't know you're my client."

He shook his head. "I greeted you in the street. I'm associated with you now, and you with me, in Autumn's memory. If she sees me with another man whose facial geometry is only a little off, she'll make the intuitive leap. That's the advantage of having a human mind rather than a constructed intellect. She can make judgment calls machine language can't."

I nodded. If a little face makeup was what stood between cancer treatments and me, so be it. "Let's get started. At this point, though, they know everything about me Adolfo could possibly tell them."

"Yes," Alejandro agreed. "So we'll also need to disguise you in other ways."

I arched an eyebrow, but I didn't object.

An hour later, I was looking at myself and wondering whether this was at all a good idea. A floor-length mirror I kept behind one of the filing cabinets showed me looking patently ridiculous.

A part of me also thought I looked really, really good.

My customary long jacket was removed and replaced with my most formal top. Alejandro went to the store for makeup and brought back the sort of thick, all-covering face paint we tend only to pull out for things like Thin Night. It was stark white and obsidian black, and he spent several minutes applying it, first with a broad brush and then a narrow one. Toward the end, I noticed he would blink rapidly when he leaned back and looked at my face, then lean in and it would fade.

"Is something wrong?"

He opened his mouth to speak, then let himself chuckle. "It's messing with my ability to recognize you," he said. "My systems are based on the same as Autumn's. It's not like I keep thinking you've been replaced with someone else while I wasn't paying attention, but there's a certain degree of cognitive dissonance." He put a few more touches on, holding open only one eye. "If I do this, it helps. That disengages some of the geometry functions. And, of course, I know at a rational level it's *me* doing this, and my reaction is a sign of success."

He asked me not to wear my long coat, so I pulled out an old surplus Naval jacket I bought at a yard sale right after I ran away from Pentz. The coat was far too big for me when I got it, and in later years, too small. I withered some from the cancer, though. Now it fit again, tight in the shoulders but baggy in the torso. At least I would get another use out of it before I went. The jacket was like an old friend. It reminded me of days that were terrible, yes, but also of my survival of them. I liked it as a trophy of hard-won freedoms.

Alejandro said it changed my profile, and then he and I spent a few minutes modifying my walk. He said Autumn's gait recognition might get me even if I wore the face paints. We practiced different footfalls, different fake limps, but they were all too tough to maintain over periods of a minute or two or three. Sooner or later I would forget and slip into my normal lazy swagger, half *couldn't care less* and half *I'm yours to fuck if you've got the scratch*. Eventually Alejandro said he knew just the thing: I needed a stick of wood in my pants. My eyebrows went up, but he waved off the dirty joke I was about to make. He went down the hall for a couple of minutes and came back with the mop the landlady keeps stashed in one of the shower stalls.

"She locked me out of the bathroom. Do you have lock picks in your fingers or something?"

Alejandro flexed one fist. "Who needs lock picks?"

"She's going to be immeasurably pissed off you did that."

"So buy her a new doorknob. Or tell her someone broke in and did it." And that was when I knew we were nearing the endgame of whatever we each thought we were doing—Alejandro's pursuit of an insane fantasy, me trying to chase down a Spiralist doc who'd dunk me on the sly—because I'd been party to a golem committing breaking and theft.

Alejandro sized up my leg and then snapped the mop handle cleanly, effortlessly even, at a particular point of his choosing. Then he knelt beside me and worked it up the leg of my pants and into the neck of my right shoe. I took a couple of steps and, sure enough, it made me walk differently. It felt like a splint coming apart—something with which I had plenty of practice one very long summer back in Pentz when I fell from a tree and broke a leg. My parents thought I was nothing more than a boy being a boy, but in fact, I thought if I climbed high enough, I would see in which direction I could escape. Like every Artie in the preserve, the only way to get better was to let my body do its thing. No bone generators for me. It was the first time I didn't hate only *where* I was, but also *who* I was.

Hobbling around my office with the mop handle gave Alejandro a headache, which he said was another sign of success. I felt a little bad, actually. He had to ask me to speak once I had both the face paint and the mop handle hobbling me so he could be sure I was still the person in the room with him. Even though he did, as he said, know he was the one making changes to me, his systems kept telling him I was someone else.

"Much like Dr. P.," Alejandro said, but he dismissed it when I asked who that was. I figure one of his designers. I kept practicing walking so the mop handle wouldn't show, an obvious angular point standing out from my leg, but soon I was too tired. It was getting late, and I was getting antsy, but I had to take a brief nap on the couch so I could regain a little of my strength before we went. Dying, I've discovered, wears your ass out.

When I awoke, Alejandro was putting the final stitches on an insert he made for my old navy coat. "It will protect you from the deep eyes," he said. "They can see through a layer of regular clothing. This is something we used to have, back in my day, to ward that off. It's illegal now, but it's not difficult to construct." He shrugged. "People simply don't take the time to learn about it. I doubt many people even realize it would work." The coat had been made heavy by what he added, but the new material was flexible. It helped fill me out in the middle. "You can carry a weapon under there, and the eyes won't see it."

"If only I had a weapon." I smiled, though. It's not that I've never used them; it's that having one makes it a lot more likely someone will get killed, particularly the person with the weapon. Alejandro and I set off from the front of my building, me with my funny walk and my face paint, and he shook my hand at the end of the street.

"You'll do fine." Alejandro reached up and tugged the brim of my hat, adjusting it. His face went blank and slack, and if he'd been a human being, I would have thought he was afraid. "Valerius." His voice was small. "Say something." He was looking right at me.

I cleared my throat. "It's me, Alejandro." I took his hand, still hanging in mid-air halfway back to his side. "It's Valerius Bakhoum."

His face relaxed, and he smiled with embarrassment. "Sorry. I guess you really will be fine."

If it hadn't been for the face paint, I would have kissed him. He looked so scared, and I can never get enough of a hard-luck case hoping I'm there to save the day.

It was probably two hours past midnight when I hobbled through the gate into Little Marseilles. It took me for-goddamn-ever to get there. I didn't want a cab to remember me as his fare, so I walked the whole way. Maybe, I was playing it too paranoid, but I like to walk the City, and by then, I was growing increasingly aware I wouldn't have too many more chances to do that.

The night was a little chilly by Autumn standards, so I was grateful for the old coat. It felt good, and the lining Alejandro sewed in kept the breeze out. I was very sensitive to chills the previous few weeks, but I've always loved them and loved them still. That night, setting out on a mad quest, the air fresh and sharp, I felt my old self again—at first. The walk was invigorating after the nap, even energizing, but eventually the shine wore off. I felt dumb for walking by the time I arrived at Little Marseilles: I had to stop and sit down twice on the way to catch my breath. Oh yes, the end wasn't too many days away now. The docs warned me about this. *You may feel fine for a long time,* they said, *but eventually you will start to weaken, slowly at first, then rapidly. That signals the beginning of the end.* They were very apologetic about it all.

I started to descend into a well of feeling sorry for myself, dragged down by a body that didn't have the energy needed for optimism, but I shook it off, stood up, ran my fingers through my hair. I could wallow in self-pity when I was dead. Until then, I wouldn't have time.

The gate to Little Marseilles was a gate in the classical sense, of course, rather than being a literal gate. A very wide arch in the stone and plaster wall created a portal with no means of blocking ingress or egress. I could feel eyes on me, though. A couple of stalks swiveled toward me as I walked up, panned as they tried to identify me, then looked elsewhere. The whole way there I listened for footsteps behind me or the whine of a big mag somewhere ahead, as though the whole City were crawling with agents of some foreign land, or of some alien time, making their way toward me to take me down. Nothing happened. I got a few stares from the face paint, sure, but ultimately Autumn is too cosmopolitan, too diverse in fashion and presentation, for people to stare at anything very long. That's one advantage of collecting three-quarters of a million people in one place: there's plenty of room to be weird because there isn't room for anything else.

I stepped through the portal, into Little Marseilles, and the sound of the City fell away. It was quiet as a Sincerity church inside. The street lamps were low, casting mood lighting more than anything else. The shadows were deep as stairs down into a human heart full afraid. As I walked that silent cobblestone street, its gutters meticulously clean, more like a painting of a street than the thing itself, I imagined those shadows as the unseen corners into which the whole rest of the world gets swept by people who live in a place like Little Marseilles.

The buildings were low, and long, and the staircases up from the sidewalks were few. Plants and small gardens reflected the land far below, but mostly the whole thing was as sterile as the rest of Autumn. The houses were long palazzos with small, round portholes and large, overhanging bay windows heavily shrouded in curtains. The rich always want plenty of windows, but they can't stand the thought of anyone looking in. The walls were more stone, a small number of permitted varieties used with enough variation for any one person to peek out a window and not see next door an estate entirely identical to his own. The result was actually very tastefully done, even artful in its architecture, but I suspected their walls were really painted plascrete. I couldn't imagine someone paying the weight of something as heavy as this much granite. The whole City would be tipped over on one side. Little Marseilles' obsession with the appearance of stone was its own punch line. The street looked pretty, sure, but no one would ever believe in it. Context destroyed the illusion, like a magic trick that wows at first but obvious after only a moment's thought.

There were more stalks on the street, of course: some attached to homes and some to lamps. They noted me, gawped as they tried to associate me with an identity, then went back to looking at whatever moved next. A wall had gotten another round of graffiti sometime when no one was watching: MANIMAL RIGHTS ARE HUMAN RIGHTS, but the letters were unfinished, incompletely outlined by someone who got interrupted by discovery.

Two blocks of semi-urban peace and quiet later, a pair of Upgrades came around a corner on security patrol. I never considered that the whole neighborhood might be a Spiralist enclave, but that certainly seemed to be the case. Spiralist charms peeked out from flowering shrubs here and there, markers of genetically enhanced plant life they like to put out as signs of their devotion. I thought again of the old Octopus I'd seen washing the wall. Spiralists have it as their official dogma that all humaniforms are worthy beings—Arties, Plusses, and Mannies—but history is chock full of religious adherents who couldn't live up to their egalitarian ideals.

The Upgrades eyed me with suspicion—slight limp, beat-up old coat wrapped around myself, big hat—and started to make their way toward me with the practiced scowls of cops approaching vagrants in all places throughout all time. "Evening, sir," one said to me, but I didn't give him time to say anything else. I tilted my head back, looked out at him from under the brim of my hat—with my weird makeup and everything—and sniffed as hard as I could.

"Yes, *hand*?" I narrowed my eyes into offended slits and jutted my chest out at him a little. "Is something amiss?"

The derisive term caught him off guard. It's what people used to call Upgrades and other only-halfway-to-Plus servants. A generation ago, it was a standard term of address that saved people the trouble of having to remember or use their slaves' names. These days it's an insult in most circles, an ironic paean to times gone by in others. A certain kind of self-absorbed asshole wouldn't hesitate to use it to put an Upgrade in his place while saying, loud and clear, *I insulted you on purpose and you can't do a thing about it.* The Upgrade's partner looked me over up and down, but the one to whom I spoke was enough of a lapdog not to look away for fear of showing disrespect to a superior.

The other spoke up. "Sir," he said, voice tight. "Our apologies, but we have duties to fulfill. What has you out at this hour?"

I let my nostrils quiver as I looked slowly at him, death stare at full radiance. "My own desires, of course. Might I not come and go as I please in the community I call home?" My voice had shifted up, and my accent had gone upper class. "Or must I go wade in the shit beyond the wall in order to have a moment of quiet with myself? Hmm?"

There's a kind of rich that lets you dress however the hell you want, and damn the eyes of the first person to look askance at you. The first Upgrade decided that must be me. As an Artisanal Human, I look my age, but if I were a Plus, I'd be a very old one indeed, and an elderly Plus could make this go hard for them. The face paint wouldn't even register as strange if I were merely an eccentric who liked to look how he liked to look.

"Apologies, sir," the first guard said, more readily obsequious than his unconvinced colleague. "We're looking for slander makers." Ah, the graffiti. Slander indeed, I supposed, to paint modestly progressive slogans within sight of wealthy isolationists. "We'll be about our business."

The other still wasn't sold, but once his partner stepped aside and I made it a meter past them, there was precious little he could do without raising his voice or touching me. He wouldn't relish what could happen if he were wrong. He stayed quiet as they watched me shuffle away. Twenty terribly long seconds later, I was around a corner and gone from sight.

I sat down to catch my breath. I wondered if I wheezed when addressing them. If so, it helped sell the show. *Thanks, cancer,* I thought with a dumb smile. Two minutes later, I lifted my head from my hands, rubbed my eyes, and looked around. Not a hundred meters away, on a corner of a small park and market square, was the very clinic I sought: the one at the corner of Strive and Tester.

Time to go to work.

13

The Spiralist Church has clinics all over the City of Autumn—all over the world, in fact, even in the Eastern Expanse, Lesser Aus, Greater Aus, and all the little places too peaceful to remember—but this one didn't look like any of the others. The others have giant glowsigns in the shape of the Sacred Helix, two-story high images of smiling people in clinician garb, all the cheapest ways of snaring anyone who walks by. Sure, they do great work, not that I know from experience. They turn a tidy profit on their cosmetic work, and they aren't shy about saying so. They trumpet how much money they've earned doing aesthetic work for clients then funneled into disease research, developing new treatments, improving life for their patients. They really seem to do it, too. In addition to the design work, they cure actual diseases and—for everybody but Arties—they do it for free. Spiralist clinics kick death square in its teeth a million times a day, charging nothing but a smile, because it's phenomenal publicity for the cosmetic side of the operation.

Curing someone's sweet old grandma of the Hamlin fits makes everybody feel good, sure, and on the way out, the Spiralists weigh Grandma down with pamphlets about a hundred ways to rewrite their own code. The motto on the outside of every Spiralist clinic is the same: "Enter in need of improvement; leave possessed of perfection."

Most clinics are open all the time. This one was no different, but they had noticeably dimmed the lights around the entrance and the only external signifier of its purpose was that ancient symbol of the Spiralists' quest for genetic ascendancy: double serpents climbing the winged staff representing humankind's inventive nature. There are plenty of reasons to walk into a clinic late at night. It's by no means a necessarily suspicious act. My close call with the Upgrades had me a little spooked, though. I wasn't sure I could pull off the snob voice and talk my way past the reception desk of an essentially private facility, even if the fancy makeup job hid my Artisanal crow's feet and hollow cheeks. Neither would I do myself any favors by hesitating or visibly dithering over what to do. No, I would have to wing it and hope for the best.

So I walked up, opened the door, and removed my hat as I stepped inside. In four hobbled strides, I crossed a lush waiting area full of overstuffed upholstery and carpet so thick you could lose a small child in it. There was an Upgrade+Plus receptionist-security-guard-bouncer in a sleek white uniform and a little paper hat that said to anyone meeting her that she wasn't that important in the grand scheme of things but she was certainly more important than *they*. What the presence of someone so meticulously engineered told me, on the other hand, was that this was pay dirt. The Church had plenty of muscle around. It didn't need to waste one of its trickier achievements on overnight front desk duty in a nice, quiet neighborhood unless they *really* had something to protect. The receptionist looked up, her eyes flaring microscopically to indicate she was surprised to see anyone, much less to see someone dressed like me, and her refusal was getting warmed up before I'd even taken the second step.

"Sir." She was going to say something else, but I didn't let her finish.

"I have an appointment with Surgeon Lee." I tried to smile broadly and innocuously. "My name is Jonas Daven." I gestured slightly, an apology of hands and pointy elbows. "I'm a little early, actually."

"I'm sorry, but we have no Surgeon Lee at this facility." Her smile barely stuck its head into the room and looked around before getting the hell out. "You must have the wrong clinic. Perhaps I can look them up for you?"

I looked around, trying to seem a little nervous but not too much so. "This *is* the Little Marseilles clinic, yes?"

She gestured at the walls, beyond them, at a city within the City and its posh population resting well in comfortable beds. "Of course."

"Oh." I blinked a little owlishly. "I'm quite certain this is where I was told to go for my appointment."

She wasn't having it, and I didn't blame her. "Well, I'm sorry, but you misunderstood." There was no chance I had been misinformed—the fault, she made clear in tone and in posture, was entirely mine. I didn't blame her for this. She got paid to keep bums out, and I was a bum. "I take it you were referred, so perhaps you should polly the referring clinic."

"That does seem the wisest option." I was making noise while the rest of me tried to think. There had to be a way past the desk. I couldn't threaten her; she had the Upgrade genetic encoding for a big frame and endless muscles and a decisive tone that all said nobody was going to have much luck trying to push her around. I couldn't charm her. The most obvious and believable lie—that I was a patient—hadn't done the trick. I hesitated for a moment, the brim of the hat in my hands as I clenched my fingertips around it.

A very quiet beep sounded, and her attention was elsewhere. I realized she had a whisper in her right ear. "Have a good day." She was dismissive when she spoke my direction, condescending, speaking as though my back were already to her, but she was the one leaving. The receptionist stood and, without further discussion, disappeared through a door I hadn't even realized was tucked behind her station.

Okay. *That* was not normal, and there was no pretending it was. A religious person might have thought their preferred flavor of gods were looking out for them, creating an opportunity where none was before, but I think at this point we all know how I feel about religion. The receptionist left for a reason, and she didn't throw me out first.

This was all an obvious setup. I'd been made, and there was something they wanted me to see or to do while I was here.

To my left was a large and heavy door proclaiming ACCOMPANIED PATIENTS ONLY in a script suggesting they smiled when they wrote it but their free hand made a fist. It had a slim window down one side to keep people from opening it and hitting another in the face, and the hallway beyond was invitingly empty.

I hobbled over and tested it. The door was unlocked.

Obvious bait. Too obvious. To take that bait would be madness. To walk into a trap this ornate was insane.

Well then, I thought to myself. *Into the trap I go.*

The thing about a trap is, you've only got two choices: avoid it, or spring it yourself. I couldn't think of a way to avoid it. One or both of two things were in this place: the truth of Alejandro's mad case, and the truth of the fruit dealer's genetic treatments. I couldn't see a path to either of them that involved avoiding this trap. I would have to spring it. Doing that might get me killed, but, joke's on them, right? I was too distracted dying to be scared of getting killed.

The hallway was like that in any other clinic, but all the hard surfaces were heavily carpeted. An upscale place like this probably didn't see as many bloodstains and other bodily fluids as the one in, say, the Shade. Where the latter was designed so every surface could be attacked with a mop or a sponge, this one gambled on comfort instead. Of course, these were Spiralists: they probably engineered the carpet out of a moss capable of releasing enzymes to consume spills.

The walls were not quite white, what I suspect my mother would have called "eggshell" had she been here to see it. There were representations of nature scenes, impressionistic, realistic, hand drawn, captured by eye, color, black and white. They weren't dupes, they were originals—the way the paper on the drawn ones was creased in the center of the ink, from the pressure of the pen, was visible on close inspection. Money everywhere, even on the walls so you could ignore it on your way to one of the half-dozen examining rooms staggered across from one another like the teeth of a zipper.

I wasn't interested in the examining rooms. There would be no secret to reveal in any of them. It wasn't like they would have a special one set aside for their illicit genetic treatments. They would conduct that hidden business in a more remote corner of the clinic. In the back, though, or somewhere, they would have one of two things I hoped I could use to secure some proof Adolfo had been bought off with cosmetic regeneration: an inventory list or a patient file. I hoped they didn't give Adolfo a codename. And I hoped I could anticipate whatever box they would try to drop around me before I got to it.

To be honest, I wasn't exactly sure what I would do with evidence if I found it. I supposed I would try to get back out and then later inform them I had proof they treated an Artie and see if that made them talk. That wasn't much as plans go, I admit, but I wasn't thinking totally straight. I was so furious that Adolfo would be selling his stupid fruit with the dark hair and taut skin of his younger self while I would be, at best, another gout of ashes in the exhaust of a City that wouldn't even notice I was gone.

The six medical chambers were all empty, their lights out, their doors open. Each had an elaborate upright display of lurid status flowers. Think of a sunflower blossom but growing out of the surface of the door like a flowering vine instead of out of the ground. When a patient was in the room, the blooms would open. The colors of the petals would shift over time to indicate things to the staff: how long since they were checked on, how soon to give medication, that sort of thing. It was all a part of the Spiralist aesthetic to make incredibly and unnecessarily complicated living things simply because they could.

The rooms themselves were lushly appointed: more carpet, thick drapes over false windows, heavily upholstered companion chairs for parents or kids who had to wait while someone else got all the attention. There was a seventh door before the end, throwing off the already-offset symmetry of the place, but it went to a restroom with a shower cubicle and a heavy smell of gingermint oil cleansers.

There was an eighth door at the very end, unmarked, kept in shadow in a way clearly intended to discourage the curious. Everything about it indicated being closed to anyone who had to ask. I reached out and pulled the handle. It held fast, but it did rattle a little when I tugged it. A closer look showed a recessed key slot built into the door near the bottom.

This had to be another lure in the trap. A mechanical lock struck me as unusual. Since when were Spiralists afraid to trust technology to control access? Where were the palm readers or eye-eyes or noses? But instead of those, they gave a lock someone could pick. Someone who didn't think to question when something was a little too easy would count this as a lucky break. This all made me nervous—were they luring me into a setup involving the law? Get evidence of me perpetrating a break and enter and then blackmail me into silence after? Only one way to find out. I reached into my coat and felt the small leather pouch with my picks in it—every good detective has them, even poor ones like me—but as I started to withdraw them from my pocket, I heard the receptionist's voice approaching the door from the lobby, fifteen unobstructed meters behind me.

"Said he would go somewhere else, but, obviously, he was making shit up," she said, her voice muffled by the door, the handle starting to turn. "He was probably hoping for an 'emergency' treatment for something big. Like they all are. If it seems like a crisis, no one will say no. Typical." I gave her credit: she did know the way it *usually* works when someone random wanders into a clinic in the middle of the night. It was all too picture-perfect, though, just like her disappearance from the reception area and the mechanical lock in a Spiralist clinic. Her tone wasn't that of one explaining a fact to another, but instead of one trying to convince herself something was okay. Would an amateur hear that and be assured they were getting away with breaking in? Was the person she was trying to convince actually meant to be me?

I ducked into the bathroom for lack of anywhere else to go. If there was a certain role expected of me, I would play along, for now. I needed to get out of sight, but I was every bit as exposed there as I was in the middle of the hallway, or would be, if they walked this far. So I kept going, slipping behind the shower curtain and pressing myself into the near corner, hoping against hope I would not be visible to her.

"How did he even get this far?" The guy talking to her had the rich basso tones of an Upgrade, probably working security or possibly doing number crunching as a head job. "You'd think the patrols would have picked him up."

Their voices got steadily closer, and I noted the carpet was thick enough they couldn't be heard walking toward me. The bad news was I would have no idea if anyone else was moving around in the place. The good news was, nobody would hear me, either. We both thought we were playing cat and mouse, but we both thought we were the cat. I shook my head. Maybe this was all a bad idea.

"Who knows? I'm simply glad he's gone. I don't need shit like that this week."

"Nobody does," the Upgrade said. They were almost to the near end of the hallway now, and I was waiting to hear them unlock the door and go through. Instead, they paused. "Hey, I'll be a minute." Great. The Upgrade needed to take a leak—or needed to telegraph that so I would let my guard down while she and he swept the place to find me.

"Sure. I'm going ahead. I need to do some prep." The receptionist made some rattling and clanking noises I took to be the door being unlocked while the Upgrade stepped into the restroom and closed the door. He didn't bother turning on the lights—he probably didn't need to. He would, of course, be engineered or upgraded to operate in the dark. I heard the clacking of things and a zipper opening and then the familiar sound of liquid relief.

The door at the end of the hallway hadn't been relocked—she'd left it unlocked for him. And then left. And now he was distracted, with his back to me.

I am definitely not too proud for a cheap shot. Always take advantage of having the upper hand, *especially* when you know you're walking into a trap.

I waited until he was done, then as he was zipping up, I slipped back from behind the shower curtain. A slight rustling sounded as I did so. I heard him make a small murmur of curiosity. Before he could turn around, I leapt onto his back, got an arm around his neck, and clamped it shut against his windpipe with my free hand. In an Artie that's a killing move—squeeze too tightly and you drop us dead, not unconscious, as you cut off the wind and the circulation of blood through the big vessels on either side of the neck. It's an ugly way to kill someone, and it takes forever, and even though there are precious few good ways to go, I think it's clear that's one of the worst.

This was an Upgrade, though, and I could tell from his frame he wasn't only a head job: he had physical enhancements, too. He had muscle and height, and I would have flirted like hell with him in any other circumstance, but right then, I had other priorities. I heard him gasping and gagging, trying to get out a groan or a yell, trying to bat at me from behind. He landed a pretty good blow in the middle of my forehead at one point, and I saw stars for long, terrifying seconds. He nearly shook me off, but I hung on, and after a little bit, he started to sag. The gasping gave way to panting and then, in time, to one long exhalation as he toppled, unconscious, to the floor of the bathroom. I rode him all the way down.

I kept my arm around his neck for a few moments, in case he was faking for me. If this was a trap, he either screwed up his part, or he was supposed to catch me here and beat the life out of me, or he was supposed to be the barrier that kept me from backing out at this point. No matter what, I had to know he was off the board entirely. I held on hard for ten more seconds, then twenty. I had to break off a few of the trap's teeth. I let go and rolled up to my feet, half-crouched, on the chance he came up swinging. He lay there. I couldn't see any details in the dark, but I could hear wind flutter softly between his lips.

To be sure he wasn't faking, I did the face-flick test. It's exactly what it sounds like: I put my thumb over the tip of my middle finger, then flicked his face right above the top of the cheekbone but not on his eye. The reflexes that sensation activates are essentially impossible to control. They're tied into the musculature and reflexes that keep us from getting jabbed in the eye, and those are *very* strongly involuntary. If someone is faking, the face-flick test reveals it. In the case of the Upgrade, I got a big fat nothing in terms of response. He was out, for real, no doubt about it.

I had no idea how much time I bought myself, but with his physical enhancements, it couldn't be much. There was a thing like a key ring on his waist, but with only one big key that glowed from within. I grabbed it, shut the restroom door behind me, then went through the unlocked door and damn the consequences. I was going to get something on these people, something I could use for leverage, and if I had to walk headlong into every trap they could imagine and half-asphyxiate every muscle-bound Upgrade in the whole Spiralist church, so be it.

Through that door was another hallway, but this one wasn't carpeted. It was tiled, clinical, with lights turned down low.

Along one side were business offices. They sat dark, but the plass inset in them showed me desks, a few plants, bookshelves, a chair for a client or a colleague paying a brief visit. They weren't fancy; they were for whatever passed for a worker bee around these parts rather than for a boss. The doors were all closed, and I didn't even bother to see whether or not they were locked. If they were open, then they were another part of the trap, and I had violated the trap's expected program by knocking out the Upgrade. My gut said I had to stay off-script to keep surprising them.

At the end was a huge door with the universal symbol for a biological hazard, the ancients' rather silly stylized sign of three large circles (the three visible phases of the moon, representing the body in various states of being well and unwell) and the miniature circle in the middle (symbolizing the spirit, which is not threatened by the purely biological but may recede or disappear if the body is too greatly harmed). I considered it a tad overwrought as nonverbal messages go, but it stood the test of time, so clearly it meant something to some people.

ENTERING BIOCONTAINMENT AREA BEYOND THIRD DOOR, said the sign. INTRUSIVE PATHOGENS MUST BE MINIMIZED.

I wondered what their version of the script said. Did they expect that to scare someone away? Did they hope that would steer me through a different set of doors, send me off in search of a way to go around? Or did they think I would see it as an invitation? Now I was thinking myself in circles. *To hell with the script,* I thought. I was too tired to play more checkers. I was already dying. What could they do to me? I'd come this far. I wasn't going to turn around now. Not when I was possibly literal meters from what I needed. Not when I was this close to finding out whatever they wanted me to think I had sweat so hard to achieve, and maybe something real beyond that.

I pulled on the door, but it didn't open. It was locked, and locked tight. That... that I did not expect. I figured the door would open, welcoming me into the heart of the trap they had lain. Pulling on the door was like pulling on a wall: they used a magnetic lock, and a tough one. Running a system like that would mean a solar garden on the roof and a lot of extremely expensive equipment. No other clinic I visited—and I went to plenty in this City in search of a doc corrupt enough to take whatever favors I could offer—had something like this. A Spiralist clinic in Little Marseilles could be expected to offer plenty of cosmetic regeneration with the light touch of luxurious service, not huge warning signs and what looked like a secure research area. The door itself suggested whatever was behind it wasn't something merely fancy: maybe something extremely dangerous, and danger was something unexpected here.

There was a box to one side of the door, affixed to the wall, and it glowed with the same red light as the Upgrade's key. I lifted the key until I heard a beep. A humming sound faded out from the rest of the ambient noise. I tugged again at the door handle, and it swung open easily, perfectly balanced.

I shook my head. I couldn't believe they thought someone would fall for all of this. But my heart surged with hope at the idea the cheese in the middle of the trap might be real after all.

The room beyond was brightly lit, with white panels glowing in the ceiling every meter or so. The lights were almost blinding after the semidarkness of the office area behind me, and I had to spend a few moments blinking to adjust. The room was massively large, with spotless white walls and lots of long, low tables or display cases or something: big rectangles, square corners, thin white sheets draped over them. It gave the room the atmosphere of a disused surgery with the machines powered down and the cancer sniffing Mannies and the antibiotic microbe vats elsewhere for the night.

There were maybe eight or ten of these draped rectangles, each encircled by a nest of pipes and hoses, phosphos indicating this or that on the wall behind them. These were treatment tanks, obviously, but why conceal them so?

Sure, this was a clinic in the richest part of town. The people around here were exactly the sort who would be willing to pay what it took to get what they wanted. We all know the Church of the Infinite Upward Spiral of the Double Helix is, behind the free clinics and the *personhood of humankind without limits* rhetoric, essentially a cosmetic factory with a fancy set of religious justifications designed to let believers find in them whatever they hope to hear. It's a pyramid scheme with some science-y inspirational posters. That's true anywhere, though. In the rattiest clinic in the Shade, even, anyone with money—and a Plus genome, no matter how basic—can get anything they want on the menu. The Church doesn't have a requirement of social standing to make its services available. Cash on the barrel and you get new genes, the end.

So maybe this was *the* clinic where even Arties could get what we wanted, as long as we had the money. Maybe this clinic worked on Mannies, too. Maybe this was the one clinic in the whole City where the rules simply didn't apply as long as you paid the cover charge. It would make sense to concentrate that sort of illicit activity in a space that was otherwise above reproach, surrounded by the best security in the City. This was a clinic I never tried. I made the incorrect assumption it was in too ritzy a neighborhood for that sort of thing. I figured this clinic probably offered plenty of off-books services and also that they would only be offered to the very top of the heap.

Still, none of this felt right in my gut, and a detective has to trust their gut above everything else. Time to pull the plug on the whole game we were playing. If they wanted me to see this, I was ready to trip the wire. If they didn't want me to see this, time to find out why—or for whom other than myself this whole charade was being played.

I stepped up to a tank and pulled the sheet aside.

I looked down at the person—the creature—in the tank, then looked up at the wall on the far side of the room. I drew a breath to steady myself. I let out that breath. I drew another. I let that one out, too. I looked back down.

Yep, I said to myself. *That's an angel all right. No doubt about it.*

Imagine the most beautiful Plus you've met: skin tone perfectly to your preference, hair of exactly the variety you like, with cheekbones you could use to hang drapes, and a look of peace—no, more than peace, of *contentment*—on its perfect features. This one happened to be of caramel skin, with long, straight hair curtaining his face and fanned out around his shoulders. His hair started out black, but streaks of gold and copper ran through it like wire string. It was hard to know, given he was laying down, but I would have guessed he stood upright at two meters and change in height. He was thin but powerfully built with arms sculpted into bulging muscle and a wide chest tapering to an athletic waist. He was genetically perfect, what people sometimes call a "floor model" because they sell the rest of us on the idea of the whole process. In sleep—or whatever state this was—his lips were slightly parted, his eyes closed, long lashes the color of cinnamon sticks not even twitching as he rested. He looked oddly two-dimensional, sort of flat, like a poorly done holovideo, but it was an effect of the thick plass of the crate he was in. Looked at edge-on, the stuff was at least five centimeters thick.

It had wings, of course. They were unformed, vestigial, maybe a meter long: not nearly long enough to let it fly. They were covered in what looked like down, as though they were new. The angel had the face of an adult but the wings of a baby. A possibility presented itself that froze me to the spot: what if this was a human being in the process of *becoming* an angel?

I hung the draping back in place and looked around the room. Seven other boxes were spaced evenly. Phosphos glowed behind each of them. None of those indicators were flat or dead, either. They all looked more or less like the ones behind this guy—this *thing*. I may not have comprehended exactly what those indicators were meant to convey, but I sure as hell could figure out that eight more or less identical displays would be for eight more or less identical creatures.

I was scared now, not so eager to look in the tanks as I had been moments before. I pulled out the length of mop handle Alejandro built into my disguise. Holding it like a long baton, I used it to lift the corner of a sheet over another tank.

Another angel. It hadn't fully formed yet—its wings were smaller, its body less developed—but, like a row of corn planted two weeks later than the rest, there was no mistaking it for something else entirely. And there were six more tanks just like these.

Eight avenging angels—the most destructive creatures imagined in our modern myths, worse than the dragons in which many ancients believed, worse than the alien invaders the High Ancients convinced themselves were right overhead, worse than the massive weapons the ancients were said to unleash on one another when they failed to handle a crisis—and a Spiralist clinic was keeping them on ice in the back like they were the second round of beer for the latter half of a party.

I turned around to—I'm not even sure what. Leave? Find a chair and sit down? Toss the joint? I needed to process this. I needed to get steady again. This was all still something they wanted me to see, right? This was all too obviously a put-on. But...

I looked from one tank to another, around the room, and then to the door.

The receptionist was standing in it. Beside her was the Upgrade I knocked out. The bruises I'd left around his neck were already showing, and he looked angry as all hell.

"Kill him," the receptionist said.

"A nice day to you, too, sister."

14

The Upgrade actually did that thing where the tough guy cracks his knuckles before stepping forward. I couldn't believe it. For a mostly brain job, he wasn't very original.

"Don't you want to know what I'm doing here?" I hoped it would buy me a second of time. It didn't. He took four more steps toward me and smiled. He raised his fist back so I had time to admire the color of his blue eyes before his forearm shot forward like it was on a spring. I dove, throwing my body as hard to one side as I could, and he barely missed me. His knuckles thudded against the plass of one of the angel tanks, and his whole arm rebounded, shaking. He cried out in pain, his voice strangled, and the receptionist yelled angry noises at him.

I didn't give him time to swing again. I took off into the middle of the room, dove under one of the tanks, and slid cleanly underneath and out the other side on the room's spotlessly micromopped floor. This place didn't merely have the dirt eating bugs around: it had the ones that distribute the designer wax behind themselves. Class all the way, baby, in Little Marseilles.

I rolled to my feet on the other side and could hear Upgrade chasing me. He still couldn't talk, probably from when I choked him unconscious, probably also from his rage at having missed with the first punch. In some part of my mind not immediately occupied with my survival, I decided he must be a calculator. I was going to get torn to pieces, possibly literally, by a pissed off bookkeeper, and the receptionist was going to watch. There wouldn't be enough of me left to scrape off the sole of a boot when this was over.

Upgrade tried to turn when he got to me, my back pressed against the wall with an angel tank on either side, but the microbial wax finish caused him to skid, and he kept going a half a meter. I saw just enough of a gap for me to jump through and go running right at the receptionist in a bull rush.

She held up a gun and pointed it at me. My whole life flashed before my eyes, and I dove again as she squeezed the trigger. I heard a pop and felt what seemed to be something banging into me with the force of a spitball at most, or of a leaf spinning out of an Autumnal tree and bumping against my chest. There was a low hum, and my special coat lined with stuff to block the eyes from catching my bioelectrical signature made a crackling noise. The air smelled strange around me as I hit the floor, like burning pleather and the atmosphere after a lightning strike, or sometimes when a mag car breaks down. It was ozone. Instead of a bullet in my chest, I had two thin strings running from underneath my torso back to the pistol in her hand.

Upgrade caught up to me, and his arrival was what actually hurt: all hundred thirty kilos of his muscled mass slamming into me in a vicious tackle. I held the mop handle up to try to defend myself, but he swept my wrist aside and pinned it to the floor as he landed on me. I cried out in pain as something snapped inside my increasingly frail body. I'd probably broken a rib. It hurt like very few things in my life ever had before: a sharp pain stabbing me in the side. Upgrade didn't seem to take it any better, though. He cried out in a strangled moan and began shuddering on top of me, grinding my broken rib and the rest of me into the floor as he spasmed and fell into what seemed to be a full seizure.

I writhed wildly under him, trying to squirm my way free. The receptionist tossed the gun aside and picked up a big book. She clocked me across the back of the head with it as I squirmed out from under Upgrade and tried to stand. I spun and tumbled, tripping over Upgrade and myself, but I managed to land on the side without the broken rib and launched myself back to my feet. Upgrade was panting and possibly unconscious under me. I scrambled for the broken-off mop handle and smacked the tip of it against the back of his head once to be sure. He sagged more completely and dove away again, skidding under tables.

One down.

God on the mountainside, I thought, my surprise so profound I went right back to the secret faith of the people around whom I'd been raised in Pentz. *She tried to juice me with a gun.* Electricity held in the hand, mech-magic like the ancients, but here, in a clinic dedicated to worship of the future through biotech science.

The receptionist produced two knives from out of nowhere—slicers like the ones Fiono and his ilk liked to use—and I knew I was in real trouble. She probably planned at first to knock me out so Upgrade could do the dirty work. Now she was on her own, and she was very much up to the task. She crouched the way a street fighter does and made her way slowly toward me.

The room had a door in the back, but the sign blared VAT-WORKS PROTECTIVE EQUIPMENT REQUIRED. I clambered up off the floor. The receptionist was still advancing. I lifted the mop handle as a weapon and struck my best *en garde* pose. Faster than I could follow, she knocked it out of my hand. It clattered against the floor.

My hands went up in the universal pose of surrender without a conscious thought. "Look, we can work something out. Let's be reasonable about this."

The receptionist took another step forward and raised the knives. Their tips were barely two centimeters long where they extended between her fingers, their handles cupped in her fists. She was good. She was the sort of fighter who could get *very* close and win.

"Seriously. I mean, what am I going to do? Tell people I've seen a room full of angels in plass tanks?" I bumped clumsily against a counter behind me, reaching the end of the line.

She was maybe six terribly slow steps from me, her knuckles white where they tightened on the knives.

"I…I'm a detective." It hurt to talk. "I came here to find out why you gave the fruit seller cosmetic treatments but your church wouldn't cure my cancer." I gulped air against the sharp point of my shattered rib. I tried to sound pitiful as I made my last pitch. "I'm going to be dead in a month anyway."

The receptionist paused, savoring the moment. She was only a couple of arm lengths away. With one swift step, she could be in range and cut me open. The jacket would probably protect me from the first slice, maybe the first two, but eventually she would work her way through, and I didn't much look like I had another ounce of fight left in me.

"Please." It was more a wheeze than a word, a whisper fighting to get out of me. I put one hand against my throbbing side, my other arm crossing my chest out of protective reflex. A phrase I'd heard before, from cops and from news stories, floated into my head: *defensive wounds.* "Please." I tried to sound a little more alive. "I'm dying and I really don't want it to be like this. I want my landlady to have to clean it up. We hate each other that much. I want my last act to be becoming her problem." I tried to smirk, thinking maybe I could make her laugh—always a good strategy, make them laugh so they'll keep you around, ask any jester from history and see what they say—but she didn't laugh.

Much worse, she *smiled.*

That door—the door into the vat-works—was only a couple of meters away. Maybe there was a roof access. Maybe there was a door into a back garden. Maybe there was a portal into the sewers. Maybe there was a mop I could use as a weapon.

The receptionist took that step and swiped the blade in her right hand in a quick arc. I flinched, back arched backward over the counter, unwittingly throwing open the jacket and baring my abdomen. The knife was so sharp I didn't feel it. I *heard* it. And I saw blood—my blood—slash out across her uniform.

The eyes of the receptionist went wide, and she hesitated, and that was her undoing. There was a big jug of something on the counter next to me. I hefted it, clumsy in my weakness, and tried to swing it at her. I didn't succeed, she stepped out of its way, but when it crashed to the floor, it shattered and sprayed across her feet and ankles. The smell was awful.

The receptionist screamed in pain and anger. I clutched my hands to the shallow wound across my guts and screamed back at her, no more than one frightened animal reacting to another.

"They didn't tell me you would bleed." Her voice was loud. She strained to speak so that it came out in a loud groan rather than a growl. Whatever was happening to her flesh smelled terrible. Strips of her skin were sloughing off. Blood was running in thin streams from spontaneous wounds. The big jug had some sort of acid in it. They'd be able to regenerate her later, I was sure, but it was awful to be in the presence of an injury anyway. Real bodily trauma like that wasn't something we saw much of anymore. I'd seen it a couple of times as a kid, on the rez, but I still wasn't prepared for the sight of sloughing flesh and raw meat and bone. The receptionist wasn't going to be able to stand up anytime soon.

I took one breath while my brain turned her words into thoughts, and everything made sense in a second.

"I want to know who put you up to this." I looked at the counter and grabbed from it a smaller, less heavy jug. I didn't know what was in it—the labels were jumbled letters, and I was no chemist—but that didn't matter. I'd hurt her with one big bottle of clear liquid. I could now threaten her with another. "And I want cancer treatments."

She wrinkled up her brow at that, then laughed at me. Her teeth were clenched with the pain, but I was still funnier than she was hurting. "Cancer treatments take hours, sometimes days. I can't simply give you a pill and make it all better. You idiot." She shook her head at me. Arties get that a lot: we're often assumed to be naïve. Those of us who go out into the world find we're more often than not the objects of condescension.

"Patient records, then. I need the files on a specific guy. And I need to know who." I shook the jug at her. "I need the name of the person who paid you to be here and do this."

The receptionist balled up her face like a fist and spat right at me, the classic slicer insult and challenge. No dice. I was never going to get information out of her.

I didn't set the jar down, but I did step to the side, around her, away from her, moving backward, never turning my back to a slicer with her knives in her hands. I recognized a little object on the counter from endless stories and videos, grabbed it, and put it in my pocket as I went by.

I didn't say another word. As a detective, my most powerful weapon was always going to be information, not my fists, not a knife, not a club, but whatever facts I had and the other side didn't. I buttoned up before I revealed anything else, stepped carefully over the unconscious form of the Upgrade, and without much of anything to show for this visit but the fear in my eyes and a gash across my guts, I backed out under the hateful glare of the receptionist.

The lab doors closed behind me, gray and featureless and turned away from me like the backs of strangers shunning my pain. I looked and found a door stop inside one of the worker-bee rooms. I grabbed four of them, total, and ran back to kick them under the edge of the doors into the lab. They wouldn't hold forever, but they'd buy me a little time.

My steps weren't entirely steady, but I half-walked, half-jogged back out of the place, trailing a little blood behind me the whole way. The front door opened at my touch, and I limped out. All I needed to do was find an alleyway—not the nearest one—and close myself up.

Then I needed to find Alejandro.

Then we had to finish this.

Never before that moment was I the beneficiary of modern medicine. I once took generic antibios, and as a child I wore a cast, and sometimes I had my teeth drilled. I experienced firsthand all the unspecific barbarisms of bygone eras. Never before did I feel a wound close thanks to adaptive paste. The thing I grabbed off the counter of the clinic was a tube of the stuff, with an applicator and a handle and a button I squeezed to make it come out fast or slow: standard issue to any paramedic and perpetually in the aprons of docs in stories. A child crying as the tube is produced to be used on them for the first time is one of those cultural tropes, right up there with their first haircut or their first stem bath. I was always told adaptive paste itched a little. It turned out it also stung. I didn't care. This was something I was legally, socially, culturally, and religiously barred from ever experiencing, and I *loved it.* I smeared a little of the stuff on the slice across my stomach and gasped as it immediately started to *work*. It tingled, and it itched, and it burned very slightly: not real pain, merely a reminder my nerve endings were there. Those all faded immediately, though, as its numbing properties kicked in. I was in the back of an alley behind a café, halfway to the exit from Little Marseilles, and I stared at my own regenerating flesh with eyes as wide as one of that restaurant's platters. Twenty seconds later, the paste was absorbed, and my wound was gone. I had a very, very pale scar where the wound was. If I spent enough time with my shirt off in Down Preserves, eventually that would go away. I ran my finger across it. I couldn't feel any pain. There was no wound. There wasn't even a greasy residue. The paste was gone. My skin was healed.

I smeared a glob, very gingerly, over the spot where it felt like a rib was broken. The paste soaked in right away, exactly like it's designed to do. Seconds later, my insides started itching. My rib knit itself. A normal person would have had a doctor make sure everything was in the right place first, but I enjoyed no such niceties. What mattered was that it stopped feeling the way a fire alarm sounds and wound down to the remote annoyance of a horn in the distance.

A couple of minutes of modern medicine and I was practically fixed. And other people got to have that *every single fucking day*.

I adjusted my shirt to cover the injury, stuck the paste in an inside pocket of my coat, and limped the rest of the way to the gate. I'd lost my mop handle, but between my rib, my bruises, the exhaustion of the last few minutes and a lifetime on my feet in shoes with a hole in the sole, I'm surprised I was able to stand. All the way out, through the gates, and down the street, I step-drag-step-drag-step-dragged a circuitous route back to where I'd been once before so I could check a hunch.

I needed to wash the makeup off my face, and I bet I knew an empty apartment where I could do so undisturbed.

When that was done, I went back to my office, took a long shower thanks to Alejandro having liberated the bathroom the night before, and changed into fresh clothes. I had business to conduct.

I left a note on my door: no point trying to be subtle now.

Get low and stay low. Look for me where we first met.
V

15

"I know all about the fake angels," I said to Solim as I walked up to his table in Misconceptions. Normally it's the job of the detective to walk into the room, point at the villain, and say, *he did it,* while holding aloft the evidence. At least, that's what people think. I didn't have that luxury this time. I didn't have a goddamn thing to my name except what I'd seen for myself, and what I deduced from it. I simply had to gamble that was good enough.

Solim continued writing with that stylus of his, on a big lotus-sized pad, until he finished whatever thought occupied him. Then, very deliberately, he set down the stylus, took a long sip of wine, and looked up at me. "The what?"

"I've been to the clinic. The one in Little Marseilles. I've seen the tanks. I've seen the fruit seller. I know what y'all were trying to do, and I think I even know why. So tell me, was the fruit seller for real? Did he actually get treatments? Or was that purely for effect, too?"

Blackie wandered close enough to take an order if I spoke up, but not so close as to intrude. I wasn't being subtle. My body language was all *don't fuck with me,* and by now I must have looked far more strung out, even more withered, than Blackie had ever seen me before. On top of the wild night, I didn't have long to live, and I was done trying to hide that fact. Death already cast its shadow across me from offstage.

"M. Bakhoum," he said very softly, "I'm afraid nothing you're saying means anything to me." He produced the tiniest shrug, a look of general pity, and moved to pick up his stylus.

I leaned forward, slapped the stylus back down against the table with my hand, and growled. "The Upgrade tried to beat my head in. The secretary gave an award-winning performance. The fake angels were very nicely done. You get my compliments on all of it, *padre*, but you didn't count on the golem hiring a detective. You thought the golem would follow the trail himself: that he would walk right into your trap. You anticipated easier prey to catch, someone already primed to buy what you were selling. It's so obvious now, isn't it? The whole thing laid out in a row, like breadcrumbs in that old story of the maze and the monkey."

Solim now set down the glass of wine. He didn't look at the hand I'd placed over his stylus and pad. He looked at me, right in my eyes, unabashed. Blackie was as still as he could be, blending into the background. One—only one—of Solim's eyebrows twitched.

"It's like everything else in our society." I lowered my voice, and I let myself smile the way people smile when they've finally given up. "We don't ask 'why' or 'how' anymore. Everyone has their place, their stratum, and we're all told how to behave, how to stay in that place, and we *do it*. We don't ask how things got this way, or why we should listen to anyone. We accept it because it's all laid out for us and that's always easier than thinking. But 'why' and 'how' are a detective's meat and potatoes, a detective's bread and jam. That's why people don't like us. That's why members of my profession are seen as impolite, as unwanted, as undesirable. It isn't because we bob up and down in the wake of cheating husbands and uncertain parentage. People don't like to think on us too long because they don't want to think about the truths we reveal behind small lies and tidy alibis. They don't like the way we won't take things at face value." I stood up, starting to relax, starting to get into my groove.

"Do you want a drink, Valerius?" Blackie was trying to bring us back to normality in one of the two ways a bartender knows how: offering to get everyone drunk.

"Sure." I was speaking to Blackie, but I didn't look away from Solim. "Something in a glass, preferably a brittle one. I need it to shatter easy into big, sharp shards."

Solim rolled his eyes and downed the rest of his wine in one swig. His chair scooted back, he started to stand—and I reached out and put a hand on his powerful shoulder. He could shake me off without a thought, like a fly on the flanks of a dog, but I was so angry and so certain I frankly didn't care.

"No. You're not going anywhere."

Solim did shake me off, then—one swat of his hand, and mine was off him. "Don't touch me, Valerius," he murmured. I had him good and pissed off, and he wasn't afraid to show me. He was, perhaps more properly stated, *afraid enough* to show me.

I smiled. "What are you going to do, knock me off? I have notes. You don't know where to find them. I know people who are always looking for an excuse to go after the Sinceres. I know people who are always looking to prove or disprove this or that about the myth of avenging angels. Sooner or later one of them will find the gap in your armor *and that will be my revenge*. You can't scare me, Solim. You can't threaten to rough me up: I'm dying. You can't threaten my reputation: I'm a detective and an Artie. The people who worship me always will, and the people who revile me always will, and nobody's in a hurry to switch teams because they've already found their *place*. I went by the old lady's place. The apartment is empty. I don't know if she really saw an angel one time or if she's the best performer the world has ever known. I suspect it's the former. But I also suspect it doesn't matter. What matters is, the setup is gone because you didn't need it anymore."

Solim still stared at me, expressionless, giving nothing away.

"I know slicers and street thugs." I was starting to breathe heavily. This was an awful lot of talking, my throat told me. "I know what they're like when they fight, what they do when they want to kill. I've seen them do it hundreds of times. The receptionist didn't want to kill me. She wanted to scare me because that was Plan B: scare me into running off and believing the 'secret' I'd found was worth killing me for. But she was scared, herself, when the electric gun didn't take me out—and a scared slicer doesn't hesitate. A scared slicer goes in for the kill. I'm guessing she was surprised the electric gun didn't take me out because it was meant for my client. He was supposed to follow the trail of clues, not me, and she was supposed to shoot him, not me. I bet it would have hurt *him* something awful. Maybe knocked him clean out. And that's what this was all about, wasn't it? You wanted to get your hands on him, or someone like him, because you want to destroy anything you can that might threaten your storybook version of the past. He goes around telling people he remembers what everything was like before the Big Belly-Up, and whether it's true or not, what if his version of events doesn't match yours and people start to believe him?" I licked my lips and waited for Solim to say something, but he didn't.

He stared me right in the eye in silence.

"There's a kind of reverence people have for golems." I kept talking, plowing ahead. "People are always up their own ass with how wise and kind and *otherworldly* the golems supposedly are, and they don't realize how literal it is when they say that: golems are, if Alejandro is to be believed, actual survivors of another world."

Blackie started to back away, receding uncertainly from the little pool of light at Solim's table. I kept talking.

"But that reverence competes with you, doesn't it? The business model of the Sincerity Church is to ensnare people with a specific kind of story you can use to beat the general public into compliance if not exactly *submission*. I don't know how you got a Spiralist clinic to work with you. Maybe you're all in this together. Maybe you blackmailed them. Maybe you're both run by the same people anyway. I doubt I have time in this life to find out. What I do know is, you want people's money, and you want the faithful not to question you when you tell them what to do, and you maintain very specific supporting narratives to keep that going: like the reservations, and families of Arties like me, and the prohibitions on our participation in modern life. You cultivate a framework of simultaneously fearing and desiring this mythical *better time*, a time before humanity knew sin, and you squeeze us of everything you need in *this* world while selling people a polished turd of a version of the *last* one.

"And then, what if everything he says is true? What if there really are others? What if they really do remember the old world? You can't let that sort of possibility hang over your head, can you? So you people took a *big* gamble and decided to wreck the last true *wonder* of the ancient world: the flying cities, the two that were left, starting with Splendor. And you set up a frame to make any survivors think an angel did it: dressed up some asshole in a very good costume and paraded him past half the Ghosts in the City figuring one of them would survive to be loaded into a golem and come looking for you."

Solim blinked, and I knew I was right. I knew it deep in my gut. It *felt* correct. It was madness, but this was religious stuff. Of *course* it was madness.

I kept pushing. "Once the Ghost was on its own in a golem body, you could fish it in with the fruit and the clinic and whatever else fake evidence you've planted around the City that I never managed to find.

You'd get your hands on a golem you could dissect and throw away. It's a line of dominoes, any one of which is a desirable outcome in its own right: fake an avenging angel attack, get a golem, maybe get to pick its brain, maybe get to knock it off, lather, rinse, repeat." I licked my lips. They were dry and tight and thin. "Even if you didn't manage to attract the attention of a golem, an honest-to-fuck ancient, you'd still get to scare the shit out of the rest of us." I waggled my head at the great Out There: the rest of the City, the rest of the world. "You'd get to trot out the death of Splendor and use it to whip up fervor or guilt or anything else by pointing to it and saying, maybe, *if it weren't for us, you'd be next*, or maybe, *look to us to learn about the ancient world before all of it is gone*. You people love saints *because* they're gone. They don't stick around to ask awkward questions or express doubt in their convictions. They hang on the wall and glare at people until those people behave. There's no better saint than a martyr, either, so you made a whole City into one. You people..." I shook my head and laughed once, very low, very quiet. "You'll probably hang the last Artie to make sure they don't get the chance to say something embarrassing about how you treated us."

Solim's hand twisted the stylus, and the fibers of its concealed blade unfurled and snapped to deadly rigidity. I was goddamn tired of knives that day. I'd seen enough of them for the rest of my life, whether that was a month or a hundred years. I would never cut food with anything but a fork for the rest of my life if I could manage it.

The blade was not a slicer's, and it did not look like it took a slicer's skill to be effective. It was long and thin and sharp as hell, visibly old, and the tip narrowed a little unevenly.

Blackie dropped his order pad and scrambled out of reach, and I was relieved to realize that meant he wasn't in on it. If it was only Solim and me, maybe I stood a chance. I was tired, though, and the fight in the laboratory took it out of me a few hours before, so I did the dirty street kid thing: I cheated. When Solim came at me with the knife, I let it catch me on the arm, biting deep into my flesh and muscle and producing a hollow *knock* when it hit bone.

The pain was absolutely blinding, but I pushed the arm toward him so he couldn't pull back and get the blade free. I grabbed his wine glass with the other hand, smashed it on the edge of the table, and jabbed a sharp edge right up against the flesh of his throat as I staggered forward into him. I wasn't cutting him open—not yet—but I was trying to give the impression I could. I groaned aloud from the grind of his stylus blade against the bone of my arm, but I kept up the fight.

The words came out of me a mealy mush, ground up by anguish and anger and strain, but they came out. "Tell me everything, Solim, or I swear to the gods I don't believe in that I will murder you right here. I have nothing left to lose. They wouldn't manage to get me to trial before I die of cancer. Tell me where to get the treatments, who to see, how to bribe them, and tell me what the fuck is going on with the fake angels and the trap you set for Alejandro. Tell me anything I've gotten wrong, anything I've overlooked, or I will slit your throat and hold it open with my bare hands while you bleed out all over this fucking floor."

Solim stared at me—no, stared through me—and then he spoke very slowly and distinctly, careful not to dig the broken glass any deeper into his own neck as he whispered to me. "You really don't see the larger picture, do you?" He paused. "Or you do, Valerius, but you see it from the other side, and only uncertainly, like a child holding a drawing up to the sun to study it in opaque reversal." Solim didn't sound angry or dismissive. He sounded like he truly pitied me. "You, the most precious of us, and you think we would do this to harm you? We don't want to eliminate you, Valerius. We already have the vast majority of you corralled. If we wanted to exterminate you, we would." He cleared his throat a little, the tiniest grunt of effort, and grimaced with pain. "You look at all of this..." We stood locked in this agonizing embrace, and he drew a breath and smiled a little, his big, beautiful, trust-inspiring eyes welling up. "All of this artifice, and you see a cage, a trap, perhaps an abattoir: a mechanism intended to ensnare and do harm. I am a minister, child. Let me show what I see in its place."

I didn't say actual words. I hissed air between my teeth and held my place against him. Solim could have flung me off. He could have killed me. He didn't, though, because my genes are a sacrifice his church has made on the altar of my life, and he was a true believer.

"I see a clockwork, child." Solim's eyes closed halfway as he spoke, and his focus softened. In his mind, he beheld the perfection of their plan and he hoped he could make me see it, too. "I see a great many teeth wheels, some large, some small, turning as intended, their coils unwinding as designed. What you see as oppression, I see as order, as control. What you see as the forced isolation of your people I see as preserving an investment. You hated the reservation? The case carved from wood and polished smooth, assembled with care over time. Your mistake is in thinking that *you* are the most important person in your life, Valerius. No one is. None of us matters. Our culture matters. Our traditions. Our beliefs. Without them, what would be the life of any one of us? Consider the kitchen of the humblest home. Do they throw all their utensils on the floor? Or do they have an organizer, and a drawer, and a little bit of order? The biologist and her insects under glass; the botanist and his pressed clippings; the worshiper with their candles in the path of a coming storm. An orderly world makes all things possible, makes all things endurable. The clockwork I see in all this does what any clock does. It turns disordered events into *meaning*. It organizes the lives of all who operate under its benevolent rule. And sometimes, once in a while, it must be taken down and *wound*, Valerius. And that is what we are doing. We are winding the clock so that it will keep running until such time as it must be wound again."

Solim didn't stop there. He kept going because he wanted me to understand that I was wrong to want anything better than what was handed to me.

I was also wrong in my theories. The angels in the plass tank weren't fakes. They were an experiment. Avenging angels were a useful story to the church, so why not try making a few? The Sincerity Church, so obsessed with genetic purity and *olden ways,* was engaged in engineering a whole new line of Mannies who would look enough like angels to scare the shit out of people. Solim told me that much in the hushed tones of the reverent fanatic, but he refused to tell me the who of it, or how they got the help of Spiralists.

The fire in Solim's eyes was a pyre ready to consume the unbeliever, and he trained those eyes on me as he spoke. He went on and on in that practiced, hypnotic voice of a Sincerity Priest with long years under his belt of leading the meditative chants of the faithful, and I could tell he was trying to lull me into inattention. He was trying to talk me into a stupor so he could turn the tables and finish me off.

But the more he talked, the more I imagined the screams of the people of Splendor as they rode their City all the way down to its violent death in the middle of the sandy wastes. I thought of the lovers who knew they were about to die and couldn't embrace one last time. I thought of the children who cried out. I thought of the Mannies who probably worked their whole lives to organize and saw it all taken away from them. I thought of the faithful of Solim's own church who futilely prayed out the last minutes of their lives. Solim's words had the ring of real and final truth to them. A jury would have believed him—but, of course, I would never get him in front of a jury. I would be left to *know* what happened and have no way to *do* anything about it.

Then he told me the treatments of the fruit seller weren't real, and that they would never give me the cancer treatments, because what was one dead Artie when you've already killed a City full of people whose names you'll never know?

"We love your kind." Solim let go of the knife in my arm and put his hand on my shoulder to comfort me. "We love what you are. And I consider it a tragedy you do not appreciate what we have given you. We made you who you are, Valerius Bakhoum. I am sorry that was not enough for you, but exactly who decided that? Not we. Not I. We live in a world of constrained possibilities. We must live with such curbs and borders. The Ancients did not and look what happened to them: death by excess and lack of foresight. I will mourn you when you are dead, Valerius, but I will be grateful to live in an era when rules matter, and roles are fixed, and so tomorrow can be predicted, and faith can be relied upon when all else has failed. There are many of us who truly understand." Solim believed what he was saying, every word. "More than you might imagine. And we are well-placed in the churches. We will one day, sooner or later, run the churches ourselves. After that, we'll run the whole Empire."

So I killed him right there, in the middle of the bar, while he talked, and Blackie didn't say a word to stop me.

When it was done, I went outside and sent Alejandro a polly. I was hungry. He owed me breakfast.

16

Alejandro didn't talk about what happened, didn't ask for the story, until I ate my whole meal and drank two cups of coffee. He insisted on the second cup. He said his primary concern was seeing me restored and the rest could wait.

"That's not true." I set the cup down after draining it and smacked my lips with deep satisfaction. It was a good breakfast, and the silence and the civilized people all around me had a palliative effect. I got some stares—for being an Artie, for being an Artie in bloodstained clothes with his arm covered in bandages in a culture where normal people, the Plusses and the Upgrades and the Mannies and the like, never had a cut more than five or ten minutes. I used the adaptive paste on my arm, like I did my stomach, but the cut was too big, too deep, for the paste to take care of it all. Some of it would have to heal on its own.

Alejandro got a few stares, too, for being a golem. Seeing the two of us together must have been like seeing a pair of unicorns gallop through with hot-pink hay in their mouths.

"Excuse me?" Alejandro's look was of pure well-intentioned incomprehension.

"My health is not your primary concern. Angels—what this case was all about—are your primary concern. I simply turned out to be the guy for the job. But you didn't pick me because I was so good with the idea of angels. You picked me because you're smart enough to want an outsider's perspective. You knew you *wanted* to believe an angel wrecked Splendor, and you wanted to have someone else sanity-check that by figuring it out for you."

"Well," Alejandro said with a little shrug of his beautifully crafted shoulder, to which I pressed my lips in a moment of ecstatic release the night before. I treasured the whiff of that experience on the breeze of recollection. "That *is* why I hired you, yes."

"But more than that..." I signaled the server for a third cup. I needed sleep, but another cup would have to do. "You didn't want *any* detective to find it. You wanted *me* to find it. You wanted someone who would go into the lion's den but wouldn't have any friends to come find him there if he never returned. Am I right?"

Alejandro settled back into his chair and crossed his arms. "Were you a difficult child? I bet you were, weren't you?"

I ignored it. "That's why you sent Talons. She felt me out for you with her too-typical story: bad boyfriend, see if he's cheating, and follow him until you know for sure. The role of the boyfriend was played by Buttercup, of course, exactly the sort of guy a less stupid detective might turn down the chance to follow into the middle of Down Preserves. Had I backed off when he went up that shaded path, or if I didn't follow him at all and told Talons what I thought she wanted to hear, great, you'd go find another dog to do your sniffing for you." I gestured with my hands, something small that said *so it goes*. "But it turned out I was the real deal. I was able to keep up with him across a complex obstacle course, and I was willing to face him alone if it meant doing the job for which you hired me. Then Talons put out the lights, and they left me there for you to 'find.'"

Alejandro didn't say anything, and his expression grew blank over the course of the seconds it had taken me to speak. If he were a human, I would have taken it as a sign of guilt. Since he was a golem, I wasn't totally sure, but I was about nine out of ten on it. Then he uncrossed and re-crossed his arms, and I was ten out of ten.

"Right." I kept going. "So you figured maybe I would actually be able to lead you to an angel, but then I'd get out of the way, or report back, or maybe get killed, and then you could go in and clean up. You were leaving all options open because you're also smart enough to smell a trap being set. You knew things were a little too easy, a little too tidy. An angel gets paraded past you just in time for the City to go boom? Too tidy by half. So you wanted someone to check it out, and you hoped you were wrong about the trap and right about the angel being real rather than the other way around. I was useful, the way the Imperial Army sometimes sends in Mutts to see if there are landmines before they march in the expensive Upgrades."

Alejandro was quiet. His face was as still as the surface of a mirror.

"Anyway," and then I drank the whole third cup of coffee at once, "thanks for breakfast, but I'm nobody's collar-dog. I don't mind that I got to slice open Solim's throat because that's only the tip of the tail on what the people who brought down Splendor deserve to have happen to them. But I'm not going to be anyone's pet."

I started to rise, but Alejandro's arm shot out and his hand covered mine on the table. He didn't move to hurt me, and he caused no pain, but he made it clear I wasn't quite allowed to leave. "Wait, Valerius." His eyes were pained. It was very skillful. A day before, I would have believed him without hesitation. Now I had to hesitate if I were going to get out of all this with my skin in one piece. "Please," he said. "Let me explain. You're mostly right, but not entirely."

I eased back into my chair. People looked over at us. The tension we were throwing off was being picked up by whoever around us had improved scent receptors, and that was true of nearly everybody. "What have I got wrong?"

"I never would have knowingly allowed you to get killed. Oh, I used you, and I won't deny that, but I never knowingly would have..." He searched for a word, licking his lips, and that was one of those human reflexes I couldn't imagine someone programming a golem to use. "I would never have *wasted* someone like you."

"Explain. What am I supposed to think makes *me* special?"

"Because you have eyes to see in an age blinded by its own heightened awareness. You give a damn when everyone else takes things at face value. You care about the consequences of your actions, but you act *anyway*. Have you any idea how rare that is? How precious? I won't claim to be in love with you, though I have absolutely treasured the moments of pleasure and intimacy we have shared. It's been a long time since anyone thought of me as enough of a man to have those times. I won't lay any emotional traps along those lines. You have *character*, and that is worth preserving."

I smirked. "Haven't you heard? I'll be dead in a few weeks."

"Not if you let us transfer your consciousness into a golem carriage." He said it just like that, as though he were asking if I wanted him to pick up my laundry.

I sat there and stared at him.

"I'm serious, Valerius. We can't make one for everybody, obviously, but we do make them. Once in a while, we seek to preserve those who might be needed to see the world through these dark times." It was a tidy bit of rhetoric, and I recognized it as such, but there was a part of my vanity that stirred at the offer, too. I imagined Alejandro and me, side by side, wading across the centuries helping humankind rise again from the ashes. I imagined myself whole again, whole *forever*, maybe with better eyes and different hair, and skin that would never grow pale with sickness.

I thought of all the money I'd save on food.

He searched my eyes, my face, and I stared right through his in response. The world he offered me stretched out ahead so clearly. I could have sat down and written it as a script for a play with every word perfect in the first draft. There was zero reason to say no. There were infinite reasons to say yes. The biggest was somewhere in my abdomen, attached to my pancreas and growing in fits and starts, dumping poison into my blood.

"No." I blinked a couple of times. "No." I said it again before I could say yes instead. Then I said it a third time. "No." That's what the ancients used to say: three times makes it real.

Alejandro stared. He didn't get up and walk away. He didn't tell me I would never have a chance to change my mind. Instead, he swallowed air, his throat bobbing. We held hands, staring into each other's eyes, while a big, wet tear rolled down my sallow face and off my jutting cheekbones and splashed in my empty cup.

"You said yourself I'm the sort of person who considers the consequences of my actions. I'm not ready to spend eternity ducking and weaving and wherever else this shit would lead. And I'm not going to let the reward for becoming a murderous vigilante be eternal life." I licked my lips, as he had done, and I started to tremble a little. He tightened his fingers' grip between mine, and I did the same. "The choices I've made, the life I've had, they need to matter. I killed that priest because someone had to, Alejandro, and I happened to be there to do it, not because I think I'm so fucking pure. If I bail out at the end and go, become someone I'm not—an eternal detective, an agent of the shadows in search of the light, stronger and faster and better than before—what am I saying? I'm ditching everything I've done, all the things I am. I'd lose my humanity. I'd lose the sense of…" I paused, closed my eyes, opened them again. "What if I forget the mortality that made me willing in the first place to kill so I could avenge those people in Splendor? What if having infinite life makes me think life isn't valuable? I'm sorry, Alejandro, but no. I'd take you home and let you bed me every night until I die, yes, and I'd let you walk out that door without looking back because that is who you are, and who I am, and I don't have to like your choices in order to live with mine. But my answer has to be no. I'm going to die, Alejandro, and I'm going to do it with what little honest humanity I can scrape together."

He opened his mouth and started to say something, but I broke the moment by standing up and walking away without another word.

It was the hardest thing I've ever done, and it hurt me more than I knew how to handle, so I went home and got drunk.

The next day I went and found Fiono and made him fuck me until my mind went blank. Then I gave him a key, and I told him he had to come back every day for a week, which he did and then some. Fiono became the medic I needed to live long enough to die without leaving an even bigger mess. He brought me some generic salve and fresh bandages, and with the skill of a street slicer who's had at least a couple of fights end in a draw, he washed my arm wound and bandaged it every day.

Alejandro paid me because golems are creatures of their word. He paid me half in Imperial money and half in street scrip because he was smart enough to know that would be more useful. The official currency went to catch me up on rent and buy a new knob for the bathroom door. I hated my landlady, sure, but she had to eat, too, same as the rest of us. I figured dying on her property was enough of a *fuck you* for both of us.

The Imperial police took about five minutes to open and close the case on Solim's murder. Blackie gave them Yuri's description, and the *rent boy slices up a priest* story was too simultaneously messy and tidy to be worth questioning. Everybody likes a little scandal that solves itself that way. I went around and paid my tab at Misconceptions, which turned out to be rather larger than I remembered. Blackie backdated a bunch of drinks I never drank, and I didn't really begrudge him skimming off the top of the end of my life like that. I owed him that and more for Solim alone. I couldn't even begin to account for all the other times I've probably made much smaller messes in his bar. Too bad I couldn't expense Alejandro for them since they were dated from before he hired me, but that's the way it goes sometimes. Blackie had to explain his ledgers to the tax man like anybody else, and that was the price of keeping them clean.

Fiono wasn't shy about why he kept coming around to check on my arm. I had food I couldn't keep down anymore, and a little more money to spend—some official, some not—and we were both a little intoxicated by the taste of death we both got when he fucked me. That's the snide version of it, though. In the quiet moments after, and when he ran his thumb across my arm to spread a little more salve on the slowly-healing wound, there was kindness there. Fiono never talked about himself or his life, but I didn't imagine it had a lot of room in it for human vulnerability. If he was ever going to have a life beyond his twenties, he needed to figure out kindness and fast, and much to my surprise, I was flattered to be a part of him learning that lesson. It wasn't love so much as Fiono learning that there was something between love and fucking, something not exactly like *respect* and certainly not *friendship*, but something that valued the humanity of each of us all the same.

I would always thank him when he was leaving, and he would take my hand, and he would look me in the eye before he let go and walked away.

Otherwise, my time was entirely my own, so I started to write this all down. I made Fiono promise to take it to Clodia once I was gone. I don't expect her to do anything about this. But I need her to know. There were questions still to answer, and someone needed to ask them. Clodia wasn't the person for that, but maybe she could find that person for both of us.

My body gave up two weeks to the day after my last breakfast with Alejandro. I started vomiting blood every morning, and Fiono was reduced to being my nurse. It was all I could do to write these few words as I lay on the couch in my office, my skin raw with sores, my vision blurring, my flesh jaundiced. I didn't expect him to keep coming around but that empathy he was learning lingered, to both our surprise, beyond the point when I couldn't even get fucked anymore. I considered not including his salacious liaisons in this memoir of my last days among the living, but I think at this point, I have to leave him in. To do otherwise would be to exclude one of my favorite instances of discovering kindness where I expected none, and that's something the world can't afford to dismiss simply because it doesn't like how it got there.

I have heard stories of a burst of energy coming to those about to die:

the invalid who rises for one last active afternoon, the mindless elder who becomes lucid and conversational the whole length of their final night on earth. I think today I must be feeling that, which means I'm about to go. I can sit up. I can write again. I can finish this story. And I can tell what a wreck my body has become: its curdled stench, its tattered feel, its flimsiness, like an old cobweb its builder abandoned when it captured no flies.

I can hear Fiono's footsteps in the hall as he arrives for yet another session of showing more kindness than I probably deserve, more kindness than he probably knew he possessed.

No, those feet are not Fiono's: they're quiet despite the plaswood floor's best efforts, as his are, but his are lighter somehow, closer together, quicker and nimbler. Fiono has the footsteps of a dancer with a knife. These are confident but not subtle.

Of course they are. Alejandro is here. He's standing in the open door, staring at me as I finish writing this out. He does not disguise his sympathy and horror at my condition. My hair has become brittle, and my skin is yellow. I look like the ghost I'm shortly due to become. Alejandro has not yet spoken, and he does not need to do so. I know why he's here: he's come to repeat his offer of making me into a golem.

I hold up a finger and go back to writing.

To be honest, dying with dignity is possibly the least dignified thing I have ever done in my life. I have run away from parents who thought they should keep me trapped on their reservation because they loved me, hidden in the woods and lived like an animal to evade the search parties sent out for me, lived and worked in the most squalid sector of a City known for its easy filth, sold my ass in the streets, blown kids with knives to buy an hour of their time, and watched a monster die ten centimeters from my face, his eyes staring into mine.

I thought maybe this cancer eating me up inside would lend my death a sense of…not of purpose, but of *causation*. At least when it killed me, I wouldn't have to ask why. Solim certainly knew why he was dying, and I think that made it easier for him somehow.

When I put down this pen and set aside this paper, Alejandro is going to ask me again if I am ready to join him in a body of plastic and mystery, to become a ghost of a different sort: one from *his* world, not from mine. I've spent the last few days watching myself slowly die and thinking about Solim's last words, the last ones I remember: *There are many of us who truly understand. More than you might imagine. And we are well-placed in the churches. We will one day, sooner or later, run the churches ourselves. After that, we'll run the whole Empire.*

There are precious few people who know that. And in a hundred years, or a thousand, there might be no one who thinks to question it.

When Alejandro asks me again if I'd prefer some facsimile of eternal life, I'm going to surprise myself.

I'm going to say yes.

ABOUT THE AUTHOR

Michael G. Williams writes wry horror and science fiction noir: stories of monsters, macabre humor, alienation, subverted expectations, and the families we forge out of friends and allies. He is the author of three series for Falstaff Books: The Withrow Chronicles, including *Perishables* (2012 Laine Cunningham Award), *Tooth & Nail, Deal with the Devil, Attempted Immortality,* and *Nobody Gets Out Alive*; a new series in The Shadow Council Archives, *SERVANT/SOVEREIGN,* featuring time travel, modern-day witches, and one of San Francisco's most beloved historical figures, none other than Emperor Norton I; and a new sci fi detective series debuting in 2019 with the novel *A Fall in Autumn*. He also writes short stories and contributes to tabletop RPG development. Michael strives to present the humor and humanity at the heart of horror, science fiction, and mystery.

Michael is also an avid podcaster, activist, reader, runner, cyclist, and gaymer, and is a brother in St. Anthony Hall and Mu Beta Psi. He lives in Durham, NC, with his husband, two cats, two dogs, and more and better friends than he probably deserves.

❀ Created with Vellum

ALSO BY MICHAEL G. WILLIAMS

The Withrow Chronicles

Perishables

Tooth & Nail

Deal with the Devil

Attempted Immortality

Nobody Gets Out Alive (2019)

FALSTAFF BOOKS

Want to know what's new & coming soon from Falstaff Books?

Join our Newsletter List
& Get this Free Ebook Sampler
with work from:
John G. Hartness
A.G. Carpenter
Bobby Nash
Emily Lavin Leverett
Jaym Gates
Darin Kennedy
Natania Barron
Edmund R. Schubert
& More!

http://www.subscribepage.com/q0j0p3

Made in the USA
Columbia, SC
29 June 2022